Warworld Gaia

Captain's Fate Book 2

Skip Scherer

ISBN 978-1-7359075-2-9 (paperback)

ISBN 978-1-7359075-3-6 (ebook)

www.skipscherer.com

www.lionknight.us

For those that read the first book and continued on.
For those that helped me on the way.
For those that dared to dream, and made the dream a reality.
This book is for you.

It takes a village to raise a child, it also takes one to write a book.

A thank you to my wife who indulges my habits, even if I sometimes leave her baffled. I don't believe I'd be so organized or methodical without you in my life. To my daughter, who has an imagination that is as infinite as the stars. You inspire me to push the boundaries of what is possible. Together, my loving family, is what makes all things possible.

To Nath, Ryan, and Bill. Once again, your insights have helped me craft a better world. While I have a cast of people who help, you three always go above and beyond. I'm proud to have you as friends, as sounding boards for my ideas, and as characters in the book. Thank you all.

To my new editor Sarah Chorn, it is so wonderful to have found you. A true professional who is at the same time both positive and in-my-face. You have forced me to elevate my writing and push me to be better. I can't thank you enough for what you have helped me accomplish. Find her on Twitter @BookwormBlues or her website https://sarahchornedits.com/

To all those not listed, I thank you all.

Contents

Act 1

You'll probably think this story is about me, but you'll be wrong.
This story is about the road home.

Chapter 1

BEHEMOTH

The *Ares* was hunting. At least that was what they had been doing when she left the bridge. Communications between engine room two and the bridge kept dropping. The damage from their battle with the Screech continued to raise its annoying head. Three enemy ships had rammed the *Ares*, leaving a crater in its hull. Systems throughout the ship had been disrupted because of the extensive damage. The moment they thought it fixed; it would find a new way to break. With comms down, messages got delivered by hand, even if Lieutenant Harumi "Jax" Brandt had to do so herself. With her injuries, she wasn't running, but she could handle a fast walk. A crackle caught her attention, and as she turned to the wall, a holoscreen popped up with a familiar face. Her best friend Rose.

Lieutenant Junior Grade Rosita Koike, the person who should actually be in charge of engineering, stared back at her. Almost a mirror image of Jax, Rose stood a bit shorter with more of a bob cut to her hair. The resemblance was so strong that people thought they were sisters. Rose was a few years older than Jax, but with the height difference, Rose was jokingly called the little sister. For an engineer, Rose was normally immaculately clean. Even when up to her neck in grease, it never seemed to touch her. Her frazzled hair and dirt marked face was a powerful testament to how hard things were right now. Her normal smile was pinched in a scowl that constantly adorned her face since the battle.

"Figured you'd be on your way. Comms are fixed again, so you can head back to the bridge." Rose said, the image crackling and wavy lines appearing. The usual life like renderings associated with the holo-screens nowhere to be seen.

"That's good. Captain also wanted to know about her special project. Wants to run it this pass."

"It's ready. Pretty sure. Abyss, I don't know. It will work. Beat me with a stick. I'll call the bridge." The holoimage blinked away as suddenly as it came.

"Okay then." Jax spoke at the wall.

Jax turned back for the bridge, her hip aching from the quick about-face. It felt better than it had for the last couple of weeks, but the pain still popped up at the most unusual times. She tried not to think of it. It brought up too many fresh wounds.

Captain Moss was dead, lost in space. While Captain Moss and her were outside the ship, fixing it, saving it from the ramming. Large portions of the engineering crew were killed with the destruction of engine room 1. So many people were lost, so many people she never had the time to meet. Lost forever to the Screech attack. She doubled her pace, as best she could, her mind having to focus on each step to keep her footing sure.

Stepping on to the Command deck, she was greeted with "Welcome back LC." From Commander Issac Haddock, the operations officer.

It was quickly echoed by the navigation officer, Commander Lilly Bard "LC!"

"Commanders." She voiced her greeting. LC was short for Lieutenant Commander. She didn't have that rank, but it seemed to give the two commanders nothing but pleasure in calling her that. She took their humor in stride, but sometimes wondered if they took the friendly mocking a little too far.

"Jax, glad you made it back so quickly," the captain said, never taking her eyes from the command table. "No need for an update. I've already had the most colorful of one from a certain junior grade lieutenant." Captain Lewis brought her eyes up and leveled them at Jax. She had the impression she was about to be dressed down, but there was playfulness in the captain's eyes that put her at ease.

Commander Gemma Lewis was officially the XO, commanding officer or second in command, on the *Ares*. She was acting captain in much the same way Jax was the acting ENG officer. By tradition, or was it superstition, ships always have a living captain. So, with Captain Ichabod Moss killed in action, Gemma had taken to the role. With her stocky frame and short stature, she stood in sharp contrast to Captain Moss's larger-than-life appearance. But her shoulders held the responsibility well.

"LJG1 Kioke can be a little... colorful... when she gets stressed. Apologies, Captain, but she is managing a lot right now. I'll talk to her." Jax said, stifling a smile while taking up position at the command table. *A lot being an understatement.* Rose was almost taking the place of the entire missing ENG crew. When something needed to be fixed, she fixed it, often before anyone knew it was broken. Not to mention the extra work, like the captain's special project.

"Captain, the Screech are starting their flight pattern again." Commander Haddock announced. "Are we trying your special gift this time?"

"All colorful language aside, engineering thinks it's ready," the Captain said, nodding.

"We can only hope." Commander Moro's tone was flat, an unspoken 'I don't think so' underling his words.

"Rose will make it work." Jax replied.

"It had better," the Captain said. "I'm getting tired of this never-ending match. I don't like being stalled." Her dark eyes scanning the command table.

The command table dominated the center of the bridge. A large holotable, capable of displaying any number of ship related information. Including the *Ares'* position in space, flight patterns, ship status and more. Currently, the entire table was occupied with only one objective, their current dilemma. To one side of the table sat a perfect replica of the *Ares*. The *Ares* looked like a shark with a large bite taken from it while it floated in the void. Its hull damage showing in perfect detail on the small avatar. On the far side of the table, at the edge of their ability to scan, floated a Screech destroyer. A destroyer that looked like a squid with too many tentacles trailing behind it. No sharp edges on the craft, the Screech hated those. It moved with eerie grace.

It always amazed Jax at the level of detail the *Ares* got from its scanners. Earth ships used a combination of telescopic, laser, radio waves, gravity lensing and radar for scanning. *Ares* had those too, but also used a kind of sonar based on qave drive technology. Quantum waves, and the reflection back, could read an amazing amount of detail over interstellar distances. Precise measurements, materials, color, and more could all be analyzed and displayed in real time. *I wished we would have had that tech on the Indiana.* Images of her old ship jumped in her head. She shook them off and kept her focus on the task at hand.

They had spent weeks hiding in the rings of an unnamed planet. Those weeks were spent on what seemed a never-ending mission to repair the damaged ship. Damage caused by a successful, yet ill fated, attack on a Screech planetary terraformer. A terraformer that Gaia Fleet simply called a Lander. The Lander along with all its support ships had ripped the *Ares* to shreds and killed a vast majority of her crew. They had been victorious, but the definition didn't quite apply to their predicament.

Those weeks were dedicated to making the ship space-worthy again. The large gaping crater of the *Ares* hull sealed despite numerous breaches. Shields and weapons brought online, and with a little hope they had then set course for Gaia. The idea of a truly safe port lifting their spirits. That hope was dashed when they found the Screech destroyer stalking them.

Under optimal conditions the *Ares* could run silent and slip away from its stalker. With all the damage to the hull, that was no longer an option, there was no hiding. Up close, the *Ares* had enough power, enough teeth, that it could still take the destroyer, but they couldn't get close. For the first time, the Screech were not rushing in, not attacking with relentless fury. They were being tactical, playing to counter every possible scenario. It was annoying.

Over interstellar distances, beam weapons were futile. The energy feeding them dissipates over such vast distances. Which left torpedoes. Torpedoes that launched over enormous areas of space, with no cover, no hope of not being detected. Launching the missiles at the Screech seemed more like a recognition that they were aware of them. The same held true for both sides. A stalemate.

The best hope the *Ares* had would be too close distance and engage, if only they could. Their primary qave drive was destroyed in the Lander attack. Which left only the secondary drive to power the entire ship. Potentially still faster, but at these distances the Screech lead was insurmountable. If the *Ares* tried to advance, the Screech would run, changing what everyone on the *Ares* knew to be their modus operandi. Too many unknowns for anyone to feel comfortable in this situation.

"Commander Moro, prepare to initiate our modified attack plan," the Captain said.

Commander Terrance Moro lifted his chin and gave a slight sniff before responding. "Aye aye, Captain." After the attack on the Lander, Commander Moro seemed to soften. His usually strict self was lost as he threw himself into the work of repairing the ship. Once they were underway, his normal attitude had reasserted itself. His "I'm better than you and I know it" attitude. It seeped through every part of him from how he spoke to how he looked. Even now, as he stood at his station, he looked polished, rested, like an ad for what the perfect Fleet officer should be. While everyone else was frazzled and worn. *Scum.*

It didn't help his attitude that nobody would refer to him as the XO. No matter how many times he reminded everyone that he was officially second-in-command. It was still Commander Moro, not XO. Jax wondered if it hurt him more to not be called XO or to hear her called LC?

Adding injury to insult, Terrance Moro also seemed at odds with their new captain's style. Captain Moss was big and boisterous, a dominant personality. He always maintained a formal bridge, with procedures and titles forefront.

Gemma Lewis was on the opposite end of the spectrum with how she handled command. Calm and friendly, Captain Lewis often seemed more comfortable using names without titles. That lack of decorum seemed to upset Commander Terrance Moro the most. *Good, it's nice to see him squirm.*

"Firing solution is ready, Captain. On your orders."

"Thank you, Commander Moro. Lilly began our attack pattern."

"Aye aye, Captain." Commander Lilly Bard said from the NAV pod. On the command table, the *Ares* increased speed and began a smooth roll towards the far-off Screech ship. It was a familiar pattern that over the last few days the *Ares* had repeated and repeated.

"Fire torpedoes," the Captain said. "Again," she added with a sigh.

"Firing torpedoes one to five," Commander Moro replied, unmoving, while he watched his screens. Mere seconds ticked away before he spoke again. "Torpedoes are away."

How long can you listen to a song before you tire of it? I'm starting to hate this one. She grabbed the railing that ran around the table and leaned in. The Screech, at least on the surface, seemed content with running the same pattern. The *Ares* we would move in, launch torpedoes, and roll out. Then attempt an intercept course on an opposite trajectory. The Screech would circle away from the torpedoes, drawing them off. Then loop away from the *Ares* intercept. At these distances, they have all the time in the abyss to make it work, and they did it well. This time, it would be different. This time, the captain's special project would change the outcome. That was the plan.

Halfway to the target, the destroyer began its move. The *Ares* began its own familiar roll, except this time the captain added a new element to the mix. A little something to change the beat. "Drop the package," the Captain said.

"Dropping package," Commander Moro replied.

Why this was called the captain's special project, Jax wasn't sure, since it had all started with Rose. Shortly after they realized the Screech were avoiding their attacks. Rose had commented that it would be great to have torpedoes with the same capabilities as the pathjackers. The pathjackers being a long-range scout probe with stealth capabilities. The captain had agreed and told LTG1 Kioke to make it an immediate priority. Rose hadn't been happy about being taken away from repairs. The captain insisted that defending the ship from the destroyer was paramount. Rose had submitted, grumbling all the while, but got to work modifying a torpedo.

Rose never did anything she couldn't do well. The project bloomed from modifying a torpedo to also increasing its range, speed, and payload.

The *Ares* rolled while the stealth torpedo dropped out of a hanger bay. The new torpedo was a monster compared to the regular ones. Increased shielding and energy dampers for stealth mode meant the greater its energy core had to be for a higher yield explosive. The behemoth sized torpedo was too big for the regular launch tubes. Hanging dead in space, it would fire its engines and then activate silent running, a quick energy spike that could be detected even at vast distances. Jax knew Rose wanted to fix that issue, but the captain wouldn't give her time. So instead, Rose devised a way to use the *Ares* as a physical shield to mask the torpedo while it activated. A quick burst of energy and then it was gone. The Screech hopefully unaware of the new tactic.

All eyes on the bridge were glued to the telemetry. On the command table, the *Ares* circled off as if to intercept the fleeing ship. The destroyer turned away, veering back on its usual course. The familiar dance playing out again.

The stealth torpedo sped in the opposite arch from the *Ares*. If the Screech held to form, they would turn back into its path and run into the punch instead of slipping away. A gamble with the hopes of breaking the monotonous standoff.

"Come on, you dirty bird. Stay your course. You know you want to," the Captain said.

"The target is turning," Commander Haddock said, his high voice running higher with excitement. "They are holding true to form. Turning away now, back on an elliptical course."

The image on the table shifted. The miniature version of the destroyer becoming the focus. A small triangle showing the torpedo curving towards it.

"Target is maintaining course. Torpedo has a lock. Fifteen minutes to impact," Commander Haddock called.

Fighting at interstellar distances was a slow game. Even given the speeds at which the destroyer and the torpedo traveled. Every minute, every second, an agonizing wait for the climax. On the command table, the holo image zoomed closer. Closer again as the two objects streaked towards their meeting. Closer, and the small triangle gave way to an image of the torpedo, its path nose to nose with the Screech ship.

Commander Haddock's updates were the only thing that broke the silence. "Ten minutes to contact." A tense filled pause that stretched forever until "five minutes." Then the longest pause of all to the last countdown. "Contact in three, two and... contact!"

The image on the command table had rammed together and paused, but nothing happened. There was no explosion. No bright flash. It could have been minutes or seconds. It was as if time had frozen. No one spoke.

Finally, Jax found her voice, and it echoed across the bridge. "Well, that can't be good."

Chapter 2

GOOD DAY

"There was supposed to be a kaboom. A great big kaboom," the Captain said as she turned a questioning stare at Jax.

"I'm checking Captain. Not sure what happened," Jax said.

"Start tracking that ship. All hands prepare for attack," the Captain said, the bridge staff moving like an efficient machine. Screens on the holotable were changed to a combat layout. Staff took the appropriate positions, each of them issuing orders to their own divisions. The air itself permeated with what could only be called the scent of focus.

Jax brought up a screen to talk to Rose. It flickered out and then popped back on. Again, the usually lifelike visage was swirling into a distorted, twisted image. The sound cracked as they spoke, the words skipping and out of sync with the mouth.

"I don't know, that's the first torpedo I've ever built." Rose Koike's face was mix a of frustration and anger. "Everything I have here says it should have worked. Rallitch fripping thing."

Jax had to stop herself from laughing. While Rose may not curse often, it often got colorful. She would create curse words on the fly, most to never be heard again. It was a common occurrence in engineering when Rose was working on machines that were causing her problems. Whispered where she thought no one could hear, engineering referred to as Roseisms. Rallitch was her newest curse word. Ever since a psychopath named Rallic had tried to kill Jax, Rose had been determined to curse his name forever. The curse had gone through several variations, rallicker, bloody ral, and more. Rallitch seems to be the one that was sticking.

"Engineering doesn't have any answers right now, Captain," Lieutenant Brandt said, turning from her friend. She suppressed her smile, trying her best to show the captain a professional face.

"Right," the captain said. "Forget that for now. Get all available power to the shield and weapons. Let's get ready for incoming."

"Aye aye, Captain," she replied, waving a bye to Rose. In the same motion, she started transferring power and preparing for battle.

"Captain, the target is gone," Commander Haddock's high-pitched voice called.

"Gone? What do you mean, gone? Did I miss something, Commander? I hate missing a good explosion."

"No, Captain. No evidence of an explosion, but after contact, the target disappeared off scans."

"Disappeared?"

"They're at the edge of our scans. It's possible that the moment we hit them, they ran away. Maybe we scared them off?" Commander Haddock said, shrugging.

"This is not a situation where I want to rely on speculation. Let's find that ship." The bridge responded and went to work. Pathjacker probes were launched and a search pattern was laid in. They searched. Hours passed. Nothing.

"We have lost a destroyer," the Captain said, pacing.

"Afraid so, Captain," Commander Haddock said.

"Stand down from battle stations. Let's resume our course home. NAV make it a wary path. Double back on our tracks, random shifts, see if we can draw them out, but make sure they're not following us. We don't want to miss anything and lead them home."

"Aye aye, Captain," Commander Bard said from the pilot's seat. "Taking the scenic route."

"Jax, any word from engineering on what went wrong with that torpedo? Can they make one that will work?"

"They're checking, Captain. One second," Jax said, looking at the blurry image of Rose. Her face contorted, twisting the snarl on Rose's face, making it larger and more menacing. The sound had dropped. Jax laced her voice with extra calm since it seemed her transmission was getting through. "Captain wants to know if you can make another one?"

Rose's voice cracked back, "Work?... crackle... crackle... I... crackle...wrong... fripping... crackle..." Suddenly the LTG1 eyes narrowed and shoved her hands off screen. Sparks flew across the holoscreen as her hands came back, filled with town wires. The wires continued sparkling, a look of satisfaction in Rose's eyes. The holoimage flickered and turned clear. The constant crackle and buzzing also dropped off. Rose turned the flashing wires from her face and through gritted teeth, she spoke. "I'll look into making another one, but till I know what happened, I got nothing." She glanced at the wires in her hands. "Comms are fixed." A cruel smile crossed her lips and the image cut out.

Jax took a deep breath, composing her thoughts, before turning to the captain. "Sorry, Captain. Engineering will have to investigate the situation further, to determine what went wrong. They will update us when they know something. They did get communications fixed."

The captain's eyes were glued to the command table. Her steel focus was oblivious to anything but the probable location of the Screech destroyer. "Any good news in a storm, I guess. Very well, let's get back to business folks. Ship repairs remain a priority. OPS keep a full staff on scans. I want any sign if there is something out there."

The bridge responded and once again began moving through their well-rehearsed routines. Jax stretched her back and cranked her neck. Long shifts were taking their toll. Her hip ached from all the standing; she needed a good stretch. Her arm and shoulder were usable, but still stiff. Now that her shift was over, she could make a quick stop at MedBay for her last check up with Doc.

She turned to leave, Ensign Ambros stepping in to relieve her. A friend who was also a member of the Rat Pack, a group of engineers who were currently the major force keeping the *Ares* running. He was usually quiet, *unless drinking,* Jax thought. On the bridge he was almost a ghost. He nodded to Jax and leaped into the ENG pod. With his bald head down, he went to work. If you blinked, you might have missed him coming on to the bridge at all.

She offered a smile as she turned to leave, when a call caught her ear. "Hey LC, come over here before you go," Commander Bard called from the NAV pod.

She worked her way to the front of the bridge and peered in on navigation. The noble-looking face of the older woman stared contently back at her. Jax wondered how old the commander was. It wasn't polite to ask anyone their age. Nanotech treatments, gene therapy and modern medicines have made long lives a reality. Lilly Bard's too-perfect skin meant she likely had very good medical treatments.

"Commander. You know you and Commander Haddock should really stop calling me LC. The joke is not winning me any points on the bridge," Jax said, glancing over her shoulder at Commander Moro. *Even if I enjoy his frustration a bit.*

Commander Lilly Bard's face broke into a smile from cheek to cheek. "My dear, I have no idea what you mean." She said, pausing to make a flight adjustment before continuing. "Besides, Terrance needs his ego checked from time to time. He's a big boy and he can handle it." Her judging eyes turned back and squared on Jax. "I want to know if you are interested in flight training?"

"Of course," Jax said, her eyes wide with excitement. "But I thought we didn't do flight training onboard ship?"

A sour look crossed the commander's face and was quickly gone. "Policies change with captains, my dear. I'm sure Captain Lewis would be happy to authorize training for you."

"That would be fabulous. I'm not sure what kind of time I'll have for it. I'm supposed to be commanding engineering after all. That and another project I might be taking on."

"Oh please. You're little more than a figurehead. Engineering can get along fine without you."

"Ouch. That was brutal." Jax face pinched a bit at the retort.

"The truth usually is. It also helps keep egos in check. It's all settled then. I'll clear it with the captain, and we can schedule it later. If not here, we can always do it back on Gaia. Approval now would be easier, however." With that, Commander Bard turned her attention back to the pod. She spoke to her co-pilot, whom she called "Gums," and went back to flying.

Dismissed, she strolled the hallways. The gray metal walls and rubberized floors giving her a sense of security. The tight spaces once made her feel claustrophobic. Now it was like they wrapped her in a security blanket. Her hand brushed the cool walls as she walked. Her route to MedBay was anything but direct. Captain Moss had taught her to know the ship, and she had embraced the idea. Now Jax took the strange ways, the long ways, the ways nobody used. She learned every square centimeter of the ship as if it were an extension of her body. She passed crew members and pushed herself to say hi to each by name and rank.

MedBay came into view. Technically MedBay 1, or Main MedBay. *Ares* had four spread throughout the ship. The other three were small med auxiliary stations used when quick care was necessary.

The hatch was open, as usual. As she stepped in, the familiar scent of disinfectant assaulted her. Ever since their assault on the Screech lander, MedBay has been bursting with activity. It was a pleasant change to see it almost vacant.

"Ah, Lieutenant Brandt, here for your final checkup," Dr. Charles said, stepping out from behind a privacy curtain. The tallest man Jax had ever seen at over two meters. His head always scraped the ceiling. His white receding hairline was never neat.

"Got to keep my favorite doctor happy." She gave him a wink and a grin.

"Yes, you do," the doctor said, motioning for her to lie down. "The nanites repairing your hip should be finished and deactivated themselves by now. How does it feel?"

The side of the bed pulsed a quick light while the doctor waved a scanning stick over her legs and hip. A holoscreen beside the bed displayed a clear picture of her inner muscles and bones. "It's a little stiff, but I stretch it out as I can. Other than that, no issues I can think of."

"Excellent. If more people would listen to me, they too could be healed." The doctor motioned for her to sit. "I think we can forgo more checks. Let me know if you experience any other problems."

Jax hopped off the table. Simple and efficient was the doctor, she liked that about him. She stood staring at him as he put the scanning stick away. Jax bounced from foot to foot. *I need to ask for his help, but should I?* It only took a moment for the Doc to realize something was amiss.

"Was there something else, Lieutenant?"

Her mouth opened and closed. Doubt ran through her. She stuttered the words and then closed her mouth. With a deep breath, she rushed her question. "Will you teach me to shoot?"

The Doctor's neck straightened as he glared at her. His already tall figure grew even taller. *I've upset him. Maybe I can leave and pretend this never happened? Make for the door before you make a fool of yourself.* Jax's feet were twitching to leave when Doctor Charles finally spoke. "You do realize I'm a doctor, not a weapons officer, correct?"

"I know. Word around ship is that you're the best with small arms and that's where I need help."

"There are many weapon specialists aboard who could help you. Not to mention VR programs. I fail to see why you are seeking my help."

"I've done the training and I've tried the VR programs. None of it has worked for me. I'm told your style is different." She stared at the doctor. "I just figured... I tend to not fit this military lifestyle. I mean, I like being here. I just need a different approach sometimes, look at things a different way, so I can make it work." Her eyes had dropped to the floor while talking. "So, can you help me?"

Time seemed to slow as the doctor stood expressionless. No words were spoken, his weighing study upon her. The doctor's eyes rolled to the ceiling as he spoke. "Very well, I will put together some lessons for you. I will contact you when they are ready, and we can arrange a time to go through them. Will there be anything else, Lieutenant?"

"Thank you, Doc. Thank you." A smile stretched her lips.

"Now if you'll excuse me, I have patients that need me."

"Yes, of course. Thank you again," she said as the doctor turned away. She spun on her toes, light as a feather.

Gliding back to her berth, she stopped for a moment before entering. The lightness of her heart turning into the beat of a loud drum as anticipation built in her core.

Her room was her least favorite place on the ship. In this dark little cell, her mind would roam, building on her inner conflicts. She worked herself to the bone, so that when she returned here, she would pass out. Go to sleep. Too long alone and her mind would be lost to tragedies.

She entered her room and, with practiced routine, sat on her bed and stared at the wall. Her mind calling up all her anxieties, all her fears. No matter how tired she was, it was never enough to drown out the faces. The faces of her crew from the *Indiana*. Her first command destroyed. The faces of the ground team who died saving her. Yet she lived on and never had a chance to thank them. She wanted to give them that, but she kept having to push the feelings down. Deeper Into her core, further so they on longer affected her. How else to manage emotions until they were buried so far away that you couldn't recall them?

She pulled her legs up and hugged them to her chest. *So many dead. So many lost. How can I let myself be happy?* Images of the Screech she had killed. A sense of pleasure accompanied those thoughts. It also sickened her. She closed her eyes and forced her head down to her pillow.

Everyone keeps telling me it's ok to live. That at some point I'll get a chance to mourn. I hope it's soon. Everyone on board makes it seem so easy.

The room was cold, but she didn't bother with a blanket. Pinching her eyes tight, Jax fought her mind for control. To clear her thoughts so she could rest, but the horrors always came back. Soon she would fall asleep, and the dreams would come. They always did. Tonight, she focused on the good that had happened today. Flight training with Commander Bard. The doctor teaching her how to shoot. That she was safe, here in this room. If she tried hard enough, she could keep the nightmares at bay. One good day to start it all and be better. Would It be enough for all the terror she felt? She drifted into sleep and a single tear fell down her cheek.

Chapter 3

SINGLE ACTION

The road to a safe port was a long one indeed. Longer still when the acting captain, Commander Gemma Lewis, was obsessed with the idea that a Screech destroyer was following them. What could have been weeks to return, was over a month instead. Captain Lewis paced in the bridge like a panther stalking prey, but no prey could be found. The fact that they made any progress back to Gaia seemed secondary. Despite it all, the day had come and in a mere six hours, they would enter Gaia space.

The captain wanted all department commanders on the bridge when that happened. She ordered them to take a break.

Not wanting to go back to her quarters, Jax's first thought was to hit the wardroom for a chai tea latte. She wondered if it was possible to hide in a corner for six hours and simply savor the drink. The mere thought of that made her warm with pleasure.

A chirp graced her ear, informing her she had a message. She brought up her wrist, waved her hand until a personal holoscreen floated in front of her.

An image of the doctor popped up with a little 'rec' in the lower corner. His recorded message played when she gave it a blink. "I will be available for your private lessons for the next hour. Should you be available, the VR link code is attached." The doctor's image disappeared. *A little warning would have been nice.*

There were several gun ranges on the *Ares*. Used mainly by corps members to keep their shooting skills sharp. Fleet personnel were also required to spend time there, but less so than the corps. All her previous firearms instructions had occurred there.

All the personal VRpods on the *Ares* were in the rec room. It was one of the oddest places on the *Ares*. Where everything on board the ship seemed planned, thought out, with a purpose, the rec room did not. Jax knew that couldn't be true, but it looked that way to her. It seemed like a forgotten piece of the puzzle shoved in when the puzzle was finished. They threw everything for personal entertainment into this single room. Left to its own devices, good enough.

The large room was clustered with various forms of entertainment. Hologaming stations, regular card tables, billiards tables, dart boards, and stacks of games waiting to be used. A mess of things with no organization shoved around as needed. A mixed group of Corps and Fleet sat at a table playing a game called Towers. A mix of cards and dice that was uniquely Gaia in origin. *I guess command isn't the only group with a little time off.* The most popular game on ship, Tower games could be found in berths, mess hall or some random corner during breaks. A simple, fast game, but one Jax had not learned to play.

Jax weaved her way around the random tables and other games. Along the back wall of the rec room was the most popular attraction here. The VRpods stacked two high, with small ladders to get to the top, they lined the wall twenty to a row. Small red lights indicated that eleven of them were in use. She didn't care for those ladders, so she walked the line to the first free ground level pod.

Entering pod eight, she positioned herself on the ergonomic seat. Lacking the cushioning of the bridge pods, she squirmed a little to get comfortable. *Don't know why I bother, won't matter in a minute.* Smaller than the pods on the bridge, each of these were designed for one person. On her right, she pressed the green holo button that cycled it on. The hatch slid shut, a dim light illuminated the inside as her body floated up a few centimeters. Engulfed by the gravity wave inside the pod, she felt the ripples down her body like a gentle massage. The chair, no longer needed, folded into the wall and the lights grew brighter and swirled. A flash of light and the blink of an eye, she went from sitting in the pod to standing in a small room.

The waiting room, the first stop in any VR experience. It was a small room with a light blue tinge meant to relax users. A simple, easy to recognize environment designed to let your mind and body adjust to the virtual world. The pod would regulate heat, sound, light, pressure, and even smell as it fully immersed you. Intended to make the VR as real as possible, the gravity wave also puts actual work into your muscles. More than a gaming experience, you could get a full workout too.

With a wave of her hand, a loading screen appeared. She accessed her personal files and grabbed the code Doc had given her. *Here goes nothing.* She tapped it with her finger and the room's color shifted. Walls warped, disappeared, and her surroundings re-solidified into a new configuration.

She was standing in the bright noonday sun. A dry wind swirled the dirt around her shoes. Around her was an old broken-down barn with an equally broken horse fence. Sweat dripped from her brow as she felt the temperature assault her skin. Her clothes were the standard Fleet officer jumper she had on when entering the pod. A wave of a hand and a quick scroll through a holo menu, she activated a Fleet baseball cap and a pair of shades. The dark blue cap and aviator-style glasses faded onto her face.

She walked around feeling like a lost tourist. A desolate place, there wasn't much to occupy her but brown grass moving in the wind. She perched against a rail post while her eyes scanned for Doc. Over a far ridge, a dot, a vague moving shape caught her eye. Heat blurred the image as it glided towards her, growing, swaggering on the trail that marked its path. The heat and dust slowly fell away, and the image came into focus. Doc arrived on a pale horse.

The horse, gray with speckles of white, trotted along. Its muscular frame and high stature appeared custom built for the doc. Doc's height was amplified to epic proportions as he rode. Reaching her, he swung down, a grace to his movements she had never noticed.

Atop of his head he wore a black sun-worn high-crowned hat with a broad brim. A long leather trench coat hugged his frame from his shoulders to above his knees. Brown pants, a black buttoned up shirt and a pale gray scarf completed the ensemble.

"Quite the entrance, Doc." She flashed him a smile.

"Of course. People often overlook a good entrance. I find it sets the mood." He didn't smile when he said it, but there was a lightness in his eyes that indicated he was enjoying himself. He lashed his horse to a nearby post. A quick flick of his wrists, his hands moving daftly to tie off a knot Jax couldn't follow. Turning back, he said, "Please, Lieutenant, in this environment, call me Dutch. I come here to escape being 'Doc' at least for a while," Dutch said with a wink.

"Dutch it is, as long as you call me Jax."

"Agreed, Jax," he said, while waving his hand to the left. "Shall we proceed?"

"I can't wait."

They walked down the fence a few meters and then crossed over a broken opening. A small table awaited them. Arranged neatly on the table was an old-fashioned pistol of some kind and neat stacks of ammo. Twenty meters in the distance, the fence cut at a sharp angle. Arranged across the top were cans of variable sizes.

Jax's face pulled back as confusion washed over her. "What's this?"

"This is what you asked for. I'm going to teach you how to shoot."

She pushed the gun on the table with her finger. "Not exactly fleet issue." While clean, the metal of the gun looked worn. As If it had been cleaned, or fired, one too many times. The handle had a dark brown, oily sheen on it.

"It's my understanding that you have trouble with modern weapons. Correct?"

She bit her lip. "I guess you could say that."

"Have you ever wondered why?"

"I've never thought about it. Should I?"

Dutch shook his head and his face pinched as if disgusted. "All modern weaponry used by Fleet are the pinnacle of firearms. Stabilization control, aiming assistance, null recoil, the perfect balance to make any soldier an expert marksman." He paused and locked eyes with her. The most she could manage was a nod. He continued, "Yet the best you have been able to achieve is a shooter rating on a single weapon. Yes, you should wonder why."

She squinted and bit the inside of her cheek. Her fists were clenched, and she pushed her shoulders back. She tried to will herself taller so she could look him square in the eyes. "Fine. Why?" she said, trying hard to not let anger seep into her response.

"Simply put, you can't surrender control."

That stopped her. Her eyebrow lifted and confusion filled her. "I don't understand what that means. I'm just aiming and firing the way they taught me. How am I supposed to fire a weapon I don't have control over?"

Dutch ever-so-gently shook his head as if it was obvious. "The gun tries to balance, and you fight it for your own balance. The gun tries to target, you want to target. You're every action is counter to what the technology wants you to do."

"And you know this how?"

"Because it's the same with me."

His head came down and the fatherly smile she remembered from the first time she met him crossed his face. He continued, "People think modern medicine, doctors to be specific, are superfluous. That technology, artificial intelligence, nanites, genetically modified drugs do all the work. They forget the humanity behind it that makes it possible. Like you, I fight against it." He stopped and turned to the table. His movements like lightning, his hand was up from his hip and firing his weapon before Jax could blink. The sound thundered in her ears, a ripple through her body, as a small can jumped off the fence. As smoothly as he fired, he placed his gun back in the holster at his side.

"So, you fire a gun to embrace humanity? Not sure that makes sense to me."

"Not humanity. Simpler times. Firing a gun requires focus, a reliance on yourself. Without the simple skills behind it, the gun is nothing. Technology is not needed to make it work well. It takes knowledge to impart those things. Though technology can increase the effectiveness, it is still worthless without the person driving it."

"So, you practice for the skill, without the technology, to remind yourself you are a person and not something else? To prove it's you and not some superfluous force? Seems like there should be other ways to do that than using a violent weapon."

"The act of firing a gun is not one of violence. I am not a violent person. I have never hurt or killed anyone with a gun," he said, pausing for a second when the most wicked of grins crossed his face. "Except the egos of some exuberant Corps members."

She was chuckling as she said, "I've heard that story. Does it bother you that I will be practicing for the both the skill and the violence it can impart?"

"I am a practical man, Jax. We all prepare the best we can to save those we care about. How you choose to use any knowledge, or skill, is a moral dilemma we all must eventually make. The better question then is, are you ready to make that choice?"

"I am. It's why I'm here. Where do we begin?"

"We begin here," he said, turning and presenting the gun to her. She took it gingerly in both hands. "This is the Army Single Action. In my opinion, the most significant handgun ever created. A gun that made everyone equal."

She smiled at the name. Army Single Action. An image of her dad warmed her thoughts. "Single action? What's that mean?"

"The trigger only drops the hammer to fire the gun. You'll have to lock the hammer back independently." Dutch said, reaching to his waist and pulling his own pistol from under his coat. Pulling the hammer back and displaying the weapon. "Creates better control and increases your ability to aim. This gun relies on you for those things, not on technology." He moved it forward and fired again. Another can pinged off the far rail.

"Well, I could always use more control in my life. So, what do I do?"

He walked her through the same basic gun safety she had heard countless times since coming on the *Ares*, showing her how to load and unload rounds. It startled her to find out that this gun had no safety switch. Once loaded, it was always ready to fire. Don't put your finger on the trigger if you don't want to fire, that's the safety. Don't point it where you don't want to shoot and so on. All simple common sense that was more serious concern when holding a weapon.

She took her stance and raised the gun. Hand placement on the ASA was so much different from her trusty NEW24. Dutch kept a watchful eye while she focused on a firm grip. Her thumb resting on the back of the cylinder felt odd, but he assured her it would be comfortable in time. Her left hand hugged the right as her left thumb cocked the hammer.

"Remember to breathe naturally. When ready to fire, hold that breath and squeeze the trigger," Dutch said, his voice gentle.

She saw the target down the sights and squeezed the trigger. Her hand snapped; her shoulder jerked back. Jax's ears rang as the noise exploded into her body. "Geez. That's more kick than I thought," she said through clenched teeth.

"The first shot is always the worst."

"Did I hit anything?" she asked, turning her eyes down the field.

"No. you went high and to the right. Adjust your sights down and have a firmer grip."

"Right," she said, setting up and firing again. A puff of dirt appeared below her target to the left.

"Target in the middle of first and second shot."

"Okay." Cocking the hammer, she fired again. Splinters burst from the fence.

"Better. Miniature adjustments now. Walk it in."

No answer from her this time. Lock the hammer. Hold the breath. Squeeze the trigger. More splinters, but closer to the target. She brought it up and fired again, the excitement vibrating through her. Nothing happened.

"You rushed it. That shot will now progress to parts unknown. Slow down. Speed will come in time. Focus now, it's your mind we must train. The body will follow."

She took a deep breath and let it out slowly. "Right. Smooth is life." Adjusting her stance, realigning her grip. *Breathe. Feel the rhythm. Lock the hammer. Sight the target. Squeeze.*

A ping echoed back from the fence as the large can tumbled away.

"I hit it. I hit it!" Her body tensed as she jumped around to look at Dutch.

"Yes, you did," he said as she jumped in and hugged him.

"Thank you, Doc., I mean Dutch. That was fantastic!" She took a step back from Dutch, the shock of being hugged fading from his face. *Lucky number six saves me again.*

"I'm not sure about amazing, but it's a good first step," he said, stepping away from the table. "You have the basics. Let me know when you can hit all the cans without missing. Then we can work on drawing. Firing from the hip and fanning."

"Fanning?"

"Another time, you have plenty to work on before that," he said. "Till then, I have my own free time to see too. The VR will keep you safe and you can replay my instructions should you need reminders. Application is the best teacher, so shoot more and think less." He grabbed the edge of his hat and tilted his head. "A good day to you, Jax."

"To you too Dutch," she said, attempting to mimic the jester. His VR image blinking out before she could complete the task.

Reloading, she raised the gun. "Cans, you are now my nemesis, and you will fall." She could feel her smile as the sound of the gun rang out. Her focus locked, she would fire again, and again, and again.

Chapter 4

SLICK SLEEVE

Her fingers hurt as she walked the dull gray corridors flexing her hand. Her shoulder was also feeling tight. *If I didn't know better, I could swear my uniform smells of gunpowder.* There was no actual smell in a VRpod of course. A trick of technology activated the olfactory nerves to simulate the experience. It might be a virtual world, but a VR pod pushed that distinction to the limit.

Once Dr. Dutch Charles had left her to her own devices, she lost all impressions of time. The hours she had spent shooting those abyss damned cans had felt like minutes. Of course, her body was in complete disagreement with that. Her hand and shoulder were feeling every second. The VRpods ability to mimic real world physical resistance was fine tuned.

The bridge was busy in a way she had never seen. People moved like bees in a hive. Multiple holoscreens littered the command table. Fleetwalkers flowed in and out, delivering messages and running off again. Each station had an overflow of staff handling checklists and docking instructions. Even NAV had extra pilots standing near their pod, keeping eyes on flight information. The stoplight was green with no other markers. Safe waters for the *Ares* had created a hectic, but enlightened, mood on the bridge.

The Operation Commander had the most of it. Issac Haddock had an uncountable number of holoscreens up. Avatars of people Jax couldn't identify stood like mini statues around the screens. The lifelike images scattered around, some were busts talking, some whole-body images waving hands, some were floating heads. He was carrying all the conversations at once. Flipping from screen to avatar and back as necessary. One moment checking with his pod staff, Lt. Commander Sharma, and Lieutenant Wisler, from what she could see, to jumping back to the screens. Jax knew the two officers only in passing. They had been on the bridge during the Lander attack but locked into the OPS pod. She kept wanting to talk to them more, get to know them, but never found the time. Their never seemed to be enough time. Other OPS personnel jumped in and out in well-orchestrated movements. The muscular ops commander was in his element and seemed to relish every moment.

Captain Lewis and Rose huddled in a corner of the table where two avatars talked to them. The avatars were wearing work vests and had their own mini holoscreens dancing around them. The avatars would point, shake heads, and make notations. Each screen had different aspects of the *Ares* displayed: damage, lists of repairs, available resources, and more.

The avatars blipped out as Jax approached. Rose turned on her, her face red. "It's about time you got here. You can deal with these pixel pushers. Telling me I don't know my own ship. Questioning our repairs. They're going to need repairs when I'm done with them."

Jax's eyes went wide and turned to the captain for support. The captain was already turning away, a wicked grin crossing her face. "Sorry I got here when I was supposed to. Didn't know we had a review team holoing in," Jax said.

Rose waved her hands in the air and the words rushed from her. "Of course not. Nobody did. Captain had me run from my station. These dim-witted fools think we can't repair the ship on our own because they are not here to tell us how? But did they actually look at the damage reports? Did they actually understand you can't repair that kind of hull damage without a repair doc? No, they don't. They think their little checklists will fix it all."

"'I'll take care of it from here. You head back to the engine room. I'll see if I can sort it out," Jax said, trying to give Rose a supportive face.

"Damn right I will. You tell them if they want to insult my repairs, they can drag their asteroid butts up to the ship and actually get their hands dirty. Screen loving fools," Rose said, stomping off the bridge. Everyone heard her triad on the way out. The echoing sound of Roseisms lasted long after she was gone.

Jax panned her head around the room and realized everyone was staring. Jax shrugged, shook her head, and went to work.

She scanned the reports the review team had sent over. Their primary concern seemed to be a list of things the "screen loving fools" thought should have been completed. The ENG crew had done it all and more, but the review team wasn't buying it. They didn't see how the repairs were possible with the reduction in the crew and the amount of damage. In her mind's eye, Jax could see how justifying each little thing would be annoying. She pushed the report away and turned her attention to the main screen on the command table. ENG could wait a moment. She wanted to see what else was happening.

Her eyes gleamed as she studied the screens. *Ares* was cruising into a new, at least to her, solar system. The planets unveiled themselves before her, small labels accompanying each. The old Earth names seemed a strange mix mash to her, and she only recognized some of them.

At the center of the solar system was a yellow dwarf star, labeled "Sun". Furthest out from the sun, three dwarf planets zipped along. Their orbits were more oval, and they crisscrossed each other. They were named Athos, Porthos, and Aramis. Next in line were two planets that looked like twins, both larger than Jupiter. Dead, rocky worlds with simple rings accenting them. These bore the names Inanna and Utu. Close to the sun was a Mercury-sized planet speeding its way around, named Savitr.

Between Savitr and Inanna was a blue and green orb that demanded Jax's attention: Gaia. Jax opened her own sub screen on the command table and zoomed in on the bright ball. Setting squarely in the habitable zone, Gaia, at a passing glance, was like Earth. Size, clouds, and color were all there. Sparkling with whites, greens, and blues. It was on closer inspection that bought out the difference.

Polar ice caps mimicked Earth's, but besides that, there was only one major continent. Gaia's very own Pangaea. Total land mass was nearly forty percent less than Earth. Islands uncountable were scattered throughout the globe. "Pretty little marble," she whispered, using her finger to trace the image. Something caught her eye in orbit, and she pulled back. "What are those? Space stations?"

"Weapon platforms," the Captain said. Jax jumped but tried to hide the fact. "Weapon platforms? But they're the size of small moons."

"Yup. Gaia is serious about its defense. Two are fully operational. The third is on the far side of the planet and almost done. Fourth one is starting soon."

The image spun in on one platform. It was over twenty-five thousand kilometers in diameter, larger than Pluto. Other statistical data scrolled on her screen. Jax blinked on the weapons section and gasped. The weapons load-out was staggering. A never-ending list of missiles, energy weapons and things she had never heard of scrolled past.

"They are beasts. Not very moveable, but they are heavily fortified. Artificial gravity tech keeps them from affecting the planet. And they use some of the same light-bending technology we have on the *Ares*, so light from the sun is not blocked. I'm sure Rose could give you a more in-depth analysis if you need it," the Captain said.

"No. No, thank you. I think this is more than enough."

She felt her stomach turning over. Bile rose in her throat. On Earth nothing like this existed, it wouldn't even be dreamed of. Try as she might, Jax could not comprehend a universe where such things were necessary. Despite what she had seen with the Screech, this seemed too much. It felt like having a hammer over your head and expected it not to fall. This was her life now, and that simple thought scared her.

"Captain, space traffic control wants us to dock at the Alpha Station," Commander Haddock announced.

"Alpha Station? Do they realize how much damage we have? I was expecting a repair dock or being passed to the shipyard."

"Yes, Captain, they are aware. I've double checked, Alpha Station is the command."

"They want to honor us for a victory," Commander Moro said, a rare, broad smile crossing his face.

Jax raised a questioning eye at the captain. Gemma Lewis met the eye with a smile that was anything but happy and a nod of the head. She seemed annoyed by the prospect.

"So be it. Set course for Alpha Station and prepare to dock."

Jax sent a notice to the ENG crew to prepare to dock. The docking checklist was ready for her, but if she had to guess, ENG was already on it. The best thing for her to do now was stay out of the way. It would still be over an hour before they could dock. While everyone knew their role, she was bored. She decided to study more.

She brought up Alpha Station. After seeing how they had named the planets, she was hoping for something more. Less than half the size of Highgaurd and Alpha Station at in a tighter orbit than the weapon platforms. What Earth called an old-fashioned space station. It had an outer ring rotating around an inner cylinder core. Ships could dock with the outer ring to transfer cargo or people as needed. A quick stopping point for goods being brought to and from the planet.

The internal docking berths are reserved for ships like the *Ares* that needed repairs. *Ares* would eventually need more work than the station could handle. A repair frame, or repair doc, would be needed to fix the hull. The repair doc would surround the *Ares* in a skeleton like web for the large-scale repairs.

The shipyard was her other point of interest, since it could also be used for repairs. It was located several hours on the far side of the Gaia solar system. Nestled near a rogue planet that they mined for materials. The massive space complex was churning out ships. Large wire frame space docks housed dozens of ships. On Earth, this complex would be automated, EVE units running the show. On Gaia, the opposite was true. While some AI-assisted units helped, the workforce was largely manual. Combat vessels were the principal work, but cruisers, shuttles, and even some Earth-style ships were being worked on. As she scrolled its ship manifest, she made a startling discovery. Two *Ares* class ships sat ready to be used. A third was in the final stage of completion. The *Menrva*, the *Perun*, and the *Segomo*.

Her curiosity peeked as she waved for the captain. "Why are they just sitting there?" Jax said, pointing at the listing. "We could have used the help."

The captain nodded as she said, "We could have. It all comes down to captains and crew. Gaia has a good number of people, but not everyone is in the military. We can build them faster than we can crew them." The captain placed a hand on Jax's shoulder. "It's why we need good people."

Jax turned to her, grinned, and gave a nod of her own. Could one of these ships be for her? She had wanted to explore the galaxy, search the stars for new wonders. This was something different, however.

The *Ares* floated into Alpha Station. Docking berth number 4 awaited them with open arms. The other inner berths all stood empty. Which left plenty of room for the NAV crew to place the *Ares* into spot. "We are docked. Mooring clamps in. Welcome back everyone," Commander Bard announced from the pilot's seat.

"It's good to be back," the Captain said. "All division commanders secure your posts and let your teams handle disembarking procedures. I've just received word that all command staff have been requested for a meeting on Alpha. You have fifteen to get into your service dress and be in air lock one."

"Yes, Captain," Commander Moro said, the glee in his voice ringing out. "We shall be honored."

Jax rolled her eyes. She was pretty sure everyone on the bridge did. Still, they filed out of command, a sway in their steps. Fifteen minutes was not much time to get ready.

In her room, she pulled her service dress uniform from the box under the bed. Folded and stored because she had never had a call to wear it.

Changing, she pulled up a full length holoscreen to use as a mirror. Gaia preferred real mirrors, but the little mirror on the wall wouldn't do. Such practice seemed silly to her. The uniform was a perfect fit. No crease or seams, the wonders of modern fabric. It was a bit too blue for her liking. She would have preferred it darker, but it was still a nice shade. Her hair was longer than when she last checked, her dark auburn locks pushing past her shoulders.

She checked the buttons down the single-breasted suit. Silver with a hint of gold and embossed with the same star as on the Fleet logo. At the end of her sleeves were the two lieutenant rank bars matching the buttons in color. The straight leg pants and black dress shoes finished it off. She grabbed the white-brimmed hat; the Fleet logo embossed proudly on its dark blue face and placed it under her arm. Much like the captain's hat on the *Indiana,* the thing didn't fit right.

Having wasted all the time she could, she made out for airlock one. Quick steps, down some stairwells, and she arrived with little thought. She stepped through the portal to the staging area for the airlock. The staging area was a large open space. Designed with military ceremony in mind, it was wide enough for personnel to maintain rank and file on the sides with a formal walkway down the middle. Used for welcoming VIP's on and off the ship. Today it stood empty, except for the command team gathered at the airlock hatch.

As she walked up stiff backed, the Captain greeted her. "Glad you could join us, Lieutenant," the Captain said, smiling. The Captain's eyes seemed to measure Jax. She realized every one of the command staff was eyeing her.

Eyeing them back, it dawned on her. All the command officers wore ribbons, medals, and stars over their left breast. Commander Moro seemed to have the most awards. On their sleeves, each of them also had cardinal-colored vertical stripes. Gemma had four, Terrance and Issac had three each. Lilly's stripes were seven deep and gold. Jax glanced at her own sleeves.

"I don't think I've ever seen a slick sleeve so slick," the Captain said, a wicked grin gracing her face.

"At least it doesn't hurt the eyes like some eye candy I've seen." Commander Bard laughed, making a small thumb towards Terrance Moro.

"Every accomplishment I have is hard earned, I assure you."

"Of course it is," Lilly Bard said. The Captain, Commander Haddock, and Lilly all suppressed laughter.

"This was all the vanityfab made for me when I was getting my uniform," Jax said, shrugging. "Was I supposed to have something else?"

"No, you're fine. Rarely do you see a command rank with so little to show for it. A 'slick sleeve', someone without awards or time served ribbons, is rare. It makes you novel," the Captain said, turning and looking at the commanders.

"Shows her experience," Commander Moro muttered, turning as if he had not said a word. Jax felt her eyes flare at him, the phoenix rising, not that he would notice.

"Shall we go?" The Captain ushered them forward.

They nodded, except for Commander Moro, who said, "Yes, Captain, we are ready." Jax didn't think his chest could get any larger.

The *Ares'* inner air lock cycled, and they walked forward. Alpha Station had extended a sealed walkway. Once the outer airlock opened, an open bridge would connect the two. A moment's pause and a hiss of air. The outer seal popped, and the way was clear. The *Ares* command team walked onto Alpha Station.

The Captain led, with Commander Moro nipping at her heels. Commander Bard and Haddock walked side by side. Jax followed in their shadows. Issac Haddock's muscular form blocked much of her view. The two commanders chatted something about Founder's Day being soon and how nice it would be to have leave at that time. Did they want to go to the Ball later? The tunnel was short, but as they cleared it, a high-ceilinged room opened around them. While walking behind the commanders obscured her view, Jax was sure it was a larger version of the receiving area. She could make out troops standing in formation, awaiting their arrival. Jax hoped she could continue hiding behind Commander Haddock.

Jax bumped into the commander when he stopped. The Captain was shouting, "What in the damn abyss is this?"

Jax peaked her head around Commander Haddock. Her eyes shot wide with realization. The formation of troops was all military police. She had seen plenty of those as a kid on Earth. The bright white armbands with the black letters 'MP' shining like a beacon.

Standing in the middle was a skinny man. Too skinny by far. His black hair slicked back on his head, a pointy chin, and a hawk-like nose. His black suit was high-collared and blended perfectly with his shirt and shoes. A shadow standing.

"These are the department heads, Commander Lewis?" the shadow asked, disgust layering each word. His hands folded behind his back; his head tilted as if listening.

"Of course. I'll ask again what is going on?" Gemma Lewis' voice growled.

"I'm Attaché Estaban. By the authority of the Gaia government, I hereby place you all under arrest."

"Arrest? On what charge?" Gemma spit the words.

"Treason," the shadow, Attaché Estaban, said. A smile oozed across his face as the MPs moved in, and the *Ares*'s command staff were marched off.

Chapter 5

PLAYING GAMES

J ax was bored.

She sat in the small brightly lit room, her chair, a table, and the chair across from her the only furniture. There were no clocks and they had disabled her ability to pull up a holoscreen. Nothing to occupy her time and nothing to say what time had passed. An MP stood by the door, a human statue, but even less animated. She remembered guys like him from her childhood. Their personalities were equal to that of a rock.

What is it with people from Gaia putting me in rooms? The whole scenario ran through her head. As a kid, the MPs did the same thing to her when she was causing trouble. Isolate her and let her sit, let the worry set in, until the 'big scary person' in charge would enter. On cue, the door sprung open, and two men entered. She sat stiffly and stared blankly at the wall. She suppressed a laugh, as she realized the *Ares* did this so much better. A dark room, strange creatures to keep her off balance, noises for distraction. The *Ares* had treated her as someone to respect, these people were treating her like a kid to bully. She fell back into the training her dad had given her.

Her dad always found her trouble with the MPs to be amusing. She got away with more than they ever knew, but even she got caught. At first, she had been scared; the MPs were good at fear. Her father believed in facing such things, so he taught her their strategies and how to beat them. "Knowledge is how you face fear, how you conquer it and make it work for you," he would say. She felt warm hearing his voice echo through her memories. He told her not to get caught, to not cause trouble again, but if she did... Life was always like a game with her father. Pitting his daughter versus the MPs was just another challenge. Jax felt ready to play this game.

The first man to enter the room sat in the chair across from her. He wore a well-tailored dark gray single-breasted suit. White button-up shirt with a black tie. His hair was styled like something from a sales advertisement. A small curly light brown lock hanging above his eyes.

The other man took up position behind the first. His bigger frame and thicker neck filled an outfit similar to Corps fatigues, but not any military look she was familiar with. His high and tight haircut might mark him as military, but there was something off. It wasn't his face, though it seemed too flat and had a nose that looked broken at one point. It was the way he stood. His balance, it wasn't like Gunnery Sergeant Locklear or Corporal Chambers, or even the MP's.

Jax kept her face blank as she sized them up. The one sitting had to be in charge, so that made the other one what? A bodyguard, or some loyal dog, brought in to look tough. She had worked with the Gaia Terrain Corps first-hand, and Jax doubted he was cut from the same cloth. She sank a little into her chair and dropped her eyes. Let them make the first move, let them think she was worried.

The master spoke "Harumi 'Jax' Brandt, you little lady are in a lot of trouble."

They really did think she was some kind of kid. The words spiked Jax's anger, but she pushed the feeling down. She dropped her head more and started drawing little figure eights with her finger on the table. "I don't know what you're talking about?" She mumbled out.

"The Command crew of the *Ares* is being charged with treason. By attacking a Screech ship so deep in Earth space, they have revealed our existence to them. The death of Captain Moss, the damage of *Ares*, it's all very bad. The treason alone warrants a death penalty."

Death penalty? She didn't have to act shocked at that revelation. Earth didn't have a death penalty; it had been abandoned a long time ago. She couldn't imagen why any civilized culture needed a death penalty. She shook her head and decided not to dwell on it now. "I didn't know that.

I fell in with them. They saved me from those Screech things. I don't understand what's going on." She said, a slight tremble in her voice.

"Oh, don't worry, you poor girl. We know this is all strange to you and what you're used to on Earth," he said. Leaning in, a warm smile crossing his face. "We don't blame you, but we need your help." He fingered his wrist and a holo document appeared before her. "DNA mark this statement that you had nothing to do with all these horrors. An innocent bystander and we'll see you removed from danger and taken care of. You can reclaim a life like what you had on Earth."

Then the game was over and Jax saw his hand laid bare. Jax was sad that it was so easy. This guy wasn't very good at this. They want her to be the naïve Earth girl and say how she was used. No subtly at all, was he really dumb enough to think that would work?

She looked up. "What was your name again?"

"Time is of the essence, Ms. Brandt. If you want our protection, we need your mark."

"I haven't read it yet," she said, leaning in and squinting at the document.

"It's full of Gaia legal speak. That will mean little to you. Trust me, it will protect you," he said, his smile growing expectant.

She hovered her hand over the document, centimeters away from making contact. She brought her eyes up quickly and locked with his. Snatching her hand away, she leaned back in her chair. "Maybe I should talk to a lawyer. I do get a lawyer here on Gaia, right?"

"Oh, this one thinks she's funny, Eli," the dog said, a snarl crossing his lips.

Eli held his hand up as if to stall him. "Ms. Brandt, you realize you're up for the death penalty here? Signing this will save you. I'm here strictly for your best interest, I assure you."

"Death penalty does sound pretty serious."

"Yes, Gaia can be a hostile place if you're not careful. Sign that and you will have nothing to worry about. We will drop all charges against you."

"I didn't know I'd been charged. Maybe I should talk to a lawyer first? That is how it works here right, or is it different on Gaia?"

"Lawyers can complicate things." Eli said, the tension in his voice rising. "I don't know how long I can keep this offer on the table."

"What happens to the command officers if I sign that?"

"It is a governmental and military matter, not something that concerns you. The *Ares* crew will be handled I assure you. Please sign, Ms. Brandt."

"It does concern me. They saved me. I've faced some pretty horrible stuff with them. And it's Lieutenant Brandt, thank you very much," she said, letting her voice rise, steel lacing the words.

The dog barked a laugh, slammed his hands on the table and leaned into her. "Look at the little Earther acting all tough. Maybe you should leave her alone with me for a moment, Eli? She'll be shaking with fear in no time."

"Fear? You think I'm afraid of you?" She tilted her head and pointed a finger at the dog. "I'll tell you what I'm afraid of. Taking an unarmed ship against three hostile vessels had me panicked. Stuck alone, fighting a terror of Screech, had me frightened." She leaned in. "Being on a warship, fighting an armada of alien invaders. Losing everything I've ever known. Oh yeah, that scared me. But you, you thick-necked rallitch, Screech-lover, don't even rate!"

The dog's nostrils flared, and he pushed his chin closer. "Wait till I get my hands on you!" he said, spitting at her.

She leaned on the table and put her nose to his. Letting the fire of her anger burn, focused on the dog. "Anytime you think you can handle it! You know, they made me a lieutenant when I decked Commander Moro. I wonder what rank they'll give me for decking you?"

The dog's eyes went wide, and he pulled back. He tried to hide it, but it was too late. They didn't know that about her. They came in here under-estimating her, thinking her an easy target. Now the game had changed, and their advantage had been lost. Jax thought her dad would be proud, but a little critical that she had lost her temper. She was okay with that.

"That's enough, Talbot. I think we're done," Eli said, when the door slammed open. She never flinched, never turned, but the image from the corner of her eye was clear. She sprang to her feet at attention, staying laser focused on Eli and Talbot. Talbot jumped, fell back a couple of steps, eyes wide. The image at the door had paused a moment to survey the room. She had only seen him on the holotable aboard the *Ares*. There he had looked frazzled and worn. Now was a different matter.

In full dress uniform, a darker blue than the service uniform. Double-breasted and so sharp it could cut like a knife. His hat with its full gold leaf decoration across the brim rested firm on his head. Admiral Bill Koonce entered the room. "I think you are done here, Mr. Dakos," he said, his voice like iron, his gaze impaling Eli Dakos. "Lieutenant Brandt, Commander Lewis is waiting for you in the hall. Let her know I will be there shortly. I have some wisdom to hand out first."

"Aye aye, Admiral," she said, saluting, giving a wink and a half-smile to Eli and Talbot. Turning sharply on her heel and toe, she marched out the door.

In the hall, Commander Gemma Lewis was pacing like a caged animal. As she rounded back, her tight face relaxed and let loose a deep breath. "Jax, are you okay?" Gemma asked, grabbing her by the shoulder.

A smile beamed across Jax's face as she said, "I feel like a kid again. That might have been better for me than all Doc's therapy sessions combined."

Gemma's face lit up and let out a half laugh, half grunt. "That's good to hear. I was having doubts when we couldn't find you right away. The rest of the team is in station Command. We'll wait for the Admiral and then join them. You sure you're okay?"

"Positive. Unlike when I first came on the *Ares* that..." She pointed a thumb over her shoulder. "Is something I know how to deal with. They should have tried harder, and they really shouldn't let me get so bored."

"Oh, no."

"Oh, yes."

"I almost feel bad for them. Who were you talking to in there? Everyone else was on the far side of the station. I got some tablet-pusher trying to scare me. I had him crying to leave before he stepped two steps into the room," Gemma said with a laugh. Jax remembered that Gemma Lewis had started in the Terrain Corps, switched to Fleet security, and worked her way to *Ares* XO. Such experience would give her a fine grasp of Gaia legal procedures.

"Someone named Eli Dakos and his guard dog. They wanted me to sign a document that would save me, but I'm sure it would have condemned the *Ares* crew at the same time."

"Eli Dakos? Wow, you got the royal treatment. He's a government representative. Came close to being the Prime Representative at the last election. What's his stake in this? I know he is strong on Gaia's independence, but why do this? Could this be a Gaia First thing?" Gemma questioned. Jax could see the ideas running through the commander's head. "If he is, then they probably thought you were some Earth refugee, or token officer, a weak link, that we picked up on the way. Get you by yourself and break you. Use your confession as leverage against us. But what does discrediting the *Ares* actually gain them though?"

"You got me. He was insistent that I sign. The way you're talking makes me feel like I should actually go back in there and break him. I'll show him a weak link." Her fists clinched, head turning back to the room.

Gemma's hand held Jax off as she spoke. "Keep it cool, Jax. I'm sure the admiral is unleashing more punishment than either of us could manage. Let him do his thing and then we'll get together with the others. Nobody attacks the *Ares* without consequences, I guarantee it."

"I hope so. This is not what I was expecting for my first visit to Gaia," Jax said, and Gemma could only nod as they waited for the admiral.

Chapter 6

HEART OF GAIA

The Admiral marched from the room and homed in on the two officers. His grim face broke into a smile. Like iron bending as he said, "I have not imparted knowledge such as that in a long time. That man is an idiot. I shall file a formal complaint with the civilian half of the High C later." The High C, was the Humanistic Commonwealth. Gaia's two-part governing structure was made up of the military and civilian sides. "Officers. Shall we proceed to the station bridge?" Gemma and Jax checked each other from the corners of their eyes and gave nods.

"Admirals first," Commander Lewis said, waving a hand down the hall. The Admiral gave a tilt of his head and the trio strolled away. The halls reminded Jax of the *Ares*. Four times bigger but the same metal gray and dark rubberized flooring. Gaia's pragmatic style stood in sharp contrast to what Jax was accustomed to from Earth. An Earth-based hallway would be two or three times larger still. With bright colors, designer floors, and the occasional work of art adorning the walls. She missed the aesthetics of it all but had to admit her fondness for the practical was growing.

The Admiral set a brisk pace to the Alpha Station command center. The double-wide portal was open as they entered. Crossing the threshold, Jax stopped and marveled. Command centers on Earth space stations were based on a classic layout. Multiple rows of workstations arranged to peer at a large main screen. It was the one part of an Earth space station that focused on usability over style. It had worked for centuries, and the powers that be felt no need to change.

The Alpha bridge was altogether different. The immense room opened before her. Its high domed ceiling showed blue skies and clouds, as if the command center was planet side. In the middle of the room, Gaia rotated on its axis. Over a story tall, the planet's avatar dominated the view. The weapon platforms, space station, and both natural moons were all to be found. Spaceships zipped to-and-fro, each orbit tracked and mapped. The planet, its entire space ecosystem, was brought to life in perfect miniature.

Closest to the planet avatar, at ground level, was a ring of standing workstations. Technicians would pull up holoscreens, perform tasks, close them, and move on. A second and third ring encircled the inner one. These levels were each elevated several meters, angling away from the center. Here technicians sat at familiar looking tables, noses buried deep in concentration.

They had entered on the fourth level, a raised platform that encompassed the whole thing. Head and shoulders above the other rings. Still, they were below the mid-point where the planet rotated before them. A generous walkway connected four platforms equally spaced around the room. Each platform had standing workstations facing towards Gaia but looked to serve more as a viewing or meeting area. Scattered people moved, worked, or watched aspects of the world as Jax took it all in.

While she stood gawking at the setup, admiral and Commander Lewis continued their walk to the right. Snapping out of her wonderment, she double-timed her step to catch up. Clustered together on the next platform were Commanders Bard, Haddock, and Moro.

Admiral Koonce was speaking. "Is that everyone, Commander Lewis?"

"Yes, Admiral. It seems only the command crew was targeted. Now, would it be possible for you to tell me why?" Commander Gemma Lewis asked while the rest of *Ares'* command gathered around.

"The *Ares* defense of Earth has sent a major shockwave through Gaia. Earth can no longer deny the existence of hostile alien forces. And if they don't know it yet, they will soon discover that some human force is out here fighting that threat. Military command and the civilian council are in a panic trying to determine a course of action."

"This is the first we've heard any of this. Why weren't we informed?" the Captain asked.

"Military command decided you had enough on your hands. You needed to focus on getting back in one piece," the Admiral said, his eyes scanning each of the officers. "You should have been welcomed as heroes. It seems other forces were at play. Someone is playing games with the *Ares* and Fleet. I wasn't even notified you had entered the system. That's a level of interference I cannot tolerate."

"Is this the Gaia First movement?"

"Unknown, I suspect so, but Representative Dakos denies he is a part of that movement. He claims he was just following the 'will of the people.' We will have to investigate where he got that idea and look deeper into Gaia First."

"If this is Gaia First, this seems more than the work of some fanatical fringe group. Interrupting Fleet communications. Getting a rep from Gaia to do your bidding. That's a lot of power coming from somewhere."

"Agreed. Obviously, we underestimated them, or certain politicians, we will correct that," the Admiral said. He stopped to acknowledge two nonmilitary personnel approaching. A woman and man moving side by side down the far walkway. The lady walked like she was style and grace personified, wearing a dark gray single-breasted suit jacket that was buttoned at her navel. The dress underneath was anything but business. Simple and black, that hugged her body like it was painted on. Her hair had a metallic shine, glistening silver, and was pulled tight with curls, topping it off. Her bold face looked carved in stone.

Jax couldn't pin down the man who was with her. He kept changing. Jax blinked and shook her head. First, he was tall and slender, dressed to mirror the lady. A few steps and in a blink and he was an older gentleman with a graying beard, wearing a knitted sweater. Blink again and his appearance matched Commander Moro's except he was wearing a white version of the military dress.

The Admiral turned and said, "For those that have not had the pleasure, allow me to introduce—" He was interrupted as the blinking man blew past him and came nose to nose with Lieutenant Brandt.

"You're Jax!" he said. Blink and he was an old Roman soldier. Gold breast plate, red cape, and a white knee-length woolen tunic. "I love your pathjackers. Marvelous idea. You should come to work for me. The things we can create together." Blink. A bald man in a business suit and red tie. "I can have contracts done up."

Jax staggered back a step. Her throat choked, trying to find the words as her mind raced. *What the abyss is going on?*

"Nath, you've startled the poor lieutenant. You should introduce yourself first," the lady said, her eyes rolling.

"Ah yes," he said and blinked again. He was half a head shorter now, wearing a tweed dinner jacket and dress shirt unbuttoned at the top. Striking brown eyes complimented his complexion. Short hair cropped close completed the sharp style. "My apologies," he said, giving a bow. "I am Nath. Of Nath Industries. Maker of technologies, fine weapons, and warships. Would you like to work for me?"

"I just floated the idea. It was Commander Urd and the engineering crew that did the work." Jax throat chocked thinking of the smiling commander. "Probably better to talk to LTG1 Koike. She did a lot of the work on them."

"Oh? I must talk to this Lieutenant Junior Grade! Are they here?" he said, his head whipping around.

Before she could answer, the admiral jumped back into the conversation. "Nath, I've told you to not pilfer my personnel. And stop switching your image. You're making me space sick."

The biggest frown Jax had ever seen drooped down Nath's face. "No one appreciates the genius of personal holo technology combined with an adjustable nano exo-suit. I am not switching images, my dear admiral. I am becoming what my mood dictates I need to be," Nath said, his hand flaring into the air, staring back at the Admiral.

The Admiral said nothing, but the look of 'I don't care' was plain on his face. The staring match stretched until Nath broke. Shuffling back to the lady, his physical appearance didn't change, but his suit returned to the outfit that mimicked hers. A last bit of defiance.

The Admiral seemed not to notice as he said, "As I was saying. You have met Nath, and this is Prime Representative Emma Gibson."

The Prime Representative, Jax's mind raced. She was basically one half of the Gaia government. Her position was like being the President of the entire planet. Along with the high marshal, who controlled both branches of the military, together they governed Gaia society. Working in unison, they decided the laws and policies across the spectrum. The military side was aided by the majors and admirals. The civilian side had representatives that covered different areas of Gaia society. Habitable areas, the space station, guilds from different industries were all repped in the civilian council.

A third party also existed, the majority council. Should the civilian and military sides fail to agree on some point, then all members of Gaia got a vote. The vote was a simple for, against or null. The people of Gaia could access everything their government did. Including the military, no secret or top secret existed here. Every official meeting recorded, every message archived, all business activities tracked. As Jax understood it, a citizen could call up and review any necessary information at any time to make their own decisions. A majority vote decided it all. Jax was amazed to learn this, the ultimate tie breaker.

PR Emma Gibson was making rounds. "Commander Moro, a pleasure to see you again. Looking as sharp as always."

Commander Moro beamed as he shook the PR's hand. "The pleasure is mine, as always, madam Prime."

Jax kept her scoff to herself. It made sense to her that Terrance Moro would be known to the world leaders. Even so, the thought still soured her mind.

The Prime flounced past Commander Bard. "Lilly."

"Emma." Lilly Bard's response was a bit tighter than the Primes, but only a bit.

"Ah Commander Haddock, your reputation precedes you. We must talk linguistics someday. You could help our council on creating a native Gaia language."

"I would be honored, but I doubt my obligations to Fleet and the *Ares* will allow much time for it Madam Prime," Commander Haddock said shaking her hand and brandishing his awkward smile.

It was now that Jax realized the PR was "pressing flesh" as her mom used to say. Her dad would say B.S., if mom was around, and not use the acronym if she wasn't. It was small talk designed to sound sincere, while actually not giving a damn. Her mom and dad attended such parties when she was a kid. Only to come home and complain about the entire situation.

Then she got to Jax. "And you must be the Lieutenant Brandt who I have heard so much about. You're almost a princess here with how famous your parents are," the PR said as her eyes weighed Jax, judging her worth, and casting her fate all in the blink of an eye. "You really must tell me the story of this middle name of yours someday. I'm dying to know. I love a good mystery," the PR leaned in and dropped her voice. "Just between us girls, of course." The PR waved her off, turning away. Jax stood staring after the PR, her mouth agape.

The PR continued, "A pleasure, all. I really wish I had the time to enjoy it more. For now, we need to speak with your XO, or I guess I should say acting captain. About your current situation. Horrible. Simply horrible. We shall see that this never happens again. You are heroes to Gaia, one and all." The PR gave a slight bow to her head. "Now, Admiral, Nath, and Commander Lewis, if you would please join me. We have a quick meeting with the High Marshal."

The Prime Representative strode off as quickly as she came. Not checking to see if anyone was following. Simply expecting to be followed. Nath fell right in step. The Admiral and commander were a few feet out of pace and needing to catch up.

What were they supposed to do now? Jax looked around at the rest of the crew. Commander Moro had turned to look out over the rail. His head tilted up, chest out like a lord looking over his subjects. She was not going over there.

Commander Bard and Haddock were huddled together and shuffled off to the side. The look on Issac Haddock's face reminded Jax of her father's face when he had upset her mom. Concern, confusion, and anger all mixed into one. *Are those two involved?* She was definitely not going over there.

She turned to look out over the image of Gaia hung in the middle of the room. A technician was at the closest workstation. The tech's hand waved and a holo screen superimposed itself over Gaia. The image was a spectacular view of light and color, the universe laid out.

Like a moth to a flame, it drew her in. She eased up to the technician, her eyes wide with wonder. Upon the universe, streaks of color flew, lines of reds, yellows, and greens. "What is this?" she asked, causing the tech to jump.

He turned and glanced at her, regaining his composure. A skinny fleetwalker with reddish brown hair, his voice squeaked like a mouse. "It's a star chart of Screech activity, ma'am. They've been acting strange since the *Ares* beat them down."

A bit of pride swelled Jax's chest. "Strange how?"

"They're disappearing from their regular patterns. When we do find them, they are evasive. They are gone completely from their more densely populated space. Very strange. Keeps us busy hunting and updating sightings."

"I see." Her eyes scanned the holo. She remembered the wave pattern they had shown her those first days aboard the *Ares*. This was similar, more expansive, so much information to process. Space was a big place, and it was obvious by this view that they were missing a complete picture. While the lines moved and updated, a sparkle caught her eyes. Faint purple dots speckled parts of the screen. "What are those?"

The fleetwalker gave a sad smile. "Those are places where we have confirmed other alien civilizations. Ones that the Screech has completely destroyed. We leave them up to remind ourselves what they are like. What they can do."

The private shook his head and continued inputting data. Jax's heart sank looking at those dots. *So many alien species we could have met. So many opportunities lost.* She began to memorize those lights. She wondered what the faces of those aliens looked like?

"Lieutenant Brandt. Jax!" Commander Gemma Lewis's voice snapped her around. The look on Gemma's face was one of icy rage. She was posed like she was ready to grab someone and spike them into the ground.

"Commander?" Jax said. Pulling back, she was afraid she had caused the commander's agitation.

"Let's go. We are out of here." The Commander stalked off. The rest of the *Ares* officers were already in step. Jax rushed up beside Commander Bard.

A whisper passed Jax's lips, "Things did not go well, I take it?"

Commander Bard shrugged as the group attempted to keep pace with Commander Lewis. The forced march continued down corridors and a lift. No one dared to speak. Entering a portal, the group came to a stop in a hangar bay.

Gathered in a circle, Commander Lewis cut to the quick. "We've been placed on leave while they investigate what happened here." Gemma could foresee the question and objections coming. She raised her hand to stall them off. "The government, both military and civilian, will look into what happened here today. They will determine who is responsible, Gaia First, or another entity. Once they have more information, they will then decide on a course of action. We are to have no hand in it."

Around the circle, stiff backs became stiffer. They heard the command and knew there would be no arguing with it. Whispers grumbled to themselves was all anyone managed.

"The *Ares* is being evaluated for repairs and figuring out a time for her return. They have to decide if we are going to be in a waiting pattern or reassigned," Gemma said, raising her hand. "This is from on high. We are on leave. We can use the time off. None of us can argue with that." From her tone, it was obvious that she had argued about it. "I should say a working leave. Some of us will still have assignments until they make decisions, and they can figure out what to do with us. Everyone gets at least a couple days to yourself. So, we'll head planet side, and you can pick your destination from there. Relax and enjoy." The last words dropped with a scowl.

Grim faces stared blankly at each other. Yes, they could use the time off, but they also wanted to fight back. To find who had set them up like this and bring to them equal retribution. It's what they were trained to do. Who they were. Those options were now denied to them and that weighed hard on their core.

Except for Jax. Her mind danced to other thoughts. "Huh. Captain, I mean Commander?" She said, trying to figure out the proper etiquette in this situation. "What does this mean for me? I have no idea where I'll be sleeping, let alone a place to take a vacation."

Gemma's face softened. "Don't worry, Jax, we've pulled a few strings. You've got a place waiting for you in the same compound as me. We'll take a bus down and I'll show you where to go. We'll be the first stop. Shall we go?" Grim nods from the officers were the only answer. They turned and made their way to the bus.

The bus reminded Jax of the *Reckless*. Except it was bigger, had more room in the seating area, comfortable counter seats, and it didn't rattle while it flew. Other than those points, it was the same. They loaded up and in no time, they were on their way.

The ride down was uneventful. Gemma and Issac sat together, talking in hushed tones. Lilly and Terrance had seats off on their own, both stone faced the entire trip. Jax sat in the back. The bus was empty except for the *Ares* officers, so she stretched out in a row by herself.

The bus touched down and Jax's eyes popped open. She had dozed off on the brief trip. She pulled up a small holo on her wrist and checked the local time. She was grateful to see it matched her mood. 01:24. Gaia's day was only forty-two minutes longer than Earths, so she wouldn't need many adjustments.

The air was crisp as they stepped off the bus. Jax followed Gemma away from the landing pad and toward the skyscraper. The engines on the bus roared as it continued on its way.

The building doors slid open as they approached. "You're on the thirtieth floor. Usually, the upper floors are for more senior officers, but like I said, I pulled some strings," Gemma said, attempting a smile, but obvious deep thoughts weighed her down.

"Thanks. I wasn't thinking too far ahead," Jax said, waving her hands around, "about this."

"You're welcome. I figured you could use something nice after all you've been through."

The lift zipped them up and Jax stepped out. Gemma stayed behind, pointing down the hall to the left. "Room is 3008. It's already keyed to you. Get some sleep and I'll see you for lunch. I think both of us can use the rest. Oh, and enjoy the view." Gemma said, this time a smile sneaking on her face.

Jax turned. "Where are you off to?"

"I'm on forty. Room 11. The compound's directory can help you find me, or anything you need. Sorry to dump and run, but I still have some red tape to work through."

"I understand," Jax said with a wave. The doors closed and Gemma was off. Jax turned and ambled down the hall.

The doors to 3008 opened as she approached, but she paused before entering. A short hall and a living room opened up before her. The basic furniture, what her dad would call Government Issue, littered the room. It wasn't a style she cared for, but she was too tired to care. Her focus shifted, the drab couch and chairs falling from her vision like a meteor shower. Past the furniture, past the large bay window, lay Soteria City.

Soteria City was the only major city on Gaia. It was a place of safety and preservation. A place where you could build a society that could defend itself, unlike Earth. That's what they had been telling her, anyway. Built in a large circle, the city unraveled before her. A giant ash tree, as tall as a skyscraper, was at its center. Around it were kilometers of farmers' markets and craft fairs, currently hidden in the night. Green, rolling hills were next, but Jax knew these were houses built to blend into the landscape. The outer rings were the skyscrapers, not the heavy metal of Earth architecture. Soft, flowing patterns that grew like artwork toward the sky. Along the edges and tops of each high rise were trees, shrubs, and other vegetation. From the sky, no city could be seen. The natural contours of the planet were preserved.

Each section of the outer ring was a dedicated space. She was in the section for Fleet, while the corps section was next door. Businesses like Nath Industries had their own section somewhere on the hub. The government and other professional offices all had their own space. All of it looking back at the center, the Heart of Gaia. The giant Ash tree was the centerpiece of the city. Standing over four hundred meters tall, it dominated the skyline. Its branches reaching out, leaves rustling in the nighttime air. *Can't wait to see it during the day.*

Her eyes drifted up from the skyline, and a universe of stars glistened before her. Jax could see every star. The lights of the city were shielded, keeping them from polluting the sky. The shiny lights twinkled and danced across the sky. Gaia's two natural moons, one half full and the other a quarter, added another layer of silver accent to the black crystalline sky. They bathed the top of the Heart of Gaia in a mystical light, like something from a storybook. "So beautiful." *I may not have chosen this place, but I did choose to be here. My life is my own and I'm starting to believe I can make this my...*

Her thoughts interrupted; her world exploded.

Chapter 7

NO BACKBONE

J ax was flying.

The shockwave hit her like running headfirst into a wall. Glass and debris slashed her face as the scenic window imploded. Her breath expelled from her lungs. She twisted in the air, pain erupted from her shoulder as she came to a stop and dropped to the floor. She could feel the wall, or table, she couldn't tell. Her whole body vibrated from the blast. Her mind scrambled, lights flashing, her ears shook with the mix of wind and the roar of engines.

Facedown on the floor, head pulsing, she turned, trying desperately to focus. *Need to orientate myself. Get ready. Fight back. This must be the kitchen island, window over there, focus.* She pushed up, an outcry escaping her lips. Her muscles felt like jelly, they wouldn't respond. Sitting was as far as she got. Back pressed hard against the island, trying to find the willpower to stand. Over the thunderous noise, bellowing into the apartment, words filtered into her head.

"... can't... still awake... hit... get her."

"...tough... Earther... if she... takes this..."

Overlapping images assaulted her vision. Blurry forms of men advancing on her, fists raining down. Jax held her hand up in a vain attempt to protect herself. To do something. Her head snapped around and she rolled back to the floor. The taste of blood filled her mouth and grunts of pain accompanied them. Her ears cleared while the rest of her body continued to fail.

"Wow. She's still not out. I must be losing my touch."

"Stop messing around, stun her and let's go."

Jax clawed her way up to an elbow and rolled over. *Get up. Get up. Get up.*

A boot stomped her chest, forcing her back to the ground.

"Where do you think you're going, Earther?" the intruder said, his voice a deep guttural chuckle.

She forced her eyes open, teeth gritting, and tried to buck him off. He laughed again and pressed his boot down harder. Dressed in black combat fatigues, a warped version of the corps gear. He pointed a NEW24 at her nose. "Should we check the little Earther for weapons? You trying to attack me?" He said, his mirrored helmet leaning in closer.

"Karl, just stun her. We have to go."

Her hands wrapped around his ankle. Fingers fumbling to clutch the heavy combat boots. Pushing and pulling the immovable object. He lifted the foot; a gasp of air filled her lungs as he smashed it back down again. The grunt, the yell, was forced from her lips. The barrel of his NEW24 punched her in the belly. Again, she tried to move; she tried to scream, and she failed at both.

"Night–night, Earther," the man in black snarled as he pulled the trigger. The pain rippled through her before sending her into darkness.

Her eyes fluttered. The brightness blinded her, double vision taking a moment to congeal into a single image. She stared into the ceiling lights for a moment, spots dancing before her. Control of her body, and the awareness of her surroundings, slowly returned. Fingers flexing, she felt cold tiles underneath. Rolling her head on the hard ground, orientating to the room. She reached out and found a handhold, hoisting herself up.

Her eyes pinched as she sat up, the pain in her chest, back and hip all flaring. The small cot she had grabbed braced her back. *They* just *dumped me on the floor.* Blinking her eyes a few more times, the cramped room came into focus. Plain white walls, with a cot and a toilet in the corner. A sturdy-looking door closed tight finished the room.

Well, this can't be good. That must be what the NEW24 stun shot feels like. All NEW24's had the capacity of shooting a nanite charged high energy pulse. The pulse would shock the person, stopping their movements. The medical style nanites would then enter the bloodstream and induce unconsciousness. Short range, only a couple meters, its use in day-to-day combat was limited. She was told that the person would be out before they felt anything, she now knew that wasn't true. Pushing herself up from the floor, every bone screamed with pain. She rubbed her hands across her face, wincing as flecks of blood stained her hand. Her left cheek was spongy.

She moved to the door; it was shut tight. Inspecting the room took less than a second. She took her jacket off, rips littered the "slick sleeve" uniform top. Holding it in front of her, she realized the left shoulder of the dress uniform hung by threads. Her ash-colored t-shirt seemed to be intact. Pulling it from her waist so she could move freely. A cool feeling pushed into her lower back. She didn't know if she was being monitored, so she left the feeling alone. A plan started to form.

Instinct took over, and she started to loosen her body. Moving her neck, shoulders, dropping and stretching out her legs, and arching her back. Calisthenics she had worked since joining the *Ares*. Drills hammered into her working judo with Commander Lewis. Focus washed over her as a course of action became clear.

She was tired, but not from her attack, rather from people underestimating her. All her pain, frustration and anger tied up like a ball in her stomach. She gave it focus; she gave it a plan. *They're not expecting you to fight back. Fighting back is all I have; I will not surrender.* She kept moving, feeling the stiffness fall away as muscles warmed up and stretched out. Her eyes, all her senses, stayed focused on the door. Till she heard a click, the door swung open. She would have an instant. A single moment in time to decide how to attack, to overwhelm her captors.

The guard entered lazily, looking for the poor Earther. The blink of an eye was all she had to decide if there was a backup coming with him. No shadows in the hall, no voices. It all registered faster than a laser in her mind. Her hand lashed out, securing his right wrist before he could raise his weapon. A grunt issued from his lips as his eyes went wide. Jerking back, he attempted to pull away. Her right hand sunk deep into his jacket. She pushed at first, matching his direction, his balance faltering, he pushed back into her. Her shoulders tensed and she pulled with all her might, turning and stepping into him. Her foot shooting out, blocking his far-right foot and her knee dropping. The guard went flying over her into the room. *Tai Otoshi! I love this throw.*

Her grip was strong, and she drove all his weight with hers behind it, into the ground. His head and shoulder crunching into the hard tiles. A deep thunk of his skull hitting the floor echoed across the small room. He yelled out, the pain exploding from him.

Her knee drove into his chest, punching the air out, cutting off his breath. She had to keep him quiet, keep him immobile. Surprisingly, he kept his grip on the NEW24. Jax sunk her wrist grip tighter and turned the gun away. She glanced at the door, a moment of fear fading as she watched it closing, not even the creak of a hinge. No back up, no other guards coming in. No alarms sounded, and only the harsh breathing of the guard broke the silence.

The guard struggled under her knee. His chest heaved, his body wriggled, trying to relieve the pressure. She reached back and grasped the bit of hope she had felt while stretching. Twenty-two centimeters of black and gray swirling colors pulled from its sheath. They hadn't even thought enough of her to check for weapons. Jax bet this guy wished he had.

She laid the blade flat on his face, its edge pressed under the crevice of his nostril. "You make a sound, and you lose your nose. You understand?" A blank stare met her question. She leaned in, her knee spiking his chest. Breath hissed from his mouth; his eyes darted around, confusion giving way to worry. She pressed the knife harder, the blade breaking the skin, her voice growling. "Do you understand me?"

He nodded, a small shake of his head, a bead of blood trickling down his face.

"I know you think I'm just a little Earth girl, but I've fought my way through a whole terror of Screech with this knife. One of you won't be a problem." He was shaking, he gulped, breathing deep as he did. "First thumb the DNA lock off on the NEW24. Slowly and keep your finger off the trigger." She kept a side eye on his hand as it scrolled the screen and deactivated the gun lock. She slid her hand from his wrist to the gun.

Securing it, she hopped off the guard. Sheathed the knife and shouldered the weapon, smooth and clean.

"Now, nice and quiet, tell me where I am?" she said, while at the same time enabling the DNA lock for herself. A few more flips of the thumb, arranging all the NEW24's settings to her liking. Not even looking at the NEW24 screens, the motion came to her like an old friend.

"Well Spring Province. Base of the Throwing Rock Mountains." The guard's voice squeaked out.

Jax stared. The Information did nothing for her. She had studied Gaia, but not its maps. She was worried about someone coming, about alarms sounding. She backed up to the door, made sure it was closed, and listened. Nothing. She let the mantra of the corps soothe her. Slow is smooth, smooth is fast. She had time to rework her plan. "I take it we flew here. Where's the landing pad from here?"

"You'll never make it. There are hundreds of us out there," he said, his voice rising. He sat up, bracing against the back wall, sandwiched between the cot and the toilet.

"I didn't ask your opinion. Where is it?"

"Screw you."

She pulled the trigger, and the red beam slashed the floor. The guard yanked back his feet, panic painting his face. The crackle of the beam combined with his scrambling feet echoed in the small room.

"You're fripping crazy!" he gasped.

She made her face look like steel. "The next one cuts you in half. According to you, I've got no chance, so I've got nothing to lose."

"Landing pad is on the far side of the complex. You'll never make it, even if you are a crazy ass Earther," he said, his voice returning to a loud whisper.

"You think I'm crazy? You're the ones attacking other humans when there are monsters out there. Monsters that don't care what planet you call home."

"Earth is weak. We can't protect them and ourselves. Better to cut it loose."

"Cut it loose? Cut it loose? Weak?" she said, closing the distance between the two. She sighted down the NEW24, targeting his head. "Do I look weak to you?"

His eyes popped with fear. His head shook ever so slightly, sweat dripping from his brow.

"You want to let billions die? Men and women? Children?"

"You don't understand."

"Oh, I'm starting to understand just fine. You're all disgusting."

"What would you know, Earther? Disgusting is thinking you live in paradise while the universe revolves around you. Being protected like babies, unaware of the dangers of life. Disgusting is being too weak to defend yourself," the guard said, raising his chin.

"Looks like I'm defending myself just fine from you." She flashed him a toothy smile. "Maybe it's you who's weak. Without Earth, this place doesn't exist."

"That will change soon. There are more of us than you know, and support for our cause grows daily. People of power seek us out because they, too, know the truth. Earth has reached the end of its time. We will be the strong that survive."

"You might not survive getting out of this room." She leveled the NEW24 at his chest.

Sweat glistened on his forehead, worry crossed his face, but his voice was all defiance. "I don't think you can. You're just a scared little girl. A stinking Earther with no backbone. You can't even...."

She pulled the trigger.

Chapter 8

TENDER FOOT

The guard's body seized; his mouth opened to scream, but only a low, guttural noise could be heard. The convulsions stopped, and he lay limp on the floor. *That was gruesome.* Jax had never used the stun setting before. *Did I look like that when they stunned me? Yuck.*

Her steps were cautious as she approached him. Kneeling, she checked his pulse, a small snort escaping his nose as she pressed fingers to neck. *Good, he's out. Better than killing him, I guess. Humans aren't supposed to be monsters. What is wrong with these people?* "Now is not the time for this," she whispered, forcing her mind back on track.

She peeked out the door. A long-whitewashed hallway greeted her. She slipped out and hugged the wall. *Slow and smooth, step-by-step, like the corridors in the Nest. I can do this. He said the hanger pad was on the far side of the complex. Go there and get out. That's the plan, work the plan.*

She paused at the doors, listening to see if the rooms beyond were occupied. If all was quiet, she would do a quick check to clear the room. Door after door was locked, so she passed them. Another hallway branched off. The one ahead looked like more doors and a dead end. She slipped down the new branch. Heavy footsteps echoed like thunder. She fingered a door; it creaked open, and she slipped in. A waft of ammonia and mildew hit her nose. Her eyes ran a quick check and spied mops, brooms, shelves of rags, and sponges. She pressed an ear to the door. The steps continued like the beat of a drum as they passed by. It took forever for them to fade.

She was out the door. Another hallway and another turn. No signs or markings of any kind to indicate where she is going. No windows to give her the hope of escaping these walls. Door after door locked, barring her way, nothing to dictate a direction. *He said there were hundreds of them. Was he exaggerating or am I missing something?*

More footsteps and she pulled back, hiding behind a corner. The NEW24 feeling sweaty in her grip. Peaking a half eye around the corner, a long hallway stretched before her. Double doors sat in the middle of that stretch, at the far end, another hall crossed the way. Guards in formation pounded down that hall. Her ears were sharp as the echo of boots faded. Returning to her previous direction, two guards stepped out of a doorway. Lost in conversation, noses buried in a small wrist holoscreen.

Jax darted down the long hall, the guards' muffled voices chasing her. They hadn't seen her, but they were coming her way. Halfway down the hall, boots could be heard from somewhere ahead of her. She had nowhere left to turn. Her mind sped as she raced for the doors. Desperation building, she gripped a door handle and pushed. The door gave way, and she ran in. A glance around showed the room to be empty, which was all she needed. Closing the entry, her shoulder bracing it, she pressed her ear close to the door. The boots continued to echo, and gruff voices grew louder. They stopped outside the door.

Her muscles coiled, her teeth clenched, as words drifted to her ear. The back of her NEW24 lifting to her forehead.

"Clark back yet? What's taking so long? He was supposed to meet us here by now."

"Probably giving the Earther an old-fashioned G1 welcome. You know how he and his brother are."

"Tell me about it. Karl almost got us caught by those fleetie fools. Such a dumbass. We'll give it a minute and if he isn't back, we'll have to trudge over there. The directors been in a foul mood, so I'm not going in there without his favorite prize."

Jax whipped around. Clark, the guy in her room, this is where he was to bring her. *To the abyss with my luck.* She scanned the room while the NEW24 kept pace. She was in an anteroom. A small fountain that reminded her of Roman architecture bubbled in the of a small, circled enclosure. Two openings on the far side branched off to the left and right.

Hugging the wall, she took gentle steps. The right archway gave way to a small room with a table setting that reminded her of Briefing Room One on the *Ares*. Only shadows filled the room, cast by dimmed lights. The next arch gave way to a hallway that curved around. Peaking as best she could, small glimpses of a room further down became apparent.

She crept down the hallway, checking her six as she went. The guards' voices faded to dull mumbles as unknown voices ahead of her took their place. Sharper with each step, the mumbles took shape and words became sentences. She stopped short of the hallway's end, before entering, she let the words fill her ears.

"...kill her and be done," the first voice said, the tone familiar.

"No. We have to break her first. Make it public. Show that even the progeny of Earth's last great General is worthless to Gaia," the second voice said. The voice was low and had a mechanical ring to it. "Show that Earth is worthless. Too many still cling to the past."

"She's just one girl, I still say remove her and be done with it."

"She's in the spotlight right now. Being on the Ares while they stopped the Screech attack. It gives her credibility. It says to people here that Earth can fight, can join us. The fools want to believe that Earth can be saved, that our original home is not lost."

The first voice was laced with disgust as it said, "Bah, she was little more than a passenger, a token at best."

"We have to show them the truth. We will break her. Make her admit that she wants her soft life back, that even death is preferable to fighting. We can use her to swing those last holdouts, bring those with doubts firmly to our side. Gaia will choose to leave Earth. I've worked hard to get us to this point. She will be the feather that finally breaks the back into our favor."

She pressed her back against the wall and ground her teeth. *Now is not the time to lose your temper, Jax.* She closed her eyes and forced ice into her veins. She saw a chance to end his, to find the powers behind it all. She needed to identify these voices.

Centimeter by centimeter, she slid from the hallway into the room. A grand living room, round like the anteroom, circulated away from her. Large paintings covered the walls like something from a museum. Vases towered over her, breaking up the spaces between the works of art. Pillars rose to support the high ceiling. In the middle of the room was plush, gilded furniture. The look of ivory and gold adorned everything. At the very heart of the area, a man donned in black was communicating with a blurry holo image.

"Should we start with old-fashioned beatings or go straight to synaptic pain Inducers?" The man in black asked.

"Choice is yours. VR mind manipulation might work better. Do whatever it takes..."

Their back and forth on how to break her continued, but Jax tuned it out. Her anger was bubbling and listening to them plan a proper time frame for her torture wasn't helping. *Damn them.* The man in black was speaking clearly, but the holographic image was blurry. Jax knew that it was because of privacy mode, which was used on Earth to prevent people from seeing the image unless they were directly in front of it. The voice could also be contained, but the two men weren't expecting anyone to be listening in.

The man in black itched at her memory. From her vantage, she couldn't make out his face. Staying low, she crept along. One pillar was only a few meters away. She could make it if they stayed focused on their conversation. Careful step by careful step, she moved towards it. She was halfway there when the room shook, the ground rippling beneath her feet. Alarms blazed. Jax froze in place, stabilizing her feet. She worked to not fall over. Was *that an earthquake?*

The man in black circled as the shaking stopped. Their eyes locking and recognition slapped her in the face. *Shadow! What was his name, that guy that arrested us?* "Freeze!" she shouted, bringing the NEW24 to aim.

The holo image blinked out, and with it, the Shadow was running. A section on the far wall slid open. The Shadow darted for the entry. Jax squeezed the trigger, the red beam lancing out. The room shook again, thunderous booms sounding overhead. The unmistakable sound of fighter jets flying low, buzzing the complex.

Her first shot wide, Jax fired again. The ground, a pillar and vase were cut down, but the Shadow continued his run. "Damn," she yelled, holding the trigger while running to close the distance. The shadow merged with the darkness beyond the opening. The door sealed and he was lost behind it.

Jax stopped short, shouldered her weapon, and let the beam fly. The ray splintered into a thousand fragments off the sealed portal. She fired another beam, to be sure. A shield had dropped on the hidden portal, and it held tight.

"Freeze!" a voice barked from behind. She stopped, closed her eyes, and raised her hands.

"Drop the weapon and turn around slowly."

She tossed the weapon and turned. Four guards, all dressed in the black pretend Corps uniforms, leveled their guns at her.

"Hey Karl, it's your Earther girl," a guard shouted, trying to be heard over the alarms.

"Frip me! Where's Clark? He was supposed to pick you up. Someone shut off those alarms. What did you do, girl?" Karl said, approaching from her left, lifting his NEW24. Another guard dropped his nose into a wrist screen and the alarms were quick to fade. Karl continued to yell, "And where's the director? Speak up, you fripping Earther, or do I need to teach you another lesson?" He tried tapping her cheek with the barrel of his gun. Jax shifted, denying him his pleasure.

"Stand still," he snarled, leveling his gun at her face.

"Karl," she said, her tone cold.

"That's right. Now where's Clark and how in the abyss did you get here?" He jammed the barrel of his gun into her chest. "Speak up. Frippin Earther!"

It had been a bad day. Her first on Gaia. Now, here was Karl. Karl, who had blown up her new place. Karl who had beaten her when she couldn't fight back. Karl who was ready to pull the trigger and end her right here. Karl a physical representation of all her anger.

She was trapped and there was nothing she could do. She brought her head up, not wanting to be meek, not willing to give him the satisfaction. She had hoped to survive a little longer and make it to another, better day. She stared at Karl, at each of her attackers, with all the malice she could. Her act of defiance allowed her to see something she had not noticed before. A way out, a change of luck.

Smiling, she said, "Tell you what, Karl. You let me go and we'll forget everything that's happened, and you can walk away."

"Ha! Hear that boys? This Earther's going to go easy on us. What do you think I am? Stupid? Tell you what, girl, tell me what I want to know, and I won't beat you again. Much." He yelled, bringing the gun back up to her eyes.

"You had your chance," she said. "You made the wrong decision, Karl. You've made a mistake only a tenderfoot like you could make."

"Tender foot? What the frip is a tenderfoot? Please enlighten me, before I fry you."

"You forgot to check your six." She said, giving her most wicked grin. *Lucky number six.*

Chapter 9

STONE DOGS

There was no pause. Her words were barely out of her mouth when shots fired, little sparks of light in her eyes.

The guards were in pain, withering on the floor, their bodies convulsing. Moans echoing into the room till finally they lay still. All except Karl. Karl turned around to face a Corps fireteam. Four guns, two NEW24's and two NEW28's stared back at him. Their adaptive armor currently showing white, gray, and black cameo. It made Karl's black version pale in comparison. The full body armor with plate shields and masks was impressive and scary. It made Jax long for the real time overlays that allowed a person to see what was underneath, as if it was a simpler soldier with weapons.

"Drop it, wannabe, or we drop you." The familiar voice of Corporal Varick Chambers brought joy to her ears. Karl snarled, but still dropped the gun while raising his hands.

"Chambers! Good to see you," she said, scooping her gun back up and moving to the fireteam.

Chambers flat cameo visor slid into his helmet and his devilish grin greeted her as he said, "Good to see you too, Jax. You gave us a scare. Thought you died when your floor became an inferno."

"Inferno? I remember the windows getting blown out, but no inferno."

"Yup, they must have done it after you left, trying to cover their tracks. The entire floor of your complex was blown. Took a scan of the rubble to figure out you weren't there. When we tried to track you, your personal locator was gone." While he talked, Chambers waved his team into action.

Two of the corps covering Karl, while the other checked on the stunned and swept the room. "Commander Haddock was a bit annoyed by that. I guess it set him off in quite the fit. Took him a while, but he broke whatever was hiding your signal and then Captain Lewis sent us in."

Jax shook her head. *These guys had masked my personal locator? That shouldn't be possible.* On Earth, everyone had a PL, Jax assumed it was the same here on Gaia. A nanite tracking unit that was placed at birth near the spinal column. PL's were only used in extreme situations to find someone or in criminal cases where required. On Earth, accessing a PL without proper authorization was a high crime. Blocking one was unheard of. It would take someone extremely knowledgeable and powerful to make that happen. *What the abyss is going on?*

"We can lay out the details later. We should go while the other teams are distracting them."

"Other teams?"

"Yup. This is a full assault. This complex is huge. Most of these wannabes are on the far side. Looks like barracks, hangers, training grounds, the works. This side is more residential. *Ares* had its full complement of corps staging an attack as a distraction. We were tasked to sneak in and get you out."

"Everyone from the *Ares*?" Jax's brows shot up.

"Yup. *Ares* takes care of its own." He winked at her. "Shall we go?"

Just like family. "We can't go yet. We need to follow the shadow."

"Shadow?"

"He was there when the command crew got arrested," she growled. "I forget his name. But he is here, and we need to get him. He has to be a key player. Can you contact *Ares* actual?"

Chambers shook his head. "No can do. With these guys tapping PLs the captain was afraid they could tap comms too. We're under communication blackout. Our orders were to get you and get out."

Jax scanned the fireteam. Corporal Chambers, two PFC's and a private. *It's my call. I may not be a captain but right now I have the authority.* "I'm changing the orders. We're going after the shadow. Do you have armor for me? And I need a key."

The faces of the fire team were wide and in shock. Except for Chambers, who didn't even miss a beat. "Roger that. Rook, armor for the Lieutenant."

"On it," said Rook, a short stocky private, more wide than tall, pulled a chest piece and helmet from his back. "Huh, you need help with this, ma'am?"

Jax fought rolling her eyes as she snatched the chest piece. "I've got it, Rook. Thanks." A quick glance showed the armor with a red dot painted in the middle, jagged rays branching out from it. Small red hatch marks circled the left arm. "Your work, Chambers?" she asked, slipping the short-sleeved armor on. The auto fit molding it to her chest, shoulders, and torso. She reached behind and pulled the self-adjust strap tighter. She gave Rook a smile as he gawked at her proficiency.

"Yup. Figured you had enough being a slick sleeve with your Fleet uniform, didn't want you to have to worry about this one."

"Really?" This time she rolled her eyes. "All I've been through, and that's what you've heard about?" she said, pulling her helmet on. A standard hard-shell top with a face shield sprang to life, the familiar HUD welcoming her. The real time overlay activated, and the group around changed from menacing, faceless combatants, into soldiers wearing combat fatigues. The corps idea was that this kept you knowing, feeling for those around you. Rook looked more boyish than Jax would have thought. Of the other two PFCs, private first class, one was slim with an oblong face, the last a lady with sunken eyes.

Chambers flashed his devilish grin. "Such things are grand entertainment in the corps."

"Wonderful. We can talk about it later. Get your key ready and give me a rundown on your team. We need to go." Jax could have gotten the info from the HUD, but a little voice of Dutch told her not to rely on the technology all the time. Jax grabbed the last pieces of her armor. Some lightweight gloves and grieves that she slapped on.

Chambers gave a rundown. "Rook and Wocheck are our tenderfoots."

"Hey!" both corps interrupted.

"Down boys," Chambers fired back before continuing, "Serph's my second and has some hard meters under the gun. Good team, but no heavy artillery, all 24's and 28's. If we hit something major, we might not have the firepower to push through."

"We'll make do, you're Corps after all." Jax flashed her own devilish grin.

"Roger that." Chambers chuckled. "What do you want to do with smiley here?" He thumbed at Karl, on his knees, hands clasps behind his head. "We can give you some time alone if you need to handle personal business."

Jax looked at Karl, his face was contorted in rage, his tongue held in check with the two corps standing over him. Jax took a step towards Karl.

Karl's eyes blazed with hatred; his mouth opened, ready to sprout curses. She never gave him a chance. His head swung around, his body twisting off his knees, lying flat on the floor. She brushed the butt of her NEW24 like it was dirty. *That was satisfying, but somehow not enough*. She leveled the gun, shooting a stun bolt into the man. Even unconscious, he groaned in pain, convulsions ripping his body. Jax couldn't help but smile as she turned from the body.

"Okay, let's get going."

"Might not be able to catch him. He has a pretty big head start at this point."

"Then we find out where he went. He's important to all this, I know it."

"Roger. Roger. I got a key." Chambers held up a frag grenade. "How you want to run this?"

Jax saw worry on the fireteam members. Having a Fleet officer, for all they knew, a tenderfoot in charge, was not going to be to their liking. They would follow the orders no matter what, but their faces were like granite as they waited for her reply.

"I'm just pointing the way. I'll leave the hunting to you stone dogs." She cringed after saying it. It was her attempt at "corps" humor, but she still wasn't sure she was getting it right. All her thoughts of Talbot in the interrogation room thinking he was a mean dog. The wannabes thinking they were hard, but they were all bark. The corps had bite, the *Ares* had teeth, she wanted to show that. *I'll never get this kind of humor.*

Chambers chuckled as a grin grew on his face. From the corner of her eye Jax saw what could only be relief cross the others corps faces. *Well, maybe I did better than I thought.*

"Stone dogs, heh, I like that. Semper A." Chambers said, nodding his head. Jax hadn't heard that expression before, but assumed it referenced the corps motto. *Semper Audax*, Always Bold. "You heard the Lieutenant, let's get going, you dogs. Rook, you're on point. Jax and I will follow. Serph and Wocheck keep our backs." The skinny Wocheck nodded, moving to the back, while Serph planted herself off Jax's back shoulder.

Jax pointed to where the portal lay hidden in the wall. With a nod and a shout, "Frag away." Chamber's arm arched overhead. A small gray metallic ball zipped away, a red light beaming its warning. The corps, including Jax, dove for cover. The explosion rocked their ears. Dust filled the room, and a metallic pang sound echoed out as the shielded wall gave way to the explosive charge.

"Frip Chambers, a little more warning next time," Wocheck bellowed.

"I like to keep you sharp. Keeps you alive." Chambers grinned as he studied the new opening.

"That's one theory," Jax said, standing beside him, she gave him an evil eye.

"Yes, it is." His smile never fading. "Let's move."

Past the ragged portal, the fireteam deployed. A hallway opened up, slanting down and curving to the right. The gray walls rushed past them as their boots pounded the hall. The overhead lights flashed by in stripes, marking their progress. Jax fell into a comfortable rhythm. The fireteam moved in column, step for step, arms reach apart, a single organism moving as one. Thirty meters they marked off, till Rook's fist raised a red "halt" popping up on her HUD.

A hatch blocked their path. Chambers signaled, his hand waving and the fireteam split. Chambers took up position on the right side of the door. Jax was tight on his shoulder. Serph moved to Rook's shoulder. With Wolcheck hanging back, Chambers nodded his head. Rook fingered the controls, and the hatch swung open. A quick check and the corps flowed in. A hanger bay opened up around them. A loading cart full of containers made for quick cover.

"Frip me, that's an Imperium 4 personal cruiser, and I think that's a CRS cruiser. Wow," Wolcheck said, envy lacing his every word. Jax eyed the cruisers as well. Recognizing them from Earth, these cruisers were the height of fashion and wealth. Sleek lines, powerful engines, great for quick excursions into space, or just arriving at a big event.

"Yup, and on this side, we have Fleet class combat ships. A couple of Drakes and a Condor," Chambers said, his head peeking out. Jax turned the other way. The ships were beautifully spaced to the left and right of the hangar. More for show than practicality, not like on the *Ares*. At the far end, the wannabes were busy loading crates on a Fleet style drop ship. Among the shuffle, Jax glimpsed a black suit in the sea of fatigues.

"Think that's my shadow. Can we take them?" she asked, ducking back down and turning to Chambers.

"Affirmative," he said, shaking his head. "Serph and Rook, you take the left. Wolcheck, Jax and I with take the right. Move together, set up a crossfire. With a little luck, we'll be on them before they know we are here. Everyone ready?"

Chambers made eye contact around the fireteam, nods greeting him. "Let's move. Go. Go. Go." They were two steps out of their cover when shouts rang out.

"We got intruders! Intruders in the landing bay!"

Their hiding spot burst into lights as the familiar red sparks of NEW24's ignited around them. Ducking back down, the corps fireteam regained its cover. "Well, so much for that plan." Chambers grimaced.

"Can't win them all." Jax smiled at him.

He tilted his head, a spark of annoyance, or maybe anger, touching his brow. "Light it up," he commanded, and the corps responded.

NEW 24's and NEW28's unleashed violence upon the enemy. Their skills homed in combat, their targets dropping like swatted flies. Jax stayed down. Her light chest armor was no equal to a full corps battle kit. *Let them hunt, you'll get a chance.*

As if on cue, Chambers called for an advance. Instinct took over and she fell in on his shoulder. They moved tight, the fast beat of their footfalls giving cadence. More of the faux corps fell as they scrambled to reach the drop ship. The wannabes had completely abandoned firing back against the well-trained fire team. Pushing each other to gain access to the ship, stumbling to make it through the door.

Another guard dropped as the door to the drop ship slammed shut. Its engines firing. The fireteam's footsteps broke into a run, a constant stream of light streaking ahead of them. Like light on a prism, the energy broke on the drop ship's shields. It rose, pivoted, its main engines igniting, and it sprinted away. The fireteam slid to a halt. A few shots of frustration chased after the drop ship as it passed the hangar doors. Jax took a few steps forward, her will taking a few extra moments to let go.

"Let's head to the pickup point. Time to get back to the *Ares*," she said with grit in her voice while she rested the NEW24 on her shoulder. She didn't hear the response to her command, lost in her own feelings. Jax was tired. She was new to this world, and she was already sick of It. Gaia was supposed to welcome her with open arms, instead she had found more monsters in the dark. Now she wasn't only fighting an alien menace, she was fighting her new home too. Too many people making plans about her life, plans that she had no part In. Time for that to change. *Time to take my life back.*

Chapter 10

ONE MORE THING

Getting out of that compound seemed like a week ago. It was only one day. However, it was sitting in this room that made it seem longer, a debriefing room at Fleet Command in Soteria City. The room was nicer than any she had been in. Larger than anything on the *Ares*, this room spoke of luxury. The deep blue walls with a matched deep gray carpet gave a feeling of being in space. Centered in the room were plush bucket seats with a red oak table that could seat twenty people. Ample standing room was also available. Placed around the walls were pictures of warships. Old versions from Earth and modern ones like the *Ares*. The Fleet logo dominated the room, behind what would be the lead chair.

Commander Lewis currently filled that chair, still acting as Captain of the *Ares*. They had occupied these seats for hours while they debriefed Jax on her ordeal. A never-ending repeat of what had happened to all the various people in charge. Legal authorities from Gaia, military police, admirals, officers of varying ranks, the High Marshal himself and now the Prime Representative. Her mind was feeling the fatigue of the constant questions. The same questions repeatedly again and again. Her answers are the same as always. Thankfully, they were nearing the end of the question chain again.

What did you do after the ship left? *Me and the "stone dogs"*, she thought that term but didn't say it saying "corps" instead, *fell into a standard two-by-two column. They made quick work of the corridors and met the Reckless for evac.* Then what? *The pilot, Hat Trick, updated us on the Ares corps assault.* What was that update? *The guards had been well armed, too well armed for civilians, but the corps had the training. Many had run once it was obvious the corps was going to overwhelm them. They dispatched those that fought with efficiency. A few were smart enough to surrender.* That's when the Reckless returned you to Fleet Command? *Correct.* Anything else you need to add, Lieutenant? *And sit here longer? Not bloody likely. Why couldn't they all just listen in at one time?* Instead of saying that, she had just replied she had nothing else to offer.

Captain Lewis and the PR chatted back and forth while Jax stared blankly at the holo image. *Maybe I can take a break for the bathroom and just never come back? Is there food around here? I'd kill for something sweet right now. By the abyss, I hope we're almost done.*

"Jax. Jax!"

Her eyes snapped over to the captain. "Sorry, lost in thought," she said. Pulling herself back up straight in the chair, realizing all the holo images were gone. "I miss anything important?"

Gemma Lewis sighed. "Just that your shadow, this Attaché Esteban, doesn't seem to exist anywhere in our records."

"How is that possible? What about Representative Dakos? Aren't they connected?"

The commander squinted, and her mouth pinched. "This is why you pay attention. We're looking into Dakos, but with no evidence linking him to Esteban, not much we can do. Nobody exists on Gaia without a footprint, which alone is troubling. Combined with the level of organization, not to mention the amount of credits needed to run it all." Gemma sighed before continuing. "This problem keeps getting bigger and we are just not prepared. Plus, they seem to have you in their sights."

"Wonderful. You once told me to keep my guard up regarding the political climate on Gaia. I didn't realize you meant it so literally."

"At the time, neither did I, but fanatics have a way of changing things, it seems. But right now, it's late and we'll have more to deal with in the days to come. I have some people putting together a safe house for you. Just hang tight and we'll get you squared away."

"I'd rather not."

"You'd rather not what?"

Jax's eyes squared with Gemma. "I was already nervous about coming here, so many changes in my life, all happening so fast. And now this." She waved her hands around the room. "I can't feel secure here on Gaia now. I would like your permission to stay aboard the *Ares* for the time being. I can't think of a better safe house. Nobody will mess with me there. Plus, I believe someone from the Command staff is supposed to be present during the repair review. Nobody likes that job, so I'll take it and make everyone happy," Jax said, rushing to get all the words out. That last part was a complete guess, but she wasn't going to tell Gemma that.

"You guessed that last part, didn't you?" Gemma said, raising an eyebrow at her.

"I study sometimes." She tried to flash her best Chambers grin.

Gemma sighed, shaking her head while speaking, a smile touching her lips. "The *Ares* would make a mighty fine safe house. You sure you want this? Gaia is going to be your life now, can't hide from it."

"I'm not hiding. I'm slowing things down. My life has changed a lot in a short time. I was finally comfortable on the *Ares* and now with people out to kill me, I think I need something stable. Then I can worry about starting a new life on a new planet."

Gemma's eyes pierced her to the core. It was the same look Gemma had when she practiced Judo *randori*, practice sparring. Processing all the moves, working the problem, finding the best plan to attack. "Fine, I'll approve it."

Jax sat back in the chair as Gemma issued her verdict. Her shoulders relaxing as if a weight had been lifted. She had prepared a list of counter arguments If Gemma said "no" but was thankful she didn't have to use them.

The Commander continued. "I believe there are some stiletto fighters housed in the hangers down here. You're qualified for them, right?"

"Yup. They're basically the same craft as the P150 I flew back on Earth. It's the craft they had me use in the VR when I got on the *Ares* to check my abilities as a fighter pilot."

The Commander nodded as she flipped through some screens on the holotable. "I remember. I also remember you not being so good with the weapon systems. Try not to shoot the *Ares*, or Gaia, as you go back and forth."

"I'm not that bad," Jax said, trying to sound insulted. Then the idea, the actual meaning of what the Commander was saying sank into her mind. "You're assigning me my own ship!"

"Yes, I am. I want you mobile and you'll be going back and forth a lot, so this way you don't have to wait on a bus."

"Sounds perfect. When can I leave?" *My own ship!*

"I just put the order in. They should have one dusted off and ready to go by the time you get to the hangar. Those stilettos mostly sit in storage since the newer Gaia designed craft have come out. You go ahead and head up. Get some sleep and take a day or two for yourself. It will give us time to look into this and to figure out what kind of training schedule to get you on."

"Oh, wonderful," Jax said, tilting her head up and rolling her eyes back.

"Get out of here," the Commander said with a lift of her chin.

"Aye aye, Captain," Jax said, standing with a smile on her face and a friendly salute off her brow.

Jax was flying. She had tried to walk the halls on her way out, but with no one around, she had broken into a run. She burst outside, ready to run to the hangar bay, and came to the quick realization that she had no idea where that was. A fleetwalker waved her down. He identified himself as Private Joel Harding and informed her that Commander Lewis had sent him to take her to the hangar. She followed the fleetwalker to a Multi-Wheeled Vehicle.

The MWV had six-wheels, each half as tall as Jax, and had a dull green paint job. Rugged and well used, it looked like a torpedo on wheels to Jax as it hummed along with its qave drive engine. She fidgeted in her boxy seat, too excited to talk on the short twenty-minute drive. While Fleet Headquarters were in the city proper, the airstrip and hangars were outside the city grounds. Once they pulled up to the location, Jax wasted no time. In one motion, she jumped from the seat, waved thanks and goodbye to the fleetwalker, and zipped into the hangar bay.

Jax found the ground crew, the group responsible for getting craft ready, standing around slightly perplexed. They thought the order to prepare a stiletto instead of a new raptor must be a mistake. Jax assured them it was correct, since she wasn't cleared to fly any other Gaia based craft. That brought a few chuckles from the crew. They had the idea that there wasn't much difference between flying the two crafts. Still, orders were orders, so they went to work.

By the time she changed into her flight suit, she had found the stiletto ready to go. Glee welled up in her chest while inspecting the craft. It even had her name and rank displayed under the cockpit. *Lt. Harumi Brandt.* Jax would of rather had her nickname on it but wasn't going to complain. She marveled at how efficiently they had gotten everything ready. Its tail number FR-06 displayed proudly was a throwback to the ship's Earth origins. Gaia ships didn't use external marking on their ships. Large ships like the *Ares* had names, small ships designations, but Gaia relied on transponders for the information.

On Earth, the P150 was a personal transport that could handle four passengers, a pilot and copilot. Popular as a personal space plane for big businesspeople and VIPs. The stiletto maintained the pilot seats, but they had stripped the passenger seating. Replaced with bench seating, that could cram six to eight corps members in a jam. On the outside, it kept its needle like profile. Except for the particle cannons and missile racks that were melded on to the hull. The weapons looked out of place on the shuttle like craft.

Gaia's raptors were smaller and less shuttle-like, only pilot and copilot, and had a better weapons load out. True fighter planes, designed to control air space and space itself. The deck crew had repeated the captain's words. Few in Fleet flew these Earth based models anymore. Now that Gaia designed fighters were available, these were obsolete. They weren't even used as shuttles since they had the dropships for that. Jax didn't care, this was outstanding.

She broke through the blue sky of Gaia and stars greeted her. Gaia amazed her as she left its confines behind. Here the universe opened before her, and all things were possible. She couldn't help but have fun on her way to the *Ares*. She banked and rolled, even hit a couple of figure eights on the way there. A few messages from flight control on *Alpha Station* checked on her well-being. She laughed her way through her answer. "All good control, just checking for loose bolts."

"Roger that FR-06, remember to level out before landing. Wouldn't want you hopping off the runway." Their words laughed in her ears.

"Aye aye. Control." She said as she thought of the tail numbers. *Well, I guess you are my own little frog hopper. Back and forth from Ares to Gaia. I don't care if you're not a big ship, you're my ship now, and you need a name, so Hopper it is.*

The landing on *Ares* was easy and came with a sense of comfort. Like a child feeling safe in their parents' arms, here she could relax all her worries. A quick chat with the ACHO, Aircraft Handling Officer, Warrant Officer Shelby. Letting him know that *Hopper* will need to be ready at irregular times and often. He was laughing at her for naming it but made it clear *Hopper* would be well taken care of.

She strode the halls without a care in the universe. This was safe. Here she could plan, and she could study. Learn more about Gaia and how the military works. For the most part, she had the ship to herself. Work crews wouldn't be in personnel quarters sections and, more importantly, on the bridge. She had time to focus and get herself back on track. She stifled a yawn and her stomach growled.

Even with reduced staff, even while undergoing repairs, the wardroom was always available. MS1 Zakar never seemed to leave. He was happy to have someone to cook for. He offered what would amount to a four-course meal. Jax, with all the care she could, talked him down to a single sandwich, a chocolate cupcake, and water. She longed for her favorite drink, but caffeine wouldn't help the sleep she wanted.

Making quick work of the meal, she headed for her berth. Exiting the wardroom, she spun as her shoulder was hit. Her right hand gripped the knife at her back while the left hand slammed Fleetwalker Percy into the hull. Her anger graced her eyes. She no longer wanted to be taken by surprise. She was not letting that happen again.

"Fleetwalker Percy, we need to stop running into each other this way."

"Yes, ma'am!" His eyes were wide as he responded, a quiver running through him. Jax relaxed both the grip on her knife and the hand holding Private Tobias Percy to the wall.

"Didn't expect to see you in the wardroom. Did you need something?"

"Yes ma'am. Not from you though, ma'am," Percy said, straightening his uniform. "I was letting MS1 Zakar know we got his shipment of spices is in, but it might be a day or two until we can unload them. They got packed under a shipment of spare parts."

"Under spare parts?" Jax asked, while Percy shrugged in response. "Well, on your way then, Private." He saluted and was off like lightning.

Jax chuckled as she strode back to her berth. *If I ever need to find something on this ship, I have to remember to talk to Percy.*

She stifled a yawn as the portal to her berth slid open. An officer's berth, the simple square room had a stiff bed, locker for her stuff, and a tiny alcove that served as shower and bathroom. She was startled to find a box resting on her bed. A simple storage box made of dull blue plastic. Used throughout the ship for various organizational needs. On top lay a folded piece of paper. Her hand grabbed the paper and unfolded it. Neatly penned letters flowed across the page. *I haven't seen a handwritten note in ages.*

Hey Sis,

Was saving this as a housewarming gift, but heard you were staying on the Ares for now. Couldn't be here when you got back. Repair teams are trying to mess up my engines. So, I thought I would leave you something to enjoy till we can meet up later. Just a few fab things for you. Why didn't you tell me you could play?

Talk later,

Rose

"Oh, my!" Excitement rushed over her as she tore the box open.

A cluster of things lay inside. A picture of her mom and dad. Pictures from her travels as a kid, her in a cap and gown graduating Earth's captain's college. Friends she had during high school and college. A picture of her on the bridge of her first pilot assignment, the *Kirishima*. So many precious memories. Her favorite images that had adorned her apartment on the

Indiana. She had thought them all lost, but here they lay real once again. Her heart swelled and tears burned her eyes.

On one of their long chat sessions, Rose had mentioned she could do this. Earth ships, she explained, took detailed scans of all passenger and personnel baggage. It was only to be used in case of lost items, or damage during transit. Rose was adamant the information was buried in the archives they downloaded from the *Indiana*. Given time, she was positive she could find it and recreate Jax's belongings. She just had to wait for the time to fully analyze the data. Jax had completely forgotten, but not Rose. *Wonderful Rose.*

Several items she had collected as a child traveling Earth with her parents flowed out of the box. A decorative stein from Germany, her maneki neko from Japan, a matryoska doll from Russia, and more flooded her memories. Her entire collection of little knickknacks from around Earth returned to her.

She pulled out her favorite jacket. Black with red sleeves. On the back was an embroidery of a quaint little Japanese village nestled somewhere in the mountains. Its silken nature was the perfect weight for fall when the weather started turning cooler. She slipped it on and pulled the zipper partway up. It was so comforting.

Her favorite mug, a large heavyweight cup with a silhouette of a sasquatch printed on it. Stopped in her hands. The original smashed on the *Indiana* when she learned of the Screech.

None of these were the originals, only fab copies, but somehow it didn't matter. To have these things back, the memories that accompanied them, to regain a bit of what she lost. Knowing they came from a friend added to those thoughts, those emotions. She wiped a tear from her eye.

Two more items rumbled around inside the box. She lifted one out; she pulled her face back, trying to figure out why it was there.

"Well, you're not mine," she said, inspecting the ball composed of thumb-sized hexagons. Jax recognized it as a vpet, an interactive toy given to children. This version given to younger kids, or those rough on toys, could be batted around with no damage. As children grew up, more advanced versions were available. They could look like anything your imagination desired; they were all the rage on Earth.

"I'm not sure whether to be amused or insulted." She spun the toy around, looking for some sign of why it was in the box. Finding only the "on" hex to activate the vpet. Curiosity getting the better of her, she pressed her thumb to it. Lights started flashing, each hex lighting up in turns. A soft melody chimed as it spun and lifted into the air.

"Greetings, Captain. It is good to see you," a cheery voice rang out.

"EVE? *Indiana*?" She gasped, her hand covering her mouth.

"Yes, Captain. I am the Enhanced Virtual Entity assigned to the *Indiana*. I must inform you I currently don't have access to my systems. I feel smaller than normal. I may need repairs."

"Oh EVE, there have been some changes. What's your last memory?"

"Last memory file shows you coming onto the bridge of the *Indiana*," EVE said, each hexagon flashing to the sound of its voice. "There was some commotion about an unidentified ship. After that my memory is blank till this moment. My internal clock shows I am missing a considerable amount of time. May I inquire what has transpired?"

"Oh my, how do I begin?" Jax said, a spark igniting in her mind. She jumped off the bunk and waved a holoscreen from the wall. Choking on her excitement, Jax knew explanations could take forever. Working with the Ares engineering crew had given her enough technical knowledge she knew she could download at least the basics faster. Tapping a few items on screen, she selected her personal files, Gaia library, basic ship layout, and all the military procedure stuff. *I'll have company when Rose isn't around and a study partner. I can finally get up on all these military protocols. It'll be like college all over again. Gaia may not like having EVEs around, but I've missed having one to help out.*

"EVE connect to this holoscreen and we'll see about getting you a proper update. Don't reach out your data connection however, Gaia doesn't like having EVE units connected to ships. I'll do a one-way copy of what you need."

"That is surprising, Captain. My EVE unit has a very high customer service rating. This Gaia seems like a strange place. I will comply. I always aim to please."

The vpet, EVE, and the holoscreen began blinking. Seeing the link established, Jax initiated the transfer. At first it was like a conversation, back and forth, but it gave way to synchronicity. The lights moved faster and faster to the point they were no longer flashing, only a bright white light. The vpet went blank, its lights going dark and its sounds cutting out. Jax grabbed it as it dropped to the ground.

The holoscreen continued blinking. Random images and numbers flashing faster than the eye could follow. "EVE?"

"Oh, my," Eve's cheerful voice rang out. "This system, *Ares*, is considerably more advanced than the *Indiana*."

"Is that a problem? You, okay? I didn't mean to download you. I must have reversed it." Jax scanned the operation on her screen, looking for what went wrong.

"Oh yes, Captain, it's that..." EVE paused. "...it will take time to integrate with this system so I may be of use to you. A week, more. I will need to enter a calibration mode for the update. Do I have your permission?"

"Can you copy yourself back to the vpet?"

"The vpet seems to have malfunctioned during the transfer. If I don't integrate with this system, its virus protocols may detect me as an intruder. I do not think I would survive. Do I have your permission to continue integration?"

"Sure" Jax said, smiling. "Finish as fast as you can and get back to me. Remember what I said before, and don't talk to anyone but me for now, okay?" Jax said, making a mental note to talk to Rose about fixing this situation.

"Of course, Captain. Entering calibration mode." EVE said. Three short, pleasant tones followed as the holoscreen went blank.

Jax waved the screen closed and hopped onto her bunk. Laughter washed over her. *Oh, I've missed having an EVE around. They can be annoyingly cheerful sometimes, but so what? Don't care what Gaia thinks, EVEs are too convenient. They are so helpful.* She grabbed the empty box to collapse for recycling when she heard something clunk inside. It seemed there was one more thing waiting for her. She reached her hand in and moved around for a moment. Cold metal brushed her fingers as she found something to grab. Lifting it out, a smile bloomed again on her face.

A little bigger than her hand, the bronze-colored cylinder was cool to the touch. Six key buttons were in neat little rows and a thumb hook on the back. Above the thumb hooks was a second tube, a mouthpiece.

Oh Rose, you silly girl. I haven't practiced this since before I set foot on the Indiana. Of all the things for you to fab for me. I thought I could practice on the long trip to Highguard, but that never happened. She was laughing while she pulled the mouthpiece and hooked her right thumb in place. The startup sequence activated.

The TruSax expanded in her hand. The buttons moving up and down, extending to their familiar positions. Small levers extended out of the body, mimicking all the classic sax controls. She pushed the mouthpiece on the neck and an "A" note sounded out, signaling the start up was complete.

The digital sax didn't look like a traditional sax. It was a slim rod with buttons. That bell shape that gave a sax its distinctive look completely missing. The tone of the TruSax could mimic any number of sax types, soprano, alto, tenor, or baritone. *I bet Rose has already set it up to my original specs. I always like to keep it a match for my traditional tenor, a tenor that is currently stuck on Earth. A tenor that is hopefully on the way here.* Given what she had learned about Gaia's ability to get her personal items from Earth, Jax continued to hope.

She pressed her lips and blew on the mouthpiece. A horrible honk, like that of a dying goose, sounded out. Her face pulled back and her eyes darted around the room.

She thumbed the volume down while closing her eyes and searching her memories. She had started playing as a child. Her mom had wanted the violin, but after a trip to New Orleans, Jax had insisted on a saxophone. Not a clarinet, or an alto, but a tenor. That is what she had heard, so that is what she had to play.

Over the years, her interest had come and gone. Her parents had encouraged her. Even giving her a classic big bell tenor for her birthday later that same year. She always treasured it, even if she didn't always play it.

Once she started training at Earth's International Space Agency, she dropped it altogether. That was until she started running long boring trips from Earth to Mars. She was the pilot, but most of the actual flying was performed by EVE on the well-defined flight paths. She had gotten the TruSax to occupy the time. Some other crew members wrote or drew pictures. She had also dabbled in those, but they never kept her interest. Sitting on the bridge with nothing better to do, the TruSax was portable and could be played quietly. She could lose herself for hours.

Her mind flooded with the past, trying to capture the skills once obtained. She moved her lips, practicing her embouchure. Then placed them once again on the mouthpiece. She felt the breath deep from her abdominals. This time, the note was pure. She held it for an eight beat and then moved through some scales. The music filled her ears and her mind drifted on the melody. She let her fingers go where they may, and her emotions powered into the rhythms.

Time blurred as she drifted the scales, till the feeling welled up and she had to let herself stop. She leaned back, a potent mix of euphoria and anxiety washing over her. *Last time I played this, I was so sure of where I was going. I never saw myself here.* She looked around the room and, for once, wasn't greeted by lost faces or names running through her head. It was just a room, not an echo chamber for her darkest thoughts. Glancing at the memories spread across her bed, feeling comfortable for the first time in a long time.

I've lost so much, but I've gained so much too. My whole life I've moved from place to place. Adapting to wherever I was. Never really belonging, just wanting to move on, and finding that next adventure. I didn't belong on Earth. I always knew I belonged in space. It just wasn't the space I thought it was supposed to be. I chose this, I've fought for it, but maybe I haven't quite accepted it yet. Time to correct that. This is your life, Jax.

"This is home."

Act II

You'll probably think this story is about me, but you'll be wrong.
This story is about friends and enemies.

Chapter 11

BLUE TOPAZ

It was the kind of day when you expected rain, but instead the sun was bright. A day where dark skies and a genital drizzle should match tears. Instead, a cool wind blew, and the occasional high gray cloud could be seen. Blue skies that would normally make for happy days were instead giving light to more somber moods.

It was late afternoon when everyone started to arrive. First, civilians trickled in, taking seats in stands erected for this ceremony. Others choose to stand, as their preference dictated. Conversations held in whispers; voices held back in respect.

The fleet and corps came next. They marched in file, creating perfect columns on the parade grounds. The echo of boots on pavement beating like a drum, a cadence, in perfect rhythm. Sharp commands, breaking the beat, turning the columns, placed each member of the Gaia military in perfect position. They stood tall and proud, to honor the moment.

As the last of the military took its place, a wave of silence washed over the civilian crowds. All eyes turned to the central podium. The metal platform, dull and gray, seemed lacking for such a grand ceremony. Those who knew, those who served, understood that practicality was cherished over pomp and circumstance.

On the left of the stage, standing in hap-hazard lines, were the VIPs. The very important people gathered to pay their respects, or at the very least, to look like they were paying their respects. The civilian government was out in full force. Representatives from each faction, and the Prime Rep herself, all nestled together. Only a single Rep. was missing, but no one was giving him any thought this day.

Moving toward the center, the Gaia Military was in stunning display. The High Marshal, Generals from the corps, admirals from fleet. Each one in full regalia, not a button out of place. They stood as if they were statues, erected long ago to immortalize an important moment in history. To the right, in a solemn line, stood the command crew of the *Ares*.

Commander Gemma Lewis, acting captain of the *Ares*, stood first. Every bit the captain in her dark dress blues. A head shorter than the rest, but her powerful form still dominated. Commander Terrance Moro was next in line. His statuesque visage, a textbook example of perfection. Commander Issac Haddock filled out the next position. Almost as wide as he was tall, Haddock's thick muscles left his custom-fitted uniform bursting at the seams. Next, in sharp contrast to Haddock's ripped form, came Lilly Bard. The navigations commander was thin as a rail, her graying hair tucked neatly into her hat. Doctor Dutch Charles finished out the line, several heads taller than all the Commanders. His usual white doctors' gown replaced by dress blues. His wild hair escaped from under his cap.

Jax stood on the parade ground, looking up at them. As acting commander of engineering, she had a spot up there. They had asked her to stand on stage, had argued she belonged there, but she had declined. This crew had been together long before she had come along. They had laughed and cried, played, fought, bled, lived, and died before she had ever known they existed. Those assembled on stage needed to represent that. She wouldn't, couldn't infringe on that.

Seeing them there now, it was clear. This wasn't her moment. She belonged, but with a different group. She had chosen to stand with what was left of the *Ares* engineering crew. Decimated by the Screech, barely a third of them remained. This was her first family on the *Ares*. This is the group that had welcomed her, embraced her, and made her one of their own. Mourning didn't come easy to her, but perhaps here she could endure.

Her new dress uniform was pressed to perfection. No longer a slick sleeve, ribbons and some silver stars decorated her chest. Awards had been handed out a few days before. Celebrate the living before you mourn for the dead, she had been told. Of all the awards she earned, on her shoulder was her most prized. A patch shaped like an old-fashioned gear; a cartoon styled rat with an atom symbol tattooed on its belly. It marked her as a part of the *Ares* ENG, specifically a group known as the Rat Pack. She wasn't sure if it belonged on her dress uniform, but she didn't care. It meant more to her than the other chest candy.

Surrounding her was the rest of the *Ares* crew. Familiar faced, shared tragedy bonding them for life. Even without names, even away from the *Ares*, she could place them into groups. The NAV team, the pilots, were the easiest. She could talk their talk and walk their walk; she could recognize a true pilot a klick away. The COM team was nice, but they were a group of introverts. More interested in data and statistics and what could be done with it. At work, they constantly pushed their heads into holoscreens. She knew some of them more by the back of their heads than their faces. The WEP team was hardest for her to categorize. Too much bad blood between her and its commander, and what they did was too alien for her at times. She hadn't built bonds with them, gotten to know their personalities the way she had with the rest of the crew.

The ceremony began like a well-oiled machine. The pression of speeches flowed like a lazy river. They listened to the Prime Representative give well practiced praises. The high marshal's encouragement to move on. Admirals and generals, each one recounting story after story of good the *Ares* and her crew had done. For Jax, the words blurred together. Her own grief welled up inside. She stood strong, but her mind wandered. She wanted to go back to her room to mourn alone. That's how it was for her. When her father died, her mom had thrown herself into work and she was alone. When her mom died, her extended family, aunts, uncles, and cousins had come, and then they had left for their lives. She had survived, had mourned, the way her mother did, buried herself in work. Pushing herself till she became captain of the *Indiana*. Till she headed out for deep space and found herself here. She was glad this time had come, but now she wanted it to end. She wanted to be alone.

Too much talking, too many people. This was more spectacle than mourning. The *Ares* crew held, so she held. When the acting Captain

Commander Gemma Lewis spoke, she tried to focus, to hear the words. Gemma talked with passion. With a heart that respected the dead, yet still inspired people's core, pushed them forward. Gaia would immortalize her words among the greatest of history. A speech to be remembered and taught to generations to come. Jax would only remember it as a vague dream.

The speeches done; the assembled military dismissed. They filed from the parade ground. Grim looks on some faces, smiles on others as they greeted old friends. Jax removed her hat and shook out her hair. Standing at attention for so long was not doing anything for her mood.

Jax scanned the crowd, looking for Rose. While Jax had hoped the day would be over after this grand ceremony, Rose let her know there was more to come. They had plans to go to the next ceremony together. This one would be private, more intimate, and a tradition for the crew. Jax's feelings were uneasy about the whole situation. She longed to skip it, to head back to the Ares.

Catching sight of Rose, who was in a huddle with Commander Bard and Haddock, she strode over. As Jax closed in, Rose saluted the two commanders. A glance at Jax with a bit of worry painting her face, and then turned and marched off.

Jax's mouth dropped open for a second as she faced the commanders and said, "Did you just scare off my ride? I thought we had leave after this, some other get together to attend?"

"Don't worry, your plans are still intact," Commander Bard said.

"We had to modify them. We're all headed to the same place. You're going to ride with us now. We need a moment of your time." Commander Bard placed her hand on Commander Haddock's shoulder, a show of solidarity. The burly commander's awkward smile was his only response.

They loaded up into a rickety, four wheeled, open top vehicle. The four seats were sun faded and had more patches than could be counted. A cone of black smoke spilled out the back as Commander Haddock sat behind the wheel and turned a key. The drab green machine rattled off with Jax in the back and Commander Bard riding shotgun.

"So, what's so important that we needed to talk?" Jax asked.

Commander Haddock held up a finger and grabbed a small white disc from his side. Sticking it to the dash, his fingers daftly entered a sequence. His eyes never left the road, as his other arm controlled the rough riding vehicle. The disc began pulsing, a dim white light radiating from the center, a heartbeat bringing it to life.

He gave a thumbs up. "All clear."

Lilly Bard turned in her seat and squared her eyes on Jax. Even with the bumpy ride, she still looked like she was standing on stage giving a speech. "You, my dear, are in a lot of trouble."

Jax laughed. "What else is new?"

"They've put a bounty on your head, a mega credit's worth," Lilly said.

"A million credits? Wow." Jax whistled. "By 'they' I'm assuming you mean Gaia First? But you're going to find them, right? Nothing to worry about, right?"

Lilly narrowed her eyes. "It's more than that. Gaia Frist has us stumped, and that's something that shouldn't be possible. Between Issac's skills and my connections, there shouldn't be any secrets we can't uncover. Nothing we can't find, but all our leads have died off."

"Even Rep. Dakos and this Attaché Esteban?"

"If I hadn't seen this Esteban person with my own eyes, I would have a hard time believing he exists," Lilly said, and Issac growled at her words. "There is no record of him on Gaia." Lilly patted Issac's shoulder, her businesslike face softening. "Dakos has connections to G1, but only the small political group we've known about. That group, while extreme by Gaia political standards, is still small. It does not have the size or organizational ability to pull off what we now know they are capable of. They're a front for the true group to hide behind."

"And we have no idea who that group is?" Jax sighed.

"None. My people are calling them Gaia Alpha."

"Who are your people? I wouldn't think a simple pilot would have that much insight into this," Jax asked. It startled her when Issac barked a laugh.

"To think of Lillian Barduke as a simple pilot. Now that's funny," he said, laughing until Lilly's eyes cut him down.

"What?" he asked. "You were going to tell her anyways."

"My secrets to tell. How would you like me sharing yours?" she said.

"That could be dangerous," he mumbled.

Lillian Barduke? Jax sat back with her mind racing at the thought. *Lilly Bard is Lillian Barduke?* It was one of the greatest stories told in history classes. The teen daughter of Earth's richest family. She was an enigma until her eighteenth birthday. When she announced to the world, she was leaving Earth. Somehow stole one of her family's lavish deep space craft and ran away into the abyss.

The Barduke family had offered astronomical rewards for finding her. Had spent a world's worth of fortune sending ships to find their only daughter. To this day, space travelers tell legends of spotting her ship only to have it disappear into the mist.

"I can tell by the look on your face that you're in awe," Lilly said, rolling her eyes. "It's not that romantic. Truth is, I was a brat who found out what her parents and grandparents were up to, and I insisted on being a part of it. So, they created a story about me stealing a ship. It had nothing to do with me. This gave them cover to move large resources to Gaia. Even the Earth government donated to the cause of finding the Barduke's lost daughter. Ships were launched, resources moved, legends were created. I got shipped to Gaia and Gaia got a large influx of supplies. Supplies that up to that point they had only received as a trickle."

"So, all those ships that went looking for Lillian, for you, were headed for Gaia. Right under the noses of those that would stop the founding of Gaia if they knew about it. That's amazing." Jax gasped. "But why the name change?"

"I was a brat. On Gaia, I wanted to have a fresh start, make my own way. That's hard to do when your family is one of the main financial founders of Gaia. So, a minor name change. Remove any record of family connections, easily done on Gaia at that time. Join Gaia Fleet and viola, new life," Lilly said, flashing a smile.

"Amazing. So, all your connections are from your family? Political?"

"Correct. Daddy wasn't happy when I changed my name, but over the years, we worked it out. Family can be such a chore."

"Is that how you know the Prime Representative?"

"I'm not talking about her, ever," Lilly said, scowling.

"Okay, so that explains you. What's his story?" Jax said, tilting her head at Issac.

"There is none. It's better that way. Trust me," Issac said, his voice dropping a few octaves from its normal high pitch. "Besides, no time to chat about me, we're here." The clanky vehicle skidded to a stop, taking a parking spot by the curb.

Jax scanned her surroundings, trying to place where they were. Confusion washing over her as she saw a sign designating this as Gaia's fleet command. This was where the officers worked their desk jobs. Intelligence flowed and where all the big decisions were made. Located in the fleet district of Soteria, this was at least twenty klicks from the airstrip and hangers. *Were we going that fat? I wasn't paying attention. This doesn't seem like a place to get together.* Jax turned to ask, but Lilly and Issac had jumped out and were heading around the corner.

"Hey! Wait up," Jax shouted, scrambling after them, ducking into an alley. The sleek modern steel on the front of the building gave way to red brick walls and a cobblestone street. A few antique streetlights dotted their path, their dim light enough to see by. The light of the late day sun completely lost here. She felt transported back in time. Lilly and Issac continued their stroll down the ancient-looking street.

The couple came to a stop at a rusty guard rail. Over their head a weather-beaten old sign, its paint faded with age, read The Blue Topaz. A crudely painted hexagonal gem filled the bottom of the sign. They dropped some stairs to a small landing. A heavy wooden door with an iron handle was sunk deep into the wall. A small half-moon-stained glass window arching over its top.

Lilly looked back at Jax and announced, "Welcome to fleet's very own ratskeller."

Ratskeller? What's a ratskeller? She thought. Then a more important thought passed her mind.

"Wait. What am I supposed to do about the price on my head?"

Issac titled his head around. "I've arranged to keep you safe. I'll explain later. Right now, we should hurry. They'll be starting soon, and I'm sure we're the last to arrive," he said, pulling the door open. Ushering Lilly in with a gracious nod of his head, they both disappeared inside. Jax could feel her temperature rising. She didn't think this was a good time to let it rest.

She jumped down the concrete stairs and caught the heavy door a second before it shut. She pulled it open and chased the couple in. Her eyes grew wide at the wonder they beheld. Her chase slowed to a walk as she crossed the wooden balcony to the railing. The barrel-vaulted ceilings rose twenty meters over her head. Twin staircases, to the left and right, swept down to an open floor. Thick wooden pillars broke up the floor. On the far wall, barrels, each one five times the height of any person, were embedded into the stonework. To the far right, an ornate bar, carved wood with a dark cherry stain, dominated the wall.

In the middle, the main floor had rows of common tables. Well-spaced to allow plenty of standing room. The long tables had long benches to accompany them. The crew of the *Ares* was disbursed throughout. Most standing, others seating, their conversations filled the hall.

To the left, a small stage, if you could call it that, only a step higher than the floor. A large brass bell, the fleet logo engraved on it, hung from a simple wooden frame. Acting Captain Lewis, Admiral Koonce, and the high marshal gathered round. This is the first time Jax really looked at the high marshal. She had spaced out at the formal ceremony. The High Marshal, Ogden Dacor, was a slim man with a lined face. He seemed of an age with Admiral Koonce, but that was always hard to tell. His dress blues were simply adorned and Jax got the feeling that was intentional.

Jax saw Commander Bard and Haddock meet up with senior members of their commands. They were smiling, shaking hands, and joining conversations as old friends. Her anger went out like a dying candle flame.

Taking a hint from the other commanders, she scanned for her group, specifically the Rat Pack.

Nestled between two of the large wall barrels, she spotted Rose. Over her shoulder, practically hanging on her back, were Fredrick Ambrose and Coleman Sales. Rose was lost in conversation with a slender man in a simple blue suit that Jax didn't recognize. *Blink*. The man changed to a balding man with a long white beard, antique circle frame glasses rimming his eyes. It was Nath, the strange man who created Gaia's weapons. Rose's face was flushed with excitement. Coleman and Freddy were wide eyed and stunned. Combined with the intensity with which Nath spoke as he waved his hands, it was obviously a high level of technical exchange was happening. Jax thought it best to avoid it.

Instead, Jax headed down the right stairs and put the bar in her sights. Bar stools were empty, the crew preferring to stand or congregate at the tables. Shuffling her way through the crowd, she said greetings as need be. Avoiding getting drawn into conversations was the goal, however.

Gossip seemed to float on the wind and touch her ears as she went. Whispers of Gaia First and what they had done to her followed in her steps. All of it damming them and commending her. Other conversations caught her ear. Some contradict themselves from one beat to the next. Riots on Earth, finding out about the Screech and Gaia. The Screech were missing. The Screech were attacking. Dacos had given a speech during a conference praising the *Ares*. No, the fool had said he didn't see the need for warships. She ignored it and swept down the bar and around its far corner. Sliding onto the last stool, she looked out over the crew. She hoped here she could be alone in the crowd.

"You must be Jax," someone said, startling her.

Jax looked up to take in a woman's age-worn face, her pleasant smile highlighting the wrinkles in her eyes. Short, cropped hair, gray and thinning offset her dusty blue sweater. She offered a firm handshake from behind the bar.

Grasping the hand and narrowing her eyes, Jax said, "I am. Do I know you?"

"Eventually, everyone in the fleet knows me. I'm Anne. I know you because I make it my business to know everyone who comes into my place. That, plus you're all over the news here, dearie, you've got something of a star about you," Anne said.

"I do? I am? I didn't know. I don't really watch the news."

Anne laughed. "You're probably better off for it. Just remember, here on Gaia, military personnel are a lot like acting stars, or professional sports players back on Earth. If you're out in public, the spotlight will be on you."

"Really?" Jax said. Anne's words had hit her like a punch to the face. Jax sank, turning to look for cameras and people watching.

"Oh, don't worry dearie, you're safe here. I don't allow cameras or news in here. This is a sanctuary, a place to relax, maybe get a taste of home," Anne said, raising an eyebrow.

"A taste of home sounds wonderful."

"What are you cravin' honey? I personally specialize in old Earth German food, but I have cooks that can cover most anything."

Jax closed her eyes and smacked her lips, childhood memories flooding her. "Ham hock, spicy sausage, red cabbage and rice." She could already taste the food.

Anne chuckled. "That's a very interesting mix."

Jax was smiling back. "Dad loved his German food, but mom insisted on having rice with every meal."

"Well then, I guess I have no choice but to make it work." She grabbed a tray with twelve shot glasses on it and set it before Jax.

Jax held a hand up and started to push the tray back. "I don't really care for whiskey and definitely not that much."

"It's for the ceremony dearie, you'll need it. The rest, if I'm not mistaken, is for your friends." Anne tilted her head into the crowd.

Jax looked over and sure enough, making a laser straight to her was the Rat Pack. "How'd you know?"

"Secrets of the trade, dearie." Anne said, tapping her shoulder while eyeing Jax's patch with a smile. "I'll see what I can do about that craving of yours. German food I can handle. I'll have to ask one of the sous chefs about the rice, however." A smirk appeared on her face as she turned and headed off.

"Lieutenant Jax!" Ensign Coleman Sales cheerfully shouted. He came bounding through the crowd. Pushing to keep up with him came Rose Koike and Ensign Frederick Ambrose. Of all the friends she had made on the *Ares,* these were the best. Rose, Coleman, who never went by Cole, and Freddy, the Rat Pack.

"Trying to avoid us, sister?" Rose said, punching Jax in the shoulder.

"Never." Jax raised her hands to wave off guilt. "I just didn't want to interrupt that deep conversation you were having with Nath."

"I know right". Rose said, beaming a smile. Freddy and Coleman also sprouted smiles like excited puppies.

"I learned more about quantum wave theory and its application in a few minutes than I have in a lifetime. I can't wait to tell you about it."

"Oh, I can hardly wait." Jax rolled her eyes.

"You should!" Rose said before all three of them began to relay information to her. She was about to plead for them to stop when a sharp whistle echoed through the room. Even Jax recognized the call to attention. The room went silent, and those who were sitting stood.

Commander Moro, sharp as a razor, brought the slim silver whistle down from his lips. Turning heel to toe, he marched to the side. Taking his place at the head of a line with Commander Bard, Haddock, and Doctor Charles.

For a moment, Jax thought she was in the wrong place. That she should be up there in that line, but a quick glance around her showed she was wrong. It wasn't just the Rat Pack that had gathered around her; it was all the *Ares* engineering crew. As she had pushed to the bar, they had followed her, as a group embraced her. Jax's heart swelled with the warmth, the kinship, the pride of it all. She stood tall with ENG, and the *Ares* crew as they watched the stage.

Commander Gemma Lewis stood by the ceremonial bell. In one hand she held a cord, in the other, a shot glass, full of a dark liquid.

"The first bell is for those that served. Those that endured the hardships of the unknown, those that survived the abyss and those that didn't. They paved the way, they set the standard for all to follow." Her hand pulled the cord and a deep, dark tone echoed through the room.

Across the room, everyone spoke, but it was a single answer that thundered. "Those that served." In each hand, a drink held high, the crew drank together.

"The second bell is for those we lost. Though others may forget, we never shall. Their names will be legend upon our memories. We are honored by their sacrifice and will continue the fight in their name," Gemma said, her voice quivering ever so slightly as the emotion trembled her words. The deep tone rang out again.

This time, each voice shouted out, giving names to those lost. "For the Captain", "For Crew", "For Engineering", "For Weapons", "For Jin Qwon", "For Angela LeMon", "For Abdul Anisis", "For Jennifer Jay", the names continued. The shouts came as one, but each one clear, all of them heard and remembered. Everyone had someone to honor. When they had finished their personal roll call, they drank. After, some closed their eyes, some held heads high, as other names continued to fill the air.

Jax watched as Gemma Lewis waited patiently on stage. She waited till they gave every name a voice, so many names, but no one rushed to finish. They would hear them all. The rush gave way to a trickle as the room went silent.

Gemma steeled herself on stage, her eyes connected with each member of the crew. Her voice projected across the hall, "The third bell is for what is to come. For the new crew, the new friends, the new battles that we will conquer. *Nos ire in tenebras. Sine timore. Sine pari.*"

Then, everyone shouted with the Gaia Fleet motto, "We travel into darkness. Without fear. Without equal."

Gemma's voice rose higher still; her drink held high. "This one is for the *Ares*. May our enemies fear the name, for she is the eternal hunter, and we are coming for them!" She yanked and released the cord. The gong boomed, its vibration engulfing them.

The room exploded in cheer. "For the *Ares*! For the *Ares*! For the *Ares*!" Around the room, the third drink was downed, and the cheering continued. Music began to play. People turned and embraced, clapped each other on the shoulder and smiles broke on grim faces.

Small groups formed as the crew shared stories, happy memories of those now gone. Tears mixed with laughter, mixed with singing, filled the hall.

With a little prodding, a little pleading, Jax left her bar stool and mixed with the crew. The inner walls to her thoughts and emotions stayed high, but slowly they fell. At first, she listened and then she added her own comments. In the darkness of her thoughts, in the names running through her head, she to found her own stories to share.

Long into the night, they didn't mourn those that were lost; they celebrated them. Jax found a way of dealing with loss she had never had before. One not born of personal pain, but based on shared hardships, on a bond forged in the heart of adversity.

Chapter 12

CALL SIGN

The strain bristled up Jax' arm as the *Ares* pressed hard into the turn. She twisted, more pull on the left, pushed harder on the right. The holo gloves wrapped around her hands. Wire frame gauntlets that signified she had flight control. The light green image pulsed along her fingers and forearms. Antigrav waves provided feedback just like in a VRpod. She could feel the *Ares* move.

Proximity alerts sounded as trailing Screech ships opened fire. Blue and green energy flashed by and sparked off the *Ares'* shield. Jax's feet pressed, turning the *Ares* like the rudder turning of a sea bound ship. Her eyes danced across the controls. Three Screech harassed her from the aft of the *Ares*, annoying in their persistence. Coming around on the port side was her target: The Screech destroyer.

Comm chatter echoed in her ear. ENG dealing with energy and minor damage. WEP announcing firing solutions and those same solutions popping on her HUD. The captain's deep voice boomed with command. Calling off targets, course corrections, and changes in strategy all coming in rapid fire. A change in course caught Jax scrambling to adjust her pitch and roll. Dropping the X-axis, looking for a broadside on the under base of the Screech destroyer.

Screech fighters came racing out of hiding. Three more attackers had joined the fight. Streaking like missiles to the *Ares'* nose, Jax's right hand squeezed on instinct. The *Ares* let loose with red death as it's TBWs, Tactical Beam Weapons, snuffed the fighters out like fireworks in the night. A second destroyer tore into her path. Her muscles flared, pushing the *Ares* down to avoid the ramming course.

Jax screamed, "Dive you—No!"

Warning screens flashed red, the entire NAV pod rumbled, sirens blazed in agony. The holo gloves burst into sparks; her hands dropped onto the counsel. *Damn.* All the holoscreens blinked out, except for one little red screen. A red screen floated mockingly before her eyes. *Mission Failure.* She leaned back in the chair, closed her eyes, tilted her head back, took a deep breath, and let out a sigh.

A voice echoed through the pod. "Don't be hard on yourself, Jax. It's only your second run. I don't think anyone has gotten that far on their second run."

"Thanks, Emitt," Jax said. Emitt was an easy-going lieutenant, who, along with his team, were currently the "Control" for flight simulators. They acted as crew, taking on the rolls of ENG, WEP, OPSs and even captain. They were also in charge of what happened in the simulation. Mission parameters, difficulty level, and of course, any random chaos that might occur.

Jax had been here all morning working on flying the *Ares*. Thankfully, Commander Bard had signed off the prerequisites necessary for simulator training. Flying an *Ares* class ship was specialty training, beyond that of a pilot. It was a highly competitive course to get into, and she had to assure the commander she was up to it. The military hates idle hands. So, they had given Jax a busy training schedule. Ten hours days working everything from class lessons on military procedure to practical training like the simulator. Her free time, what there was of it, was for her own personal projects. It had started a day of the memorial and now the weeks were blurring together.

The first part of the morning was basic flying, turning, rolling, hitting way points in space. Moving a ship of this size through space was not what she expected. You had to think ahead, working maneuvers ten to twenty steps out. The size and mass of the ship had to be considered. You had to plan a turn into an opening before an opening existed. There was a delay as the controls worked to carry out the commands.

"I shouldn't have shot those ships, right? That brief delay to start my turn means I missed my window and caused the collision," Jax said.

"Correct." Emitt's voice echoed in the pod. "Those ships were too small to affect your flight. They would move or your shields would brush them off. The Screech might be suicidal, but you throw something as big as an *Ares* class ship at them, they still move. If need be, the WEP team would have handled them. Weapons in the NAV position should be a last, only, when necessary, option. The second destroyer was cutting you off. You had several paths to avoid them, but you rammed them for a change. Trust your team to do their job, you do your job."

Work the plan, Jax. Even if it felt good shooting something. Jax's own thoughts chastised her. "Got it. Can I make another run?"

"Sorry, Jax, we have a couple more pilots scheduled. Got an opening this afternoon if you want it. One of the officers broke their arm, had to cancel their time."

"Awesome. I'll take a long lunch and be back then."

"See you then, Lieutenant," Emitt said.

The lights in the pod came on as the side hatch slid open. Stepping out of the pod, she stretched her hip; it was healed but sitting still for long periods made it stiff. She heard the pod hum as it reset to its standby position. This training simulator was a combination of a NAVpod, VRpod, and good old-fashioned mechanics. It had all the gravity control capabilities of a VRpod but used a practical set-up for the actual flight controls. Hydraulic arms attached around the pod's shell, capable of moving the pod any number of ways. Gaia Military had the belief that virtual training just isn't the same, so where possible they went for real life effects. *That's the theory.*

Suspended a good ten meters off the ground, Jax worked her way down the metal stairs. The stairs were portable, pushed into position when needed, removed while in use. The metal frame clanked and swayed under her feet.

She turned to the exit when a technician caught her eye. Wearing gray work overalls, head tucked into an electric switch box. It didn't seem out of place, but goosebumps creeped over Jax's skin. Maybe it was simple paranoia, but she had ignored these feelings before. Images of Rallic flashed through her mind. She turned to introduce herself, get a better look.

"Lieutenant Brandt, Commander Bard asked me to retrieve you. Please accompany me to hangar four," a loud voice rang in her ears. She jumped, turning to find its source.

Standing before her was a stiff-backed lieutenant. His blue gray flight suit was obviously used but fit him like a fine suit. A bit of 5 o'clock shadow dusted his strong jawline. Dark eyes, below the perfect military haircut, dug into her.

"Oh, okay. I was going to lunch, but that works too—huh, lieutenant?" Jax said, forcing a smile to cover being surprised. "'And you are?'"

The man's chin rose, and his neck turned. A small crack and pop sound echoing out. Chills ran down Jax's spine. They always did when she heard that sound. At the base of his neck, small tendrils moved. A sailing ship at full sail crested his collar and sank again as if into the depths of an ocean. Live tattoos were available on Earth, too. Available, but still rare. Normal tattoos could take hours, live tattoos could take days. Inserting nanite ink into the skin, a person had to wait for the nanites to bind with the derma layer of the skin. You couldn't move until the process was complete. The time varied, but could take from twenty-four to forty-eight hours for each application. While they could sedate you, many who got the work done considered it a badge of pride to do it on will alone.

"They call me Ray Hammer. The commander is waiting," he said, turning to stride away. He didn't bother to look to see if she was following.

She double stepped to keep up with his long stride. "So, Ray Hammer, huh? How'd you get that moniker?" Jax asked. Taking classes on base, she had found many of the walkers to be like this fellow. A bit obsessed with the rules and regulations made them tough to talk to. Finding something they enjoyed talking about was the key to breaking through that. Pilots all had a sense of pride, and they loved their call signs. You had to earn a call sign, not take one. Pilots could talk for hours about their callsigns.

He side eyed her without breaking stride while he said. "I don't like leaving things to chance, so I often hit targets with twice the recommended munitions. Commander Bard thought Ray Hammer appropriate." His eyes shifted back, his head tilted up, and Jax could have sworn his chest puffed out a bit. He fell silent.

They entered the hangar where Commander Bard was instructing. When on Gaia, Commander Bard was a guest instructor for all combat pilots. Her abilities as a pilot gave her a legendary status in the Fleet. Getting her stamp of approval on your training was a serious feather in someone's cap. When she taught a class, combat pilots would fight for the right to join.

The commander stood behind a portable holotable with a flight helmet perched on one end. Her class sat in folding chairs; faces locked on the commander's every word. Eight officers of varying ranks filled out the front rows. Ten training cadets filling in the back rows. While they structured the class for the eight combat officers, cadets could silently attend. Commander Bard enjoyed having an open class. Her lessons could help pilots of any level.

Two holo fighters zipped around in front of her, playing out the scenario she described. A Gaia SAF-14, space and atmosphere fighter, chasing a Screech fighter. The holo images zipped through a mountain range.

The SAF-14 was the main Gaia fighter. The gray metal plane, a sleek triangle, with a slight curve of its wing, zoomed across the screen. Extremely nimble, with tactical beam weapons and a typical load out of six target guided missiles, the ship was built for these situations. Even with that, as the holo ended, the SAF-14 lost the Screech fighter on a tight turn. The Screech fighters were more maneuverable, the Gaia fighters more flat-out speed. The mountains gave the Screech a distinct advantage.

"So, any other options?" Commander Bard said. The officers' heads all dropped. Obvious that their previous answers had not solved the problem. The cadets' eyes narrowed as the scene played again. "No? What about you, Lieutenant Brandt?" Jax's eyes drew back as the class turned to look at her. Commander Bard's face sparked a mischievous eye at her.

Composing herself, she stopped behind the last row of chairs. "Goal and parameters of the problem?" Jax said.

"Seek and destroy. You saw the SAF-14 tailing the Screech fighter. The Screech escapes or has been able to destroy the pursuers in all previously offered solutions," Commander Bard said, waving a hand over the class. "You've seen enough to know what you're dealing with. Now stop stalling. You have ten seconds."

"Pull up and gain altitude," Jax said. She pulled up a wrist holo and connected with the training holo, feeding her commands to the SAF-14. "Fire a missile, two actually, as you go." The holo SAF-14 launched the missiles. The missiles were quick on the tale of the Screech fighter, catching turns as it zigzagged through the mountains. The SAF-14 lifted its nose and made for the skies. "When the missiles force the Screech out of the mountains, attack from a higher elevation. No need to chase it through narrow corridors. Put the fight where our strengths out match theirs."

On the holo image, the two missiles harassed the Screech fighter. Pushing the Screech to go faster, taking tighter turns. On a left bank turn, the first missile exploded harmlessly. The next hit a wall, its shock wave forcing the Screech to climb or smash the rock face next to it. Blue skies surrounded the top of the mountain range as the Screech fighter cleared it. The SAF-14 swooped in like a predator born and required tone. Target locked, it fired on the vessel, mini ruby beams striking out. The holo Screech sparked and then faded out with the destruction.

"An example of thinking outside the box. Give the lieutenant a hand," Commander Bard said, slowly clapping her hands. Around the room, the officers and cadets joined.

As the clapping calmed down, a voice overlapped the noise. "It's an interesting solution, but can someone really come up with this in real time? Thinking outside the box seems much easier when your life isn't on the line. No offense to Lieutenant Brandt. We all know her record on the *Ares*. I don't recall her having any actual combat flight experience. Theories don't win fights."

Jax's eyes narrowed on the lieutenant. *Try telling that to the corps. Theories have worked pretty well keeping me alive. But he does have a point. I'm still new to flight combat.*

"Excellent point Lieutenant Rogers," Commander Bard said. "Which is exactly why I brought Lieutenant Brandt here today."

A chill ran down Jax's spine.

"Her path to being in Gaia Fleet has been an irregular one. She's already doing simulation runs with *Ares* class ships." Commander Bard paused. "She has excellent training both as a regular pilot and in space. Ample flight time. She has tested off the charts in almost everything we have thrown at her. I've personally bypassed her on parts of our more advanced training. She is easily top one percent here — well top three percent definitely." Commander Bard gave a wicked abrupt laugh and smile. The Officers and cadets let their own chuckles mix in.

Jax could feel the hairs on the back of her neck rise. If her eyes could shoot fire, they would be doing so now.

"However, there is one test that no one, if they want my certification, gets to pass on. Especially if you're flying an *Ares*-class vessel." The little smile became a full-on toothy grin as the Commander said, "You have to pass your ASM test."

It startled Jax for a moment, her mind racing. In all her studying, she remembered seeing that acronym. She had to take a moment before it came to her. Air Combat Maneuvering, a dog fight. Regaining her composure, she said, "I look forward to the opportunity. I guess we'll schedule that soon."

"I'm ready right now. Unless you don't think you can handle it?"

Jax eyes locked on the Commander. The pilots whipped around in their chairs. Was it sympathy in their eyes, or were they waiting for a wreck to happen? Jax found she didn't care; she really didn't want this right now. She willed ice into her veins to cool the igniting embers. *It's a problem, work the problem.* "I'll need a Weapons System Operator. I don't have one assigned."

"Ray Hammer is available. I'm sure he'd love to step in," Commander Bard said.

Jax glanced at Ray Hammer as he stiffened and his eyes narrowed. He nodded. Looking back at the Commander, Lilly Bard's face had the look of a guilty child who just got away with something.

"I'll go get a flight helmet and get ready, then." Jax said. Stalling for time was the only plan she had. Her flight helmet was on the far side of the compound. She wanted all the time she could get.

"No need," Commander Bard said, grabbing the helmet from the table.

"I've had one prepared for you." The commander tossed the helmet over the seated pilots' heads.

Catching it easily in two hands, Jax said, "Thanks."

She heard a low growl and she turned to look at Ray Hammer. His whole body was pinched, rage bottled up. Following his gaze to her hands, she turned the flight helmet's face from him to her. It looked new, all shiny and bright. She hadn't needed one of these on Earth; they weren't needed in non-combat aircraft. Fleet pilots called them "Bone Domes" which she found funny.

The skull part of the helmet was a dull white with a light blue front shell attached over the forehead. It was there that she saw what had caught Ray Hammer's eye. Neat letters in bright red type. A call sign of her very own. Something everyone here had earned over years of training, and she had just been handed one. A call sign that she never wanted to explain to anyone, ever.

Her eyes flared as she brought them back up to the commander. All attempts to soothe the flames were now lost. Commander Bard's wicked smile ignited Jax's anger more. She knew that made the call sign that much more ironic, but she didn't care. She had worked so hard to leave the past behind, and now it was being thrown in her face. One bad instance when she was thrown in the brig, a mistake now immortalized.

Fine. You want a fight? I'll give you a fight. Jax tightened her jaw to stop her from saying something she would regret. *Maybe it's time Lillian Barduke got an ego check of her own. I'll show you what 'Fire Fist' can do.*

Chapter 13

HAMMERHEAD TURN

Jax stomped around the SAF-14, doing her preflight check. Pilots weren't responsible for maintenance, but another set of eyes looking for trouble was always a good thing. Thankfully, the checklist that ran through her head from Earth was like what they used on Gaia. Nothing leaking, visible condition of the outer hull, tires, no tools left behind by maintenance, outer panels that shouldn't move—don't, it was a simple list to follow.

She tried to use the familiar routine to calm down, but it wasn't working. She wanted to beat the commander badly. Ducking under the plane, finishing her inspection, she came face-to-face with Ray Hammer. His hands crossed, the right holding his flight helmet, his head tilted to the left. Impatience dripped off him like sweat on a hot summer day.

"Can we get on with this, please?"

"I don't rush inspections. I imagine going against Commander Bard, it's going to be chaotic. I don't want anything unexpected to happen."

"It won't matter. This will be over quickly."

Jax's jaw clenched as she stared him down. "I get it. You don't think I can handle it. I'm just some Earth pilot or some Delta Sierra. You hate that I was handed a call sign and didn't earn it. I don't have the training to be here. Really, I've heard it all," she said, tilting her head. "But I know how to fly. I may not know about Gaia, or all this military stuff, but this"—she waved at the plane—" I know. How about doing the unique thing and giving me a chance first?"

Silence stretched between them, and a storm brewed between their eyes. He struck first. "You really think that is what this is about? A call sign? My brother is right. You are an arrogant little thing."

Brother? The tilt of the head, the jawline, his nose, the better than everyone's attitude, it all dawned on her. "Your Terrance Moro's little brother." she said, giving a slight shake of her head. "So, you're not mad at why I got my call sign. You're mad that it's a reminder to everyone about what happened between Terrance and me. That's just wonderful. I'm sure it's all public information now anyway, with the way Gaia works. Everyone already knows, so why the frip does it matter?" His leveled eyes didn't break from her. She didn't break either.

"Your ignorance is astounding. Not all information is public," he said, rolling his eyes. "In your case, at the time, you were not an official part of the *Ares* crew. Nor a citizen of Gaia. You were also not on duty, they regulated it to a personal matter. Your personal time is not public record. My brother has shared the details with me."

"Great. While I'm sure his tale is exceptionally accurate, it's only one part of the story. Not that you'll give me the benefit of the doubt, huh? I didn't choose the damn call sign anyway, Commander Bard did. How about this? I'll never talk about it. No one will ever know about it. Then you and I have no problems," Jax said, flashing him her most wicked smile.

"I am a Moro. It doesn't work that way."

"I'm a Brandt and I don't give a damn," Jax said, her phoenix eyes flared. "I don't live up or down to your preconceived notions of me. I don't care about you, your brother, or the bloody call sign for that matter. I have a fight to win, and you have been assigned to help me do that. Can I count on you, or are you incapable of doing the job?"

Ray Hammer's face pinched, and his eyes narrowed. "I never lack in my duty. I agreed to be your WSO and you shall receive nothing but my best. It won't matter what we do, you're nothing but a grape. An easy win. You will get shot down just like everyone else. Accept it."

"I don't believe that," Jax said, turning and climbing the portable stairs to the cockpit. "Every problem has a solution." She settled into her seat and then paused for a moment. *Was that my mom's voice coming out of me?* She shook her head and started her take off checklist.

Ray Hammer dropped in the seat behind and continued. "I have never heard of anyone landing so much as a single shot on Danger Zone. She single-handedly wrote the book on fighter combat. She is just that good."

Danger Zone? The Commander's call sign. Well, that's just—damn, that's a great call sign. No, stay focused Jax, work the problem. I need a plan. "How does she do it?"

The conversation died as they finished preparing for flight. Gaining clearance to launch, Jax fired the qave drive engines. The engines sang a high pitch whistle. The whistle faded into the hum qave engines are known for. Vertical thrusters ignited, landing gear retracted, and the craft drifted into the air. Spinning the nose around, engaging the horizontal thrust, the SAF-14 zipped off.

The dueling grounds were up past the Twin Mountains. A clear airspace reserved for this specialized training. Now on their way, Jax asked her question again. "How does she do it?"

"What do you mean? She out-flies you and shoots you down," Ray Hammer said, his voice echoing in her helmet.

"No, I mean specifically, how does she do it? Everyone, no matter how good, has things they favor. Set strategies, patterns. You know her fights better than me, so think. How does she win?"

Before he could respond, Danger Zone's voice piped into the cockpit. "Hey Fire Fist, about time you joined me. Maintain your altitude, I'm ten clicks out from you. I've sent over the bubble for our encounter. Since I'm playing the Screech, you can follow me in. Once you enter the bubble, we begin. Hope you're ready for it."

Jax heard the humor in Danger Zone's voice. *Damn her.* "Ray Hammer, we're out of time. We've only minutes. Give me something."

To the left of her HUD, a red zone appeared covering much of the landscape. The top of the bubble crested at eight kilometers and expanded outward beyond what the eyes could see. A tracking beacon popped on the HUD. Currently, a small blue triangle, the read-out listing Danger Zone (HOSTILE). Once in the zone, it would change to red. The commander was flying a SAF-14, a real time overlay changed her fighter to look like a Screech fighter. The pieces for their contest were all in place.

Ray Hammer's voice crackled in her ear. "In all the confrontations I can recall she likes to toy with her opponent first. Let them get tone on her, then cut away or drop back before you can fire. Once she's on target, I have never seen anyone escape."

Wonderful. She likes to play with her prey before eating. Jax brought the SAF-14 to a following distance of two hundred and fifty meters. Aligning to Commander Bard's craft.

The training zone fast approached. Jax's mind raced, everything she had seen Commander Bard do on the *Ares*. Stalking the Screech to make attack runs. Fighting their destroyers, flying through the swarm to attack the Lander. A thought rang in her mind.

"Which way does she veer off?"

"What?"

"When she attacks, she'll pan right, but go left. She victory rolled the *Ares* left as well. Does she do the same when she falls back?"

"I think she's done both."

"But she'll favor one. Which is it?"

"I don't know. Left, I think."

"High or low?"

"I don't know."

"Best guess, damn it!"

"High."

As she heard his answer, Danger Zone's ship crossed into the zone. The Commander's voice taunted them, "Let's go, Fire Fist, I'm waiting."

Jax punched the throttle. "When we hit the bubble open fire, if you miss, try to miss low. I want altitude for what I have planned. Force her into the sky. Don't blink. Our best shot will come up close."

"Close? What plan? Please tell me you're not going to do something stupid." Ray Hammer protested from the back.

"No time," she said as their ship crossed the edge of the zone.

Danger Zone's craft accelerated into action, evasive maneuvers, jinking the craft around. She dropped and rolled to the right. Jax struggled to keep pace. The commander dodged left and right, up and down, a veritable showcase of low-flying skills.

Jax's SAF-14 TBWs, tactical beam weapons, burst into action. The roar of the cannons vibrated through the plane. She knew it was computer simulated for these matches, but it felt real. The lights flashed away from her and, unfortunately, danced around Danger Zone.

The planes zipped around mountain peaks and into valleys. A roller coaster of altitude changes that kept Fire Fist and Ray Hammer pressed into their seat.

"We need her to gain altitude!" she said.

"Get me a shot! You have to line it up!" Ray Hammer shouted back.

They rocked and rolled skimming evergreen trees. Danger Zone pushed the low altitude combat to its limits. Split-second decisions popped in Jax's head. Her muscles tensed, jaw clasped tight, her mind narrowed on flying, on keeping on target. Lights would flash as Ray Hammer worked the cannons, but it was never enough. They could not land a clean hit. Cresting a ridge, Danger Zone shot into the air and Jax cursed. She had expected a low-cut turn. She could feel her scream ripping her throat as she pulled back on the yolk. Hands aching, gripping the flight stick, correcting to follow the commander.

Danger Zone leveled out a kilometer below their limit. Playing dodge ball in the sky. Ray Hammer let loose missiles. Danger Zone's counter measures snipped them from the sky. She danced left and right, barrel rolled; all simple skills, but done with an expert's hands. Fire Fist and Ray Hammer fired volley after volley. Matched the commander move for move. Still, Danger Zone skimmed away.

Jax found the rhythm forming. The flight corrections became easier, her pacing of the commander on mark. Lines on the HUD flowed smoothly, dialing the Screech ship in to target. While Ray Hammer handled the guns, her instincts felt the Screech fighter coming into her sights. In that blink of an eye, she hit the brakes. Pulling back hard on the yoke, her fighter plane eyed the sky. She pushed the reverse thrusters to max, tried to push them beyond. The thrusters were used for space flight, not atmosphere. Jax didn't care she wanted to move backwards, against the plane's wishes. The fighter creaked and moaned around her as its ability to fly forward stopped. A hesitation, a fragment of time, and the fighter started to drop.

In that same moment, Danger Zone hit the brakes. Angling up, hoping to drop back behind Fire Fist. Jax wanted to scream at Ray Hammer, tell him to fire, fire away, but the split second was gone.

Sparks flew. A rumble ripped through the craft. Had she seen the nose of her fighter scrape the other craft? No, that was Ray Hammer on the cannons. Her mind raced to order the rapid thoughts, catching up to alarms sounding in the cockpit.

"Fire Fist! What's going on?" Ray Hammer shouted from the back.

"Our engines have stalled!"

"Is that possible?"

"No, it's not!" Jax flattened the SAF-14 out, now falling like a leaf. The fighter began to spin. "Mayday. Mayday. Mayday—" Jax started over the comms. A loud crackle echoed back in her ears.

"Comms are down. Systems are non-responsive. I'm shut out of the startup sequences. All systems lost. We need to eject," Ray Hammer said.

"Agreed," Jax said. "Bailout! Bailout!" They both pulled the eject lever. Nothing happened. "Oh, come on!"

Ray Hammer pounded on his council. "Now what?"

"Hang on, I'm going to push us into a glide and head toward the outer base runway. Get the landing gear down."

"On it," Ray Hammer said. "We have enough altitude to make that?"

"We don't have any choice."

Jax worked the rudder while fighting to keep the craft's nose up. Back and forth she pushed it, fighting against the rotation of the plane. The spinning stopped, and she pushed the nose into a dive. Altitude falling like a rock. Gaining speed and angling the plane towards the distant runway. Ships rarely needed full runways anymore. Thankfully, they were still around for emergencies.

Grunts and whispered cruses issued from the Ray Hammer as he said, "Landing gear is jammed."

"How's that possible?" Jax said.

"How should I know? This whole plane is bent. Hold on." Banging echoed from the backseat. Jax assumed Ray Hammer was breaking open a service panel.

"It looks like something melted on the manual release lever. It won't budge," he said.

The landing gear was a gravity-based system. Remove the lock and the gear drops and secures into place on its own. A simple mechanism that should be foolproof. Perfect for emergency situations.

"Can you bang it loose?"

"With what?"

"Here," Jax said, reaching inside her flight suit and grabbing the knife from her back. Tossing it over her shoulder. "Catch."

"You keep this on you?"

"You can always use a knife."

She had the feeling he was shaking his head at her but was otherwise silent. A few moments later, the clash of metal on metal filled her ears. Banging, curses, grinding metal filled the cockpit.

The plane was in a glide; the altitude dropping faster than Jax wanted. The runway was in sight, and they were five-by-five on their approach. Closer, the runway creeped up on them. The landing gear stayed up and Jax's anxiety grew. The kilometers became meters, dots in the distance took on form. "We're going to land!"

"Got it," he shouted. "Landing gear down!"

Her teeth gritted; eyes wide as the familiar sound of the gear locking into place graced her ears. The jolt of the plane hitting the ground shook her to the bone. Jax pressed hard on the manual brakes. The brakes squealed in protest, forcing the craft into a simple roll and stop.

Popping the canopy, the sounds of sirens and trucks rumbled at her. Ray Hammer dropped first and Jax scrambled after him.

They walked from the fighter, a smile on her face, a scowl that stretched from ear to ear on his. Removing her flight helmet, she said, "Why so glum? We made it."

"My brother is right, you are reckless, ill-trained, and a danger to those around you."

"Reckless? Maybe, but ill trained? I saved our butts back there."

"Which wouldn't have happened if your so called 'plan' actually followed tested and approved air combat tactics."

"Oh, please. I didn't cause the plane to stall, qave engines don't fail like that. We were sabotaged. Even a Moro should be able to see that."

His chin dropped and his eyes flared, "I'll tell you what I see —" he said, when a commanding voice snapped them both around. Ray Hammer snapping to attention. Jax stiffened but fell short of proper formality.

"Erratic turns and last second decision making. Chaotic combat tactics, and a blatant disregard from standardized training," Commander Bard said, her eyes weighing them down. Both Lieutenants quivered as they waited for the dressing down to continue. A long moment passed till the Commander continued. "I loved every minute of it!"

Jax smiled and kept a small laugh from escaping her lips. Lieutenant Moro, Jax realized she hadn't gotten his first name, stayed stoic.

"You almost caught me with that last attack. Guess even I can get a little complacent with my attack patterns. That won't happen again," the Commander said, turning to Jax's fighter. Around them, emergency vehicles arrived. The Commander's flight class came running up. "But what happened after that?"

"The SAF-14 stalled after Lieutenant Brandt's unique combat maneuver," Ray Hammer said stiffly.

"Qave engines don't stall like that," Jax said.

"It could have stalled."

"It didn't stall," both Jax and Commander Bard said together.

"I've been flying qave based craft longer than you've been alive," Commander Bard said, looking at Ray Hammer. "And Jax's mom basically designed the qave engines that are currently in use on Gaia. If we tell you they don't behave like that, then they don't behave like that. Is that clear, lieutenant?"

Ray Hammer tilted his head. The cracking noise from his neck sounded angry as he said, "Understood, Commander."

"Good," Commander Bard said, turning to look at the SAF-14. "I'll have this quarantined and get it inspected down to the atoms. You two can take a break, but be available. I'm sure the formal inquiry will need statements. Cross statements and statements explaining the statements before it's all done. Dismissed."

Jax and Ray Hammer saluted and turned to walk off. They made it only a meter before the entirety of Commander Bard's flight class swarmed them. Cheers and congratulations rang out, pats on the shoulder jostling them both.

"What's all this for?" Jax asked, having to shout over the commotion. "Pretty sure we lost like everyone else."

A bright-eyed lieutenant, the same one who had questioned her before, shouted back in her ear, "Oh, you lost. Commander Bard blew you out of the sky a few moments after your hammerhead turn. But your guns ripped up her wing something furious."

A confused look crossed Jax's face, forcing the lieutenant to continue. "We've never seen anyone hit her before! That's a win in our book!"

Jax's eyes gleamed, and she started laughing. *Score one for Fire Fist*! She joined in the celebration as the crowd of pilots danced their way off the runway. She caught glimpses of Ray Hammer among the crowd. Another uptight Moro, another pain in her side, yet even his grim visage had broken into a smile.

Chapter 14

DRAGON'S LAIR

The door opened as Jax approached, and she strode in. The quaint little house, set only a kilometer from the Heart of Gaia, was welcoming. From the outside, it was like other examples of Gaia architecture. Blending in with the landscape, grass, trees, and shrubbery flowed from the yard to the roof. Seen from overhead, you would never know it was here. Looking straight at it, bay windows and a heavy door greeted you. On Earth, they would call this kind of house a rambler.

"I'll be out in a moment!" Rose shouted, her voice echoing down the hallway. "Make yourself as home!"

"No problem. Take your time," Jax shouted back, even though she wanted to shout, "hurry up we're supposed to go when I got here." Jax was on time, 1000 hours sharp. On the ship, Rose was always punctual, in her personal life, not so much.

I hate being late. If we set a time, we should be on time. She tried to let the thought go. Jax was anxious, excited, and scared all at once. Too much time hiding, working on the *Ares* had fried her nerves. They told her days ago it was safe to get out now, Gaia First on the run, but it still felt strange. This was supposed to be a fun day. She tried to focus on that. Her mind wasn't having it, though, and her thoughts were a jumble. Needing things to do on the ship, she had been watching the news. There were two new channels on Gaia, and both were abuzz about the raids on the Gaia First complexes. She checked constantly for information on the sabotage to her fighter. She had informed Commander Bard about the person watching her at the simulator. Was that something real or her imagination? *I feel in the dark with my own life sometimes.* She played with the idea of contacting Sebastian Moro. He had been here longer, maybe he was in the loop? Could she trust the brother of Terrance Moro? *I wonder what other Moro's are out there to torture me? I could use another chai. One just wasn't enough this morning.*

She hung her hoodie and kicked off her shoes. Then arranged them neatly by the door and stepped into the house. The living room, with kitchen beyond, met her. Her mind continued to run through thoughts unbidden. The Doc's new lessons were driving her crazy. She stretched her finger, thinking about them. She turned the finger stretched into fingering keys on the sax. *I need to work on my altisimo more.*

Her mind startled when she saw where she was. A smile broke across her face as she observed her best friend's dwelling. Rose had described this room to her many times, and her plans to do more. Jax hadn't understood what that meant. She was still confused because she couldn't imagine Rose doing more with this room. Rose's very own dragon's lair.

It unfolded before her like a scene from a holovid. Small and large statues graced every available space. Wizards and dragons predominate among them. The occasional other mythical creature sprinkled here and there. *Unicorns, griffons, and centaurs, oh my.* Each space occupied; each space planned to make the most of the display. A couch sat unassumingly in the middle, the coffee table in front showcasing a castle siege, complete with both armies. A large painting of a multi-headed dragon locked in eternal conflict with a speck of a wizard sat above the mantel, dominating the room. From the dragon's mouth spewed fire, ice, lightning, purple chaotic energy, and green acid. All of it together bordered on chaos, but the technical mind that was Rose gave the room to order.

Jax wandered around the room inspecting each piece, each scene, in turn. Wizards fighting dragons. Dragons fighting knights. Castles assaulted by orcs and goblins. The attention to detail was astounding. Each scene pulled you from reality into Rose's imagination. *Works magic in the engine room, lives with magic at home.*

The only thing that didn't seem to belong was an antique roll-top desk. Pushed into a quiet corner away from the kitchen, windows, and any other distractions. While well-polished, the cherry wood showed chips and scratches from decades of use. Deep drawers made up the left and right legs. The rolltop was a quarter down. Nooks and cubbies filled with various knickknacks, peaked from beneath. Stacked neatly, dead center on a leather pad, were stacks of printed paper. *Actual paper!* Neat words on the first page stated:

"Dimensions Lost by Rosita Kioke."

Rose's fabled manuscript. Rose could tell or listen to a story for hours on end, but she never talked about this. Jax had tried to pin her down, get the details of this epic story she was writing, but Rose held fast. This was Rose's work in progress, her first novel. Jax's hand *caress*ed the pages.

Jax longed to open the document and start reading, but knew her friend wouldn't want that, yet. Jax forced her eyes away. Instead, she focused on the little notes stuck all over the desk. Some had details like "Brund has blue eyes, Brunnd has brown eyes," "The twisted path is straight on a full moon." Others asked questions like, "What has value? Gold? Gems? Something else?"

Jax wondered why Rose didn't simply upload everything to a holo terminal? Jax never thought Rose was against any kind of technology. Probably because of Gaia's weird ideas about AI. It simply didn't make sense to her. She was using a virtual upload, and EVE, to keep track of Gaia news, study military procedures, and helping gather data on the Screech. How did people get along without them?

That reminds me, I need to ask her about EVE. Got to fix that soon. She and Rose were supposed to have been spending more time together. Instead of being on the Ares and helping with repairs, however, Rose was stationed on Gaia. Helping Nath with weapon revisions and working through ways to improve the Ares. Nobody wanted what the Screech had done to the *Ares* to ever happen again.

A larger piece of paper stuck under the corner of a smaller square had "Names" written across the top. Curiosity won, and she slid the paper out, just a little, and began to read.

Fri'drick A'msden.

Fritz Brose.

Federico Ambroggio.

Roos - Use same as above.

Roisin — Use same as above Rosaria — Use same as above.

Rose Ambross.

As she read the last name, Rose's voice drifted over her shoulder. "I'm ready, let's — what are you doing?"

Jax turned, pinching the paper up and wiggling it, a wicked grin on her face. "Why didn't you tell me? I can't believe I missed this. It's so obvious now."

"Give me that," Rose said, snatching the paper from Jax's hand. She shouldered past her to place it on the desk.

"The way you always sit near him when we were all hanging out. You work the same shifts too. How'd I miss this?"

"I don't know what you're talking about," Rose growled.

"Oh please. Now that I think about it, that night we were drinking in my room, I could of swore you wanted to—"

"Jax, you can't tell him," Rose said.

"He doesn't know?"

"Of course, he doesn't."

"I thought you liked guys with long hair?"

"I do. It's just—" Rose said. "I don't mind the hair so much. I like the way he talks. The way he is so focused on his work. He listens and understands everything I talk about. He can really be delightful. He doesn't annoy me like some people."

"Oh, you got it bad."

"I do."

"You should tell him."

"I can't. We work together. I'm his senior officer. It's too complicated."

"I can't believe you didn't tell me," Jax said, pushing Rose's shoulder.

"It's not like you've shared all your deepest secrets with me, Miss I Hate My Middle Name."

Jax's lips pursed, and she dropped her chin at her friend. Rose raised hers, eyes locked in defiance.

"Fine," Jax said under her breath. Eyes darting around the room, double checking that they were alone. She leaned in and whispered ever so gently in Rose's ear.

Rose's face pulled back; her nose pinched like she had smelled rotten eggs. "That's not great, but I don't —"

"Look it up."

Rose raised an eyebrow. Lifting her wrist and opening a holoscreen off her bracelet. A few flicks of the fingers, a moment reading. "Oh, that's horrible. What were your parents thinking?"

"It wasn't a mutual thing, it—" Jax turned away. "I don't want to talk about this. I know your secret and now you know mine. Can we get to this festival thing now?"

"Absolutely!" Rose said, the edge gone from her voice, cheery tones returning. "As soon as you change your outfit."

"What's wrong with my outfit?" Jax said, looking down at her clothes. She had blue jeans that stopped at mid-calf. A gray pleated shirt with three-quarter sleeves that hung past her waist. With her white tennis shoes by the door, she was ready for the day. She knew the day would be pleasant, but the night was a little cooler. Planning for the whole day, she felt like she had achieved the right balance.

"Founder's Day is a party. You look like you're going on a walk with your grandma."

"I thought we were shopping first?"

Rose sighed. "Yes, open market. Then lunch. All the music stages and events kick off in the afternoon. Once night sets in, the kids go home, and the adult fun begins. Normally I would just go in the afternoon, but since this is your first Founders, we're doing it all. Just not dressed like that."

"I think I look fine."

"Do you look like me?" Rose said, raising her hand and striking a pose.

Jax pulled back and took her friend's outfit in for the first time. Rose's dress sparkled, the colors shifting as she moved. Reds to silver to pale blues. It showed too much leg, and its spaghetti straps gave way to a V-line too deep for Jax's liking. Jax had to admit, however, that with the bracelets, earrings and makeup, her friend looked good. Jax had seen a white dress-style jacket and high heel shoes by the door that she was sure completed the ensemble. Wear the jacket during the day to be more proper, take it off to party at night.

"Did you cut your hair?" Jax asked. She had missed it at first, styled back from Rose's face.

"Yup. Got tired of everyone confusing me with my ugly big sister," Rose said with a mischievous grin. She squinted at Jax. "Did you cut your hair?"

"Yup."

"It looks the same."

"Of course. Do you know how long it took me to find a hairstyle I like?"

Rose rolled her eyes, laughing all the while. Taking her friend by the arm, she ushered her to the bedroom. Rose's bedroom was a sharp contrast to the living room. Mild gray walls surrounded a queen-size bed. A simple nightstand with a single holo picture, Rose and her parents toasting some event. Her parents were both engineers and worked at the shipyards, building Fleet vessels. The room felt more like a berth on the *Ares* than a place called home.

Rose waved her hands and a full body holoscreen slid from the wall. Another gesture and an exact image of Jax formed on the screen. A few more gestures and Jax's clothes faded. Leaving the image standing in Jax's underclothes.

Jax pushed her friend's shoulder. "You don't have to do it like that."

"Quiet," Rose said, raising a hand. "Let the master work."

A small holoscreen popped in front of her. Fingers flying through lists and images. Smiling and finished, she flung her selection at the screen. Jax's mouth gaped. A black bustier that made a bikini look big. Skintight shorts with metal buttons on the side. All of it overlaid with a black lace dress, if you could call it that.

"No. Just no."

"Oh, come on. You're looking good. You should show off some of that muscle you've got now. We can add a day coat for the market, of course. We'll fab it with temp controls to keep you cool. It will be fabulous."

Jax shook her head, her friend's fashion boldness a bit of a shock. "No. Definitely not," she said, opening her sub-holoscreen.

A few moments later she updated her holo preview image. Black pants, a white V-neck blouse, a short midriff jacket.

"Boring," Rose declared, and the back and forth started. Rose would change, and Jax would change. Rose would shorten, tighten, and expose. Jax would lengthen, loosen, and cover. They fought, and they laughed till the last image.

"Still think the pants are a bit tight," Jax said, but was smiling at the image. Form fitting black pants, a black strapless top that stopped a few centimeters from her waist. Sleek shoes with wide heels. *Love those shoes.* A semitransparent red jacket to set the whole thing off.

"Oh, please. Show the booty, sister. You've earned it," Rose said, punching her in the shoulder. "Let me have the vanityfab print it. We'll get you changed. I'll do what I can with your hair and makeup."

"Hey!" Jax protested.

Rose ignored her protests, laughing the whole time, while she started to pull on Jax's hair.

"No complaining. Let's get going. It's party time!"

Chapter 15

FOUNDERS' DAY

There were only two official holidays on Gaia. Winter's Requiem, which occurred on Gaia's winter solstice. It was a somber holiday, with friends and family gathering to enjoy each other's company. It also launched the Gaia New Year, with people giving thanks for all they had. Founder's Day was the opposite. It started on the summer solstice; it was also more than just a day. Music and parties were part of a week-long celebration. Celebrating the original founding of Gaia and establishing its military. The end of the event led to a grand ball.

Rose usually just went for the music, but this year she wanted to treat her friend. That meant showing her the works and that included getting to the event. Rose wanted to arrive in style, set the mood for the day. Instead of a quick ride in a rapid transport or catching a ride on a fleet vehicle, she had arranged something a little more spectacular: the horse-drawn carriage that awaited them as they exited the house.

It was like something from a storybook, something a queen of old might ride. Large silver wheels, the main riding area blue with silver and red trim. The fancy metal work falling short of being pompous. The horse was a robotic marvel. The horse's sleek, white metal skin glistened in the sunlight. Every muscle sharply defined, taking it from reality to the edge of fantasy. Its programming was flawless. It snorted, reared its head, like an actual horse would. It mimicked a horse in every way. Rose mentioned it was programmed and not an AI or EVE unit. While Gaia used AI when necessary, medical mainly, they avoided it if at all possible. Jax wasn't sure she got the difference, but didn't want Rose to go off on some technical rant, so she closed her lips and went for a ride.

On top sat an actual driver. A rarity on Earth, with positions like this being filled by EVE units, here it was the norm. He was wearing a sharp black tux with what Jax now knew to be a top hat. A small beard hugged his face as he merrily moved the coach along. They took a scenic route, a quick trip through the neighborhood and then along the central park. Jax gawked out the window. Noting the number of people playing in the park, the stages set for the festival, and the stands for the market. Rose buried her nose in a small holoscreen messaging friends they had planned to meet later.

Stopping at a drop-off at the market, Jax froze as Rose hopped out.

"I know the carriage is fabulous, but the market is over here," Rose said.

Jax peeked over Rose's shoulder, the noise of the crowds filling her ears.

"I want to go. I need to go. It's just that Gaia hasn't exactly been welcoming to me so far."

"You worried about Gaia First still?"

"A bit, I mean I thought I wasn't but now that I'm here—"

"I thought you talked to Commander Lewis, and she gave the all clear."

"I did, sort of. I messaged her. She messaged back that Gaia First is being dismantled. It's all but finished. Security would be on high alert and precautions were in place. I don't have to be restricted to base anymore. I wish I could have seen it, been a part of it. The news seemed to say the same thing, so —"

"So, you wanna go back? We can find a holo movie to enjoy. There's a hot new holovid by Rupert Ho, a Gaia director, I've been wanting to get into. Popcorns on me," Rose said with a smile.

You need to get out more, Jax. All you do is study military protocols, watch the news and study the Screech. "No, let's go. I'm dying to see what Gaia's about," Jax said, pulling the overcoat around her like its own dress. The jacket would keep her cool, and she wasn't ready to be in party mode yet.

On Earth, Jax had only known farmers' markets at local events that happened on closed streets in small dedicated spaces. On Gaia, an entire quarter of the outer ring circling the Heart of Gaia was used. The immense

tree dominated the landscape and surprisingly didn't block the light. Gaia
used the same adaptive cloaking field technology the *Ares* had for a verity
of effects. The shops nestled around the giant tree were a permeant fixture
that operated day in and day out. A great place to find some unique items
or fresh local food. Shops that housed local farmers, outfitters, artisans,
and goods of all kinds. Trading posts that hawked Earth's eccentric goods
could also be found. This was the primary place for anything you needed.
While you could fab things, or have things delivered, people on Gaia had
embraced an old concept of getting out and meeting one other. For trading their crafts and *wares* and shopping for things in person. Jax danced
through the market like a kid through a candy store.

She wanted to see everything. Not a booth was missed. Rose joined in,
but would also let Jax roam on her own. Rose spent her time checking her
holo for events and messages. For her, the market was a standard thing; it
lacked the excitement Jax found in it.

At first, Jax held back, buying anything. She didn't want to carry it all
until she learned the greatest thing ever. All the shops delivered anywhere
on Gaia, or to ships in orbit. That changed everything.

The first thing she bought, a memory from her past, were flowers. Growing up, Jax's mom loved flowers. No matter where they moved, one of the
first things dad always did for mom was to fill the house with flowers. Not
so much the kind of flowers, but the colors; red, blue, and green. They
couldn't live anywhere without flowers adorning the place.

Jax's nose filled with the aroma of the bouquet cupped in her hands.
A mix of reds, purples, and yellows. Blue and green reminded her too
much of the Screech beam weapons, so she avoided those. Red wasn't her
favorite, but they so reminded her of her mom. On Earth, these flowers
would be lilies. These Gaia varieties had the same six segments, but the
six petals were shorter and wider. She handed the bouquet back to the
vendor. Tapped her bracelet and waved a small holoscreen to the vendor
for payment. She was happy that Gaia used the same base ten credit system
that Earth did. The payment also contained delivery instructions. All the
items she bought today would be delivered to *Hopper* for her trip back to
the *Ares*.

There were paintings, glasswork, pottery, and all of it was handmade. The quality of work surpassed anything Jax had seen on Earth and far outstripped what a fabricator could do. Fascinated by everything, she window shopped her way through the items. She couldn't justify cluttering up her room on the *Ares*, but she so wanted to. She passed by shops for home improvement, farming, and the like. Stopping once to chat with a nice old couple about their homesteading booth. Living in the wilds of Gaia, roughing it without modern conveniences. Dealing with native plants and animals yet to be discovered. It was more intriguing than she dared imagine.

Clothing vendors had a large showing, too. Each booth showcasing styles from old Earth, Modern Earth, and Gaia originals. All were accepted and embraced, mixing and matching, trying hard to create original looks was the norm. Jax got caught up in new outfits and styles. She and Rose laughing and arguing about their choices. Jax splurged on clothes. She still didn't have her stuff from Earth and military clothing just wasn't enough. Shirts, shoes, pants, shorts. If it was wearable, she was buying.

Then came the food, the wonderful food. Earth staples were in abundance, stalls serving classics from America, China, Germany, Africa, Japan, and so many more. Several vendors often worked together, offering small plates with a sampling from each place. The ladies balanced plates across their arms, eating from dozens of differing offerings. During the samplings, Jax discovered a new favorite treat. A Gaia original that the locals called a gerry.

The gerry grew on a native tree, similar to an Earth maple. It had a hard shell, like a walnut. You couldn't eat them raw, you had to soak them in alcohol for a day and then deep fry them. The alcohol would burn off, leaving a crispy edible shell. Inside there was a gooey paste that screamed cherry. The Gaia cherry, gerry, was a perfectly sweet bite sized treat. Best eaten hot out of the fryer, but you could eat them cold, so Jax ordered a bag of them to take back to the ship.

They spent those first few hours eating and shopping their way through the market. Early afternoon gave way to sunshine and blue skies. The friends found themselves in the park around the Heart of Gaia. Here,

families, kids, couples, loners laughed and played, relaxed in the afternoon sun, or picnicked. The plan had been to eat lunch here, but all
the snacking changed the plan. Instead, they found a bench to rest their
feet. Rose buried her nose in a holoscreen, checking in with the Rat
Pack–Freddy, about meeting up later. Jax stretched her feet and watched
the people in the park.

On Earth, the seasons dictated fashion. Each season would see three,
maybe four, dominant trends that everyone followed. There was the
occasional rebel, but vanity fabs made it easy to keep in step. On Gaia,
it was something else completely. Here it was a cornucopia of style, plus
the kitchen sink. Fashions from Earth's past; bell-bottomed pants, track
suits, short skirts, long formal gowns, and more. Mixed in was what Jax
could only think of as Gaia originals. Color shifting cloths and skin, live
tattoos playing out scenes, hair that flowed, changing shape, length, and
style as it did. Together, it overloaded her with its array of expressions.
She loved it.

People played games, baseball, cricket, dodgeball and more. Smaller
games could be found on picnic tables, chess, towers, dicing games and
anything you could imagine. Kids laughed and played as they ran in the
park. Vpets chasing after them. They mimicked everything from a dog,
cat, bird or even the more fanciful like a bear, lion, a winged horse, or
unique creatures from their own imagination. Jax wanted to sit and take
it all in. To enjoy the people enjoying their lives, laughing, and playing.
Rose had other plans. Rose was ready to dance.

"We have to go! The music is starting. My favorite DJ is up first. I almost
missed it!" Rose said, grabbing Jax's hand and hauling her off.

Jax's feeble attempts to hold her friend back were met with an increase
in speed. The festival part of this day was on the far side of the Heart
of Gaia. It took time to round the gargantuan tree. Coming to the far
side, stages appeared, impossibly close to one another, from Jax's view. A
moment of confusion until a pop echoed in her ear as Rose pulled her
through the first sound shield. The music boomed from the stage. It was
then she realized that each stage sat in its own sonic shield. You could be
centimeters from one stage and never hear it till you crossed the threshold.

The first stage they hit was what Earth called MPOP. Multilayered Pop Music. Lyrics and music from several songs were overlapped and played at the same time, creating a whole new sound. Masters of the craft could warp several songs into an entirely new song. Words meshing, beats changing, to play something completely unique. The dancing was as fast as the music, as the two sisters joined the flow.

Stepping through the next sonic shield, the fast MPOP gave way to rock ballads. Another pop in the ears and acoustic guitar filled the air. Another pop and old Earth jazz brought pleasure to Jax's ears, but Rose rushed them on. *Pop.* Heavy thumping bass with screams for singing. *Pop.* Synthesizers produced sounds never heard by human ears. Jax and Rose laughed and danced their way through them all. The afternoon hours became a blur to shifting music, dancing, and singing. They found friends they knew and would merge with them for a while. Even Freddy and Coleman rushed by, carried by a group of three kids. She assumed they were Coleman's kids, but with the varying crowd, who knew? As easily, they would break off on their own dancing to their own beat. There were always new friends to find, fresh groups to join. You never had to be alone.

Exhausted and sweating, the next pop led not to music, but to words. Unfortunately, the words were not a play or poetry, as was being performed on some stages. This was a speech. A political speech. Jax paused as she focused on the Prime Representative. The PR wore a light blue suit, her hair a gold metallic that glistened in the setting sun. She was finishing a line about the Screech and how they were homing in on the now elusive enemy. A clear transition to the strength of Gaia and how they were equipped to handle any situation. Words of hope that inspired and drew applause from the crowd.

"Come on, Jax. This is boring," Rose said, grabbing Jax by the elbow, trying to pull her along.

"Just a sec," Jax said, resisting and holding up a finger. "I need a break and I want to hear this. Despite what Commander Bard thinks, the Prime Rep seems clever." Jax could feel Rose roll her eyes at her.

"Fine. I'll contact the boys and make sure we're still on to meet up later," Rose said, pulling a holoscreen off her wrist.

You want to see if Freddy is still coming. Jax smiled at the thought. The crowd cheered again as the PR made a point about the strength of Gaia. The speech flowed from talking about the Screech to building the infrastructure of Gaia. All of it subtly showing the strength of the PR's leadership. *She's good at this. Reminds me a lot of how Commander Bard talks.*

Breaking from the PR's demanding presence, Jax scanned the other people on stage. She was sure those surrounding the PR were important, but outside the major players, she was lost. She was watching the news and could follow along well enough, but on her own the faces were a mystery. Until she noticed him, the one person she could identify, Representative Dakos.

"What the abyss is he doing up there?" Jax said, not even trying to hide her disgust.

Rose glanced from her holoscreen and focused in on Jax's problem. "We may not like him, but Dakos is still a pretty popular Rep. He's always around when the Prime is. Her term is up in about a year. He's gunning for it," Rose said.

A Prime Representative could have three three-year terms. Emma Gibson was at that limit. Jax didn't care about that, but Eli Dakos as PR? That would suck for the *Ares.*

Rose went back to her messages. Jax looked around the stage for her other "favorite person." Beyond Dakos was a stern-looking beauty in a deep blue dress that matched the Eli Dakos suit. The lady's eyes drifted from watching the Prime to watching Eli. From news feeds, Jax recognized her as Eli Dakos wife. That wasn't who Jax was looking for. Down the steps, she spotted him, mean mugging the crowds. Decked out in his wannabe corps gear. Black fatigues, they lacked the adaptive technology of true corps gear. Talbot Blocksburg, broken nose, and permanent scowl, stood like he was the most dangerous man in the universe. Jax shook her head at that thought when another figure caught her eye.

Beyond the dog, a small head peeked out. It pulled back as quickly, hidden now behind the back of Talbot. The hawk nose, the slick hair. In Jax's mind, there was only one possibility. *The Shadow.*

"Hey, that's Esteban!" Jax shouted, pointing her finger.

"Where?" Rose asked, her head whipping back up.

"Right behind Dakos' bodyguard, just right of the stage."

"I don't see anyone. You sure? There are a lot of interns running around. Maybe it's one of those."

"No. It's got to be him, hiding in plain sight. Arrogant frip."

"I still don't see him. What do you want to do?" Rose said, her head craning around for a better look.

"I don't know — wait, I don't—" Jax's gaze darted between the stage and Talbot. "Why's Dakos coming offstage?"

It was subtle, Dakos one minute waving, smiling at the crowd. Kissed his wife and whispered in her ear. She scowled but held her ground. He glided back behind some other Reps. Down the side of the stage and his dog had moved in to screen him from the crowd.

"We need to follow—" Jax said. That's when the stage exploded.

The Prime Representative, the other Reps, everyone on stage, flew like rag dolls into the air. Screams broke out through the crowd. A buzz filled the air as the sound shields all winked off. More booms vibrated, the screams cutting into the darkness. People, clutching friends and family, scattered, desperately looking for a safe direction to run. The sound of gunfire mixed in. The distant "thumping" that came from weapons like the NEW24. Flashes burst into the panicked crowds, people dropped, they trampled some while getting away.

Another explosion turned Jax around. This one closer, her head ducking on instinct. As she came up, her eyes met the barrel of a gun. The face behind it was all-too familiar.

A face she had seen somewhere on the *Ares*. A face she had seen as a technician at flight school. The face of a person passing through the crowd in the market. She should have investigated earlier. Trusted her instincts more. It was too late for that. Too late for anything. The muzzle flashed.

Chapter 16

BUBBLE HEAD

Jax's eyes went wide as she felt the heat brush her ear and singe her hair. A grunt from behind whipped her head around. A man with a similar pistol dropped to the ground. Jax turned back. But instead of finding a gun to her face, the lady was scanning the crowd.

"Who are you —" Jax said, when her side profile finally jogged her mind. "You're Lieutenant Wisler. You're the one who's been following me. What's going on?"

"I doubt you saw me," Lieutenant Wisler said, a hint of annoyance lacing her words. "Commander Haddock assigned me to shadow you. Keep you safe. We need to get you out of here." Lieutenant Wisler grabbed Jax's arm and attempted to drag her. An explosion rumbled in the distance; gunfire lit the air, screams adding to the chaos.

"No," Jax said, ripping her arm away. "We need to help those people."

"I have orders from Commander Haddock."

"Commander Haddock is not here. Meaning as engineering commander, and being on site, my orders supersede his," Jax said, catching a wide-eyed Rose from the corner of her eye. Jax tilted her head at her friend. "Told you I studied."

Lieutenant Wisler's lip curled, and her glare was hostile, but she acquiesced. "Fine. You're the boss. What are we doing?" she said.

Jax pulled up a holoscreen from her jacket. "I can't get a signal. Can anyone get comms?" she said, looking first at Rose and then at Lieutenant Wisler. Both shook their heads as they closed their own holoscreens.

"We'll need some firepower then. What do we got?" Jax asked.

Lieutenant Wisler held up her NEW9 with a look that said, that's it. Jax looked at Rose, who was already pulling the gun off the body Wisler had shot. A pistol like a NEW9 was all the body produced.

"There's a militia station less than a block from here. We can gear up there," Rose said, offering Jax the pistol. Jax shook her head and waved for Rose to keep it. The officers were off and running.

The insurgents were reigning gunfire at any random moving target. Clad in the mock Corps combat suits, they met with little resistance. Civilians could be armed on Gaia, but it was a festival, so few were. Anyone caught brandishing a weapon or fighting back got targeted and eliminated. The insurgents were causing as much damage as possible. When civilians weren't offering easy targets, they fired into stages, buildings, or even in the air. Lights flashed, people died, and explosions ripped the ground, it was utter mayhem.

The three officers weaved through the crowd and stayed out of sight as much as possible. They yelled for people to take cover, to hide, but panic had set in. The civilians ran the wrong way and were cut down. They were trampled as others pushed to make their own getaway. In the short block to the militia station, dozens of bodies lay dead, men, women, and children. The attackers were relentless.

On Gaia, same as Earth, there was no armed police force. A first responders group made up of medical, emergency rescue, or mental health handled most issues. Earth had some non-lethal restraints for desperate measures or specially designed EVE units. On Gaia, the military could open carry their weapons in public and were trained to handle deadly situations. In rare cases where military personnel were not available, the idea being an alien invasion, not public unrest, there was the Gaia Militia. Gaia Militia could comprise active military, retired military, or civilians with the proper training. They scattered militia stations throughout all cities or townships. Each station was fully stocked with weapons and military supplies. Someone could only access them in emergencies and by command military or authorized militia members.

Sitting on the edge of the park, this militia station was a blocky building with a heavy metal hatch. It would look more at home on the *Ares* than it did on the picturesque landscape of Gaia. Heavy fortified walls would act as sanctuary while they prepared. Rose pushed on the hatch, but it didn't budge. "It's not open yet. Jax. You have command. You'll have to declare an emergency and open the doors," Rose said.

"Right," Jax replied, stepping up to the door. "Lieutenant Harumi Brandt, Engineering Commander *Ares*. Declaring a state of emergency. Open the doors." There was a long pause, and nothing happened. She was about to ask if there was something specific she was supposed to say when it clicked and slid open.

The officers rushed into a neat cube of a room that had eight shelves running down the middle. Each shelf and all the outer walls were expertly packed with armaments, standard first aid, AI Med Packs, and safety gear. A few benches with storage lockers underneath sat at the far end of the shelves.

"One minute and we're out. Let's move," Jax said.

On the double time they grabbed their gear, shedding clothes and donning the body armor. A step down from what the corps normally wore, this armor's default color was a murky yellow. It offered all the protection of regular Corps armor, but did not have the increased strength, or fully adaptive qualities of full kit gear. Grabbing weapons as they went, Jax and Rose picked NEW24's from the wall.

"24's? Really, ladies, isn't that a little pedestrian? Don't you think we'll need a bit more than that?" Lieutenant Wisler said. She stood looking ready to go, a NEW28 cradled in her hands. She had her NEW9 strapped to her side. A grenade launcher hung off her back hip.

Jax noticed that Wisler's looks had changed, too. Her round cheeks more angular, her long hair, straight a moment ago, was now darker and braided.

"I'm an engineer, not a ground pounder. This I can use," Rose said, attaching an energy sling and letting the weapon shift to her back.

"Same," Jax said. "I'll grab some grenades if we need them. Also, I want everyone to take —"

The door opened and four men came storming in. In a fluid motion, the three officers' guns were leveled at the lead. The lead man's hands rose. "I'm

Salvatore. Salvatore Feo, militia commander. We're here to help. Would have been here sooner, but it's chaos out there."

Jax's HUD identified each of the men, little pop-up boxes pointing to each of them and turning green. Salvatore Feo, Corey Singali, Xavier To, and Ryan Clay. The read-out showed that Feo and Clay were retired corps, while To and Singali were listed as militia soldiers. Read outs continued to list their training, achievements, service records. Jax dismissed it all. They were qualified, and they were here to help. That was enough. She asked with hope if any of them had comms? Shaking heads dashed any such hope.

"Suit up, corps. We have work to do. Make sure everyone loads up on AIMPs and regular medical too. Mission is to protect and serve," Jax said, glancing around at Rose and Wisler.

"Aye aye, ma'am," the four soldiers replied. They looked a bit out of shape, round around the middle, but they moved with practiced efficiency.

In thirty seconds, they were ready to go. "Ma'am," Salvatore said, "Xavier and Corey are just soldiers, but are far from tenderfoots. Ryan and I have only been on vacation for the last two years. We're ready."

"Excellent, Salvatore," Jax said, smiling. "I'm Jax. That's Rose and Lieutenant Wisler."

"Call me Brooklyn, since it seems the militia likes to use first names," Lieutenant Brooklyn Wisler said, a look of annoyance crossing her face.

"We are more friendly than the corps in that manner," Salvatore said with a grin that would give Chambers a run for his money.

Jax ignored it and pressed on. "Salvatore, your best two on point. The other two guard the tail. We head into the hot spots. This is your arena. You call the details."

"Frippen A," Salvatore said.

Forming their lines, the new militia squad stepped outside and emerged into madness. Fire erupted across the park as small groups tried to fight back. The insurgents, while wild, had them outgunned and out armored. Explosions rocked the park, sparks and debris flying into the air. Small groups of attackers roamed and caused destruction wherever their eyes fell. Ryan, Salvatore, Jax, Rose, Brooklyn, Xavier, and Corey were like a laser looking for a target. They didn't have to look hard.

A group of three roaming insurgents crossed their path, hunting easy prey. They found death as the newly formed militia group opened fire. More roaming groups moved through the park and the militia was on the hunt. They were rough, sloppy at first, doubling up targets, out of position to cover, but still they succeeded. Targets were cut down and civilians were ushered to safety. With each encounter, they became a force on the battlefield.

Rounding a jungle gym, thankfully devoid of bodies, they found a large group of insurgents. The group of eight, dressed in full black combat gear, were firing shots at a large utility shed. Not advancing, they seemed to make sport of the situation. Firing, laughing, congratulating each other as they worked the pattern again. Screams rose from the shed. In the doors and windows, hunkered down behind the building, people clutched each other in a vain attempt to be safe.

No command was given; they didn't need one. Together they opened fire, and the militia reigned deathly light on the enemy. The insurgents never saw it coming, never had a chance to respond. Lost in their morbid game, they lost their lives.

"These are not soldiers, these are cowards," Salvatore said. "They seek to terrorize, to spread fear, and nothing else. They are disgusting."

"Agreed. They deserve to be put down," Brooklyn said, her words like ice. She turned to Jax. "You know with armored opponents pulse works better. That beam you keep using might take time to cut through."

"I know. I know," Jax said as she pushed through to the sheltered people. Battered and bruised, none of these people were spared wounds. Burns, cuts, bruises, and fractures could all be found. Horrified eyes adding to the already bleak situation. Inside and around the shelter, families hugging children, couples supporting each other.

"Salvatore, who's your best medic? I want them to peel off and help this group. Guard them until more help arrives."

"Got it. Xavier, you're up," Salvatore said. Xavier wasted no time in finding the most critical to help. Calling for others to join the medical efforts, the people rallied. Militia members passed out AI med packs to those willing and able to help. As they made the people as comfortable as possible, Salvatore sent Corey to scout the area. "Safety first." He said to Jax, and she could only nod in reply.

They finished placing the survivors in the best set-up they could. While Xavier worked, a few citizens with the proper training took up his arms and started a guard duty. It wasn't much, but it was the best they could do for the moment.

Corey ran back. "We got a large group pushing into the business sectors. Looks like they have a heavy technical," he said. Technical, or nonstandard tactical vehicle in military speak, is an improvised fighting vehicle.

"That might be where the signal jam is coming from. Techs could carry the comms equipment necessary for that," Salvatore said.

"Well, that's our target then. Suggestions?" Jax asked.

Salvatore paused. "We don't want to get caught in a group. Depending on what kind of armament they have, we could get taken out in a single shot. Let's split our force and come at it from two angles." He pointed to the left and right, angling his hands as if they were circling around. "We can set up a crossfire and expose them. These guys don't seem too highly trained."

"Sounds good," Jax said. "Let's divide down military lines, Fleet one way, you ground pounders the other."

That got a chuckle from the militia members as Salvatore leveled a salute at the Fleet officers. "Hunt well, Fleet," he said. The three militia members were off at a trot.

"Let's go," Jax said, starting her jog to the left. Jax checked the comms out of instinct. A crackle in her ear echoed the loss of comms as the militia group moved off. Up close, the suites allowed for natural voice communication, but now that was lost.

Brooklyn came up beside and pushed ahead. "With the way you two shoot, better if I take point." Jax nodded her head in agreement, forcing down a growl in her throat. Brooklyn's words reminded Jax of Commander Lewis' bluntness, but without the charm.

Heading out of the park, the group trudged through the broken ground. Tangled, burned bodies could be spotted in amongst the rubble. There was nothing to do for the dead, so they pushed on. Smooth and confident, the group advanced. Quick glances at the second team kept them in step. Running a parallel course, they all cleared the park into the business sector. The large open roads between buildings, designed so small craft could fly between them, kept them far enough apart so the comms were still down. Salvatore would wave hand signals and Brooklyn would wave back. Jax and Rose got the basics of it, most being stop, go, and wait.

Rounding a corner, Brooklyn stepped back and pressed against the wall, hand signal waved for the other two officers to stop. She peeked around and snapped back.

"Two heavy vehicles with armor welded on. Heavy slug throwers on top. They have a group of civilians pinned down. They're fighting back, but hopelessly outgunned. Worse news is we got full kit insurgents and I think a bubble head," Brooklyn said.

Damn. Full kit would be like her Klick-Klick armor from Roost I. Head to toe armor, enhanced strength, sensor equipment, the works. A bubble head was something different. She had to strain her thoughts. The thick four-wheeled vehicle is called a bubble head because of its dome-like top. A mobile combat operations center, MCOC. Occupied by four to six people, a mobile tank on wheels. It had comms, scanners, everything an entire battalion would ever need. Heavy on armor, but lacking weapons, they would rely on other parts of a combat group for offence. It was beyond any weapon they had to combat it.

"I don't think the corps has even had one of those in action yet," Brooklyn said. "What the frip is going on?"

"Figure it out later. We need to take it down," Jax said. "Let me see." She peeked around the corner. A short road to an open square lay before her. Two groups of terrorists were at play. Group A was attacking the blockaded civilians. Group B was hanging back, protecting the bubble head. If the B group got involved, they could easily take out the blockade. Like in the park, they seemed resigned to terrorizing tactics rather than engaging. As she pulled her head back, Jax caught sight of the militia team. They were crossing the road further down and then backtracking. They held at a building across from her.

"Militia team is signaling that they are holding, boss. Awaiting commands. What do you want to do?" Brooklyn said, hiking a thumb at the other group.

"What's under the roads here? Are there basements like where the Topaz is? I remember something about Soteria City having a complex underground?"

Brooklyn shrugged, but Rose spoke up. "All Soteria's high rises have underground utility tunnels. A whole network used to run the city and keep it clean. That space is used for utility lines, maintenance, or storage. Some go several stories deep, some only one or two."

"So, if we blow the road out from under the bubble head and bury that thing, will that be enough to put a stop to whatever it's doing?" Jax asked.

The other two officers' faces went blank. They turned and stared at each other as if silent questions were passing between their brains.

"I don't know," Rose said. "That might work. There's enough metal and concrete, it could interfere with its ops. Hard to say without actually knowing how they're doing what they are."

"We'll have to concentrate all our grenades under the truck. The militia too. That might punch through," Brooklyn said, but her face looked unsure.

"Great, let the militia know and hand me all your grenades," Jax said. She began linking them, pulling a wire from one to another. Push one button, they all go.

Brooklyn started to hand sign the militia, while Rose said, "Why are you taking the grenades? You're no demolition expert. I ought to be able to figure it out better."

"There's no time to figure it out. This isn't going to be a precision run, more a dump and go brute force kind of thing. Besides, you and Brooklyn are better shots and I'm getting pretty good at running." Jax flashed Rose her best smile.

"We're ready," Brooklyn said. "They think you're crazy, but they're game. They think we'll be spotted once we step out, so we'll fire first to draw attention. When we cover, the militia will open fire. That's your cue to go. Hopefully, we'll get enough crossfire and confusion to keep the runners safe."

"You got all that from hand signals?" Rose gave Brooklyn an incredulous eye.

"I'm very good with my hands." Brooklyn smiled.

Jax heard Rose mumble some roseisms under her breath. "Let's do it."

The three officers stepped to their firing line and opened up on the terrorist. Brooklyn landed fire directly on one of the full kit opponent's chest and shoulders. Bursts of energy fragmented and blossomed out in all directions. Rose, while not as accurate, fired with a speed hard to match. Her volley forced the insurgents to scatter before they could effectively take cover. Jax's red beam added to the maelstrom, burning lines in the ground, on the bubble head and across the armor of a few.

As the fleet officers ducked behind the buildings, the return fire came with a blaze. The corner wall shattered, debris spraying as the terrorists did their work. The militia stepped in and let loose their crossfire. All three of the soldiers were deadly accurate. Screams erupted from the enemy as several of the full kit wannabes fell to superior gun fire. Jax doubted the men inside were dead but knew from experience that getting hit head on could still rock your world.

There was a pause when she had to kick herself into the run. Her NEW24 swinging on the energy straps to her back. Her muscles flaring, she longed for a full kit of her own, the increased strength and speed. All she had now was her own grit and determination. She leaned heavily into her stride. Shots zipped past her, not at her, but at the enemy. Rose and Brooklyn's attempts at providing cover fire, but the distraction was minimal. Enemy fire ripped at her feet, gravel spraying up around her. She dived and rolled.

She tumbled once and her feet slipped. She slid on her back, bumping into a concrete planter that decorated the sidewalk. Fire from both sides danced around her, her friends covering, the terrorist unleashing their full fury. She pushed her back down, willing herself to be as small as possible. Through squinted eyes, pulses of lights flashed over her head and around her. Moments passed, and they forced the enemy to take their fire off her and focus on her friends. A grunt and a bump as Salvatore dropped in next to her. Her heart skipped a beat at his sudden appearance. Deadly fire returned to their position, pinning them down.

"I shouldn't have eaten those deep-fried tacos earlier," Salvatore said. Energy blasts exploded the surrounding gravel.

"Let's hope it's not a last meal."

"Roger that. What's the plan?"

"I was hoping you had an idea."

Salvatore nodded his head and held up one finger. A deep breath, and as their fire team returned fire, popped his head out of the makeshift cover and ducked back down.

"I think we can make the back wheel of the bubble head. We'll go together with the cover fire," Salvatore shouted as the fire fight seemed to increase. "Once we get there, drop your package under the back wheel and I'll hit the front. Then we run like the abyss itself is chasing us."

"Sounds like a plan," Jax shouted back. "On your 'go'."

"You're on my six. Ready—" Salvatore said, pausing. "Go!"

Salvatore looked out of shape, but Jax had to push to keep up with the big, retired corps. Cover fire streaked past them, counter fire from the terrorists peppered their steps. Salvatore's shoulder flared. He yelled and spun. Jax tackled him forward, and they slammed into the rear of the bubble head.

"You okay?" Jax said, trying to examine his shoulder.

"I'll live," he said, brushing her off. With a grunt, he unslung his NEW24 and fired some shots around the bubble head. Jax followed suit. There was no shot under the tank, a large wheelbase and under-plating giving cover. Up close, the bubble head was bigger than she realized, towering easily twice her height.

"Cover me!" Salvatore said, moving around the tank, headed to the front tire. He fired as he went, and Jax burned a beam around him. A full kit opponent stepped out, only to be blown back by Jax's beam and Salvatore's own expert shots. Salvatore made the front tire, kneeled, and glanced back over his shoulder. They both unslung their packages and, with a nod from Salvatore, tossed them under the wheel well.

They were yelling and screaming as they pushed into their run. On Jax's HUD, a small screen showed the tank behind her. She couldn't help but watch as her legs pumped. Fire raged around her and Salvatore as the terrorists and militia increased fire. A flash and smoke filled her rear screen as the tank's wheel lifted, rocked, and concrete exploded out. Screams erupted, and the blast's shockwave smacked them in the back.

Salvatore hit and slid on his side, smashing into a curb. Jax rag-dolled, arms flailing, she managed to tuck and roll sideways, bouncing up over the curb. She yelled again as she forced herself to her knees, turned into a crouch, seeing the tank on its side. Its wheels were bent at wrong angles, the bubble head laying sideways in a crevice created by the munitions. Their plan had worked, but not enough. Jax yelled again, the beam lashing out at the ground by the tank. She willed it to punch through.

A shot grazed her left shoulder and bits of armor and skin went flying. Her right held strong, the beam turning the ground red with heat. Salvatore was picking her up by the waist, pulling her to safety. The beam cut out; a cracking sound as loud as thunder filled the air. Water and sparks began shooting out around the bubble head. Underground utilities bursting from the assault. Then the tank fell. The pair stumbled into an alcove of a building, laughing as their legs gave out and they pushed their backs to the wall. A happy chirp rang in her ears as comm channels reopened.

With a few flicks of her eyes, Jax opened communication, hoping it was all enough. Hoping to get a response. "This is Lieutenant Brandt. Can anyone hear me?"

"Lieutenant Brandt! This is Hat Trick. Good to hear from you."

"Nice to be heard. Give me a sit-up, we've been cut off. I'm with a militia team."

"You and us both, Lieutenant. Up till a moment ago, we had no comms, no way to mark targets. Nothing. Complete blackout. Corps squads are moving through the city, but it's been slow going. What's your status?"

"We just downed a bubble head and are currently outgunned by insurgents. Could use some help here."

"Damn, Lieutenant, that's a story I can't wait to hear. Sit tight. We've got comms and targets popping up. Teams are inbound. Stay safe and we'll have you home in time for a nightcap."

"Roger that, Hat Trick. Lieutenant Brandt out."

Salvatore and Jax stared at each other for a while, unbreakable grins on their faces.

"First drink is on you," Salvatore said.

"Damn straight it is," Jax said. "Damn straight."

Chapter 17

SIMPLE ENOUGH

S he sipped the whiskey the same way she had the last one. She was gaining a taste for the strong aroma and dark flavors. This was a local vintage, a twelve-year, that had a hint of vanilla and a bitter aftertaste. Normally she wouldn't care for that, but today it matched her mood.

She was hanging out on her favorite seat at the Topaz. Her favorite jacket hung open, its black with red sleeves usually brought a bit of joy to her, but not today. She didn't want to brood alone on the *Ares*, so she brooded alone at the only other place she felt safe.

Mid-week, several other groups spread out across the ratskeller. It was quiet. Light conversations were the rule of the day. Music was in the air. A group had formed on stage for an informal jam session. Individually, they were good, but it was obvious they didn't play together much. Missed beats and tempo changes were common. The music was mellow and helped her organize her thoughts.

The cleanup of the Founder's Day attack was efficient. Too efficient. Several days later, only minor signs of the attack could be found in the park and city. The news had gone back to covering the strange habits of the Screech and Earth. Politics seemed to have dropped off the radar for some reason. It could almost have been a dream. Gaia had a more open news and information system than Earth. At least it was supposed to. On the surface it did, but she felt like she knew less.

The more that happened to her, the more she realized she just didn't know what was going on. She lifted her drink to take another sip. A shimmer appeared in the corner of her eye. Putting her glass down, squinting to focus. The shimmer appeared human shaped and got sharper as it moved closer. As details came into focus, a large man in a dark brown trench coat walked towards her. A matching fedora pulled down over his brow didn't conceal the goofy grin below. A grin that could only belong to Commander Issac Haddock.

"Neat trick," Jax said as the commander took a seat next to her.

"Yes, it is. A personal silent running field like what the *Ares* has. Great at a distance, but up close it breaks down," Issac said.

"So, am I cloaked too? Or do I look like I'm talking to myself?"

Issac gave his classic awkward smile and placed a white disk on the bar. "To anyone at a distance, you look like you're talking to Mr. Falls. A kind, retired Fleet of a man. He's known to visit the Topaz regularly and strike up conversations in any way that suits his fancy."

"A real person?" Jax asked.

"Absolutely. I'm sure you'll meet him at some point. He'll even remember talking to you. He mostly rambles on about starship specs, should anyone ask."

"What about Anne? And what is this thing?" Jax asked, pointing at the white disk. She was tired of being angry, of being attacked. She sat here at the bar, trying to control it all, keep it under control. The appearance of Commander Haddock had put that in jeopardy. She could feel the emotions bubbling up again.

"Anne knows more than most, but most importantly, she knows when not to know," Issac said. As if on cue, Anne came by and dropped a fresh whiskey on the rocks for the commander.

She eyed Jax, realized she was still nursing hers, gave a nod, and moved on.

"More secrets. More secrets that impact my life that no one tells me about," Jax said, some of those bottled emotions slipping out.

"There're no big secrets here. We're trying to keep you safe. The *Ares* too. I know the attack was hard —"

"Hard? Hard?" Jax interrupted. "I don't really call having a gun put in my face, again mind you, hard." Jax said, the anger building. "I thought being injured again would be hard. Nope, I've gotten so used to being injured I don't really notice it anymore. I thought I would find shooting people hard, but nope, not that either. When did that become easy? These are humans and I pulled the trigger on, as easy as shooting any monster."

"Well, they are monsters. It's just not the kind you're used to. We all must do what we can to stay safe."

"Safe, now that's a funny word to me. Seems I'm in the crosshairs a lot more than others. People keep telling me I'm safe, just to find out I'm not. Why is that Issac? Why?" Jax said, voice rising.

Issac's mouth opened, but it choked for a moment. Words lost on the tip of his tongue, Jax took the opening and continued. "If I'm a part of this, why don't I know more? Why do I feel I'm just bait for others' plans? Why is your little spy still following me?" Jax tilted her head, indicating a table behind her. "No big secrets, my ass." She sipped whiskey and set it down. Her eyes were glued to it, the only thing holding back her rage.

The moment stretched while Issac took a sip of his own drink. His head nodded slowly a few times, then said, "Brooklyn will not be happy you spotted her again. She prides herself on blending in."

"If it makes her feel better, I didn't know it was her till you walked in. If she was a threat, I'm sure you would have handled her first or we wouldn't be having this conversation."

"Very astute. You don't seem too worried if she had been trouble."

Jax gave him a side eye and then pulled the left side of her jacket open. Issac got just enough of a glance to identify the Army Single Action resting under her armpit.

A couple small nods and he said, "Not my personal choice for a side carry. I'm assuming you can fire that antique?"

"I'm feared by cans everywhere," she said, a wry grin breaking on her stern face. "Not so antique, however. Rose made it for me. Shoots like the ASA I practice with in the VRpod, but all modern construction. Bullets use a qave energy cell, not as fast as a MEG, but close. Nanite core bullets are programmable so they can stop on impact, pass through, or explode."

Issac whistled. "Nice, always better to be able and protect yourself than to rely on others."

"Yes, it is. Like it's better to not have so-called friends ignore your questions."

His drink was halfway to his lips, and he stopped. "Fair," he said, placing it down. "Let's start again. Everything on the table. First, these disks are customizable, usually digital interfaces for computer systems. Mine's a bit more you might say, blocks listening, detects active threats and more. I have—access to certain tech from a previous life."

Jax rolled her eyes. "You're still leaving things out."

Issac pinched his lips. "Maybe we should start with something else then?"

"Was I bait at Founder's Day?"

"No. The information we had said Gaia First, or Gaia Alpha, was done. There were raids capturing key people, accounts seized. It was all very convincing."

"I didn't see anything about that in the news."

"I thought you didn't watch the news."

"I'm living on a warship with nothing but time on my hands. I'm doing a lot of things to kill time. Don't change the subject."

Issac nodded. "Best way to control information is make everything available. Show people what you want and leave what you don't want in plain sight on the table."

"People don't think you're hiding anything, so they don't look at it."

Issac picked up his drink, held it up to Jax like a toast, nodded his head, and took a slow sip.

"Who has the power to do that?"

"List is larger than you would think. People of influence, leaders of industry, certain government officials."

"Officials like Dakos?"

"Yes. We've found some flimsy, I have to admit, threads linking him to everything. That's actually why I'm here to talk to—"

Jax held up a hand and cut Issac off. "I'm not done yet. So, you didn't use me as bait, but I'm still being baited. Maybe not in the physical sense, but you have been using me. I'm some kind of political pawn, right? I remember Gemma mentioning something to me once, but I think I'm just starting to grasp it."

"We're in the military. We're all political pawns."

"Don't play word games with me," Jax said, swirling in her chair to stare the big man down. "Why was I not made a pilot on the *Ares*?"

Issac took a deep breath, sat up straight, and turned his face to her. A look of sadness and submission crossed his eyes. "You are the daughter of two of the most important people in recent Earth history. At least, that's how Gaia looks at it. Having you join the military, embracing it, was a huge public relation boon for those that want Earth and Gaia to work together. Being a pilot is too dangerous, only serving in the corps is worse. Placing you in engineering was to keep you safe."

Jax lifted her chin, closed her eyes, and ran her fingers through her hair. "I'm such an idiot. A naïve, fripping idiot. Here I am thinking I'm fighting the good fight, doing what's right. In reality, I'm a doll on a shelf."

"Naïve maybe, but don't sell yourself short. You've run into danger when others would flee. You've saved more lives because of your actions than we could calculate. We may have been trying to keep you safe, but you've defied us at every turn," Issac said, a gentle grin crossing his face.

Jax couldn't help but chuckle and shake her head a bit. "What about Roost I then? That wasn't very safe."

"Yeah, a lot of debate about that one," Issac said. "Captain Moss was good at politics. When the mission came up, he thought it would be a good chance to build you up, give you military cred. Up to that point, you were kind of a mixed bag of good and bad."

Jax's memory flashed, her time on the *Indiana* encountering the Screech, her breakdown after. "Yeah, I didn't transition into fighting, war, deadly situations very easily. It was terrifying. I should have done better."

"It's always terrifying and everyone thinks they'll do better the first time," Issac said, holding his glass up. This time Jax obliged him, holding hers up and clinking them together. They both took a slow sip. Issac continued. "We all thought Roost I was going to be a cakewalk. We had seen abandoned Screech facilities before, usually stripped of everything. We thought we had caught them at the end of stripping this one. Minimal personnel, easy pickings. Gemma was supposed to see if they could capture one of the smaller drone birdies. We've never done that before. Everything went wrong with that mission. Everything."

"Damn straight it did."

They sat in silence, nursing their drinks. Too many memories. Anne came by to check on them, offering to refill the drinks. Issac said no and Jax held her hand over her glass. She caught Anne's eye and mouthed the word "chai" to her. Anne smiled and headed off.

"So, what did you want, Mr. Haddock?" Jax asked. It wasn't proper military protocol, nor was it a friendly address, but it was a throwback to simpler times, and she needed that right now.

"You're right, you need to be included, not protected. We're about to do something stupid and we want you to be a part of it. I'm pretty sure you'll want that, too."

"And by 'we' you mean?"

"Gemma, Lilly, and I. Too many leaks in the government, too many possible threads that could get back to Dakos. So, this will be an off-the-book mission, using only people we can trust."

"Mission?"

"We think we've found a base, a command hub, on the outskirts of the city. Our traces are thin, but they all lead there. They are all our own sources, nothing in the normal chain of things. We only need one piece of solid evidence, and we can bring it all down."

"Going to be hard to attack a target in the city and not have anyone know we're coming," Jax said, raising an eyebrow.

Issac smiled. "We have a distraction. In two days is the military ball. We've made it known that the *Ares* command plans a grand entrance. A little showmanship has become tradition, so no one should second guess it. Before we arrive, we'll detour and hit our target."

The military ball, where Gaia Fleet and Gaia Terrain Corps come together to celebrate everything martial. In actuality, a birthday celebration for the founding of both branches of the Gaia military.

"I'm surprised they're still having that with the attack that just happened."

"Us too. The Prime put an advisory council on the matter. That council was quick to recommend we show strength and solidarity. Prove that we as a people will not be intimidated. Can't change what we do because of a few terrorists. So, they decided to hold the ball. The military command tried to fight it, but all the representatives pushed back. Elections are soon and they don't want to look weak."

"Dakos on that advisory council?"

"No, but some members have deep business ties with him."

"Figures. I hate politics," Jax said.

"My experiences have me agreeing with you. So, I take it you're in?"

"Yeah, I'm in. What do I need to do?"

"Dress for the ball. I recommend full dress uniform rather than a dress. Fits better under the kit."

"I didn't even realize I had the choice, but good to know."

Issac smiled. "I'll let you know which hangar we're staying at before you come down from the *Ares*. We'll have everything ready to go."

"Sounds simple enough," Jax said.

"Best plans are. Let's hope it stays that way," Issac said, getting up from the bar. "I still have a few things to arrange. Sit tight and watch your back."

Jax barked a laugh. "That's all I do nowadays. Before you go, Issac, just tell me one thing."

Issac's eyes glared from under his hat. "Okay."

"This isn't just another case of you using me again. Manipulating me to work for your goals. This is on the level?"

Issac Haddock took a moment to adjust his hat, his eyes lost in shadow. A small grin, not his goofy smile, but rather a wicked grin, the kind of grin that spoke of something darker. Then he said, "Of course I'm manipulating you, Jax. It's what I do. The big difference this time is you know I'm doing it." He didn't wait for a response. He just turned and walked away. With each step, he faded away like he was never there.

Chapter 18

THAT EASY

J ax walked into hangar four. The full-dress uniform brought confidence to her stride. Not long ago, the thought of a meeting like this would have pushed her forward, forcing her into a rush. Not today. Today, she didn't care if she was first or last. Today was a day of endings and that was all that mattered. The hanger, usually full of activity and ships, was oddly sparse. Two twin dropships occupied the hanger. *The Reckless, my old friend* Jax thought, joined by the *Bucephalus*. Scattered around the two condor looking ships were groups of fleet and corps.

"Jax! Over here." A familiar voice called. She turned the see Corporal Chambers waving her over. "I've got your kit ready to go," he said.

"Good to see the crew," she said as she donned the battle kit. A full kit this time, she was glad to see. Fully enclosed, adaptive armor, enhanced strength, the works. It's dull black default color, shifted to generic gray as it came alive. Auto adjustments, tightening and moving into position, fitting her body. She had preformatted defaults now. The suit was ready for her. The last couple of adjustments she made on her own, auto formatting, could only do so much. Notching her helmet at her hip, she slung a NEW24 around on the energy straps. The black light from the strap pulsating inward, swung the gun to her back, and she was ready to go. Last check and she saw the armor shell had switched to a basic city cameo. Her personal markings appeared over the armor. A crackling energy where she was shot on the chest. stripes serving missions on the *Ares*, tick marks for kills. Finishing her last checks, she scanned the hangar.

Her "stone dogs" were all present and accounted for. Commander Haddock said they had only chosen those they could trust. This was a good start in her opinion, but who else was going on this "off the books" mission? A case of déjà vu washed over her mind as she saw some old familiar favorites. The Gunnery Sergeant, Gunny Locklear or just Gunny, was huddled up to the side. With him, the acting Captain of the *Ares*, Commander Gemma Lewis. It had been a while since seeing Gemma in person, or the Gunny, for that matter. Seeing them both now brought a sense of comfort.

A couple of corps members, who Jax didn't know, checked gear nearby. The third group surprised her, but probably shouldn't have. Commander Terrance Moro stood like an immaculate, dark-haired statue. If Jax didn't know better, she would swear he was posing for a legendary holopic. Maybe an ad for some blockbuster holovid. Next to him stood his brother, Lieutenant Sebastian Moro. Only a hair shorter than his brother, he was just as imposing. Easily recognizable as brothers, especially side by side. While Terrance looked like something out of a storybook, Sebastian had a rebel quality that Jax couldn't quite put her finger on. A tilt of his head, a shifting of weight, the way he was cradling his weapon. All minor, subtle things, but they set the brothers apart.

A transport cart, empty of equipment, sat idly behind them. Leaning back in one seat, sleeping, was Brooklyn. Jax doubted she was actually sleeping. More likely, she was well aware of everything happening around her. Standing next to the cart, a fleet lieutenant was performing multiple checks on his NEW24, a never-ending series. Jax recognized him from the *Ares* bridge but struggled to recall his name. Amon—something. He was one of Commander Haddock's people.

As if waiting to make an entrance Commander Haddock strode into the hanger. Besides him was a lean man, with slick backed hair, a blue buttoned up long sleeve shirt kept pace beside him. *Blink*. The slender man changed into a wide-eyed boy and ran straight at her.

"Jax!" Nath sang out. "So great that you made it! I was afraid you wouldn't come. I feel like I know you now, Rose, and I have talked about your pathjackers often. Really, you should come work for me. I have big ideas. You have practical ones. Rose can put it all together. Oh, the wonders we could work. I'm so on your team."

Jax's mouth was agape, as she tried to find a response to the rapid-fire words thrown at her. Thankfully, she didn't have to as Commander Lewis spoke up. "Nath, you're on Bravo with Commander Moro. We need your computer expertise on the data center. Charlie team is securing the roof. You're not needed there."

"Bravo already has a computer specialist. Commander Haddock told me Lieutenant Wisler is more than capable," Nath said, pointing a finger at Brooklyn. Brooklyn lifted an eyelid in response, but closed it again. She wasn't getting into this conversation. "I need to stay close to Jax, keep her safe. She's targeted a lot in these kinds of situations. She is like a sister to Rose." *Blink.* Nath changed into an adult wearing a toga with a golden crown. Lifting a hand high in the air. "Rose, who is so sweet, so intelligent, the muse to my mind, the light of my eye, whom I would never see harmed in body or core." *Blink.* Nath was a classic old Army general with a large corn-cob pipe. "I will protect all those she *cares* about. I shall see them safely home to friendly shores. So, I shall join her team."

Gemma Lewis could have melted steel with the look coming off her face. Her jaw barely moved as she spoke, the words coming slowly. "Nath, you are the only government insider we have. With your technical knowledge, your insights are necessary to find the evidence we need. You cannot change teams because you want to. That's not how this works."

"I'm not military. You can't tell me to do anything." *Blink.* A child again, his arms crossed, nose in the air. "I will be on whatever team I want."

"Nath!" Lewis shouted when Gunny put a hand on her shoulder, leaned in and whispered in her ear. A few moments later, he stepped away and Gemma stared Nath down like fury personified. "Fine," she said, forcing the word out. "Change of plans. Nath will join Charlie team. That means Alpha will kick in the front door and Bravo will assault from the top of the building. Non-lethal, if we can. We want prisoners. Secure any tech, especially personal databases, and any access hubs." She held her hand up and a holo image sprung out. A squat eight story building appeared and started to rotate. It matched the architecture found all around Gaia, tree and shrubs mixed into modern steel and glass. "Charlie team will use the loading dock to enter from the lower level." Gemma said, the image spinning around and holding. The holoimage went transparent to show a long tunnel dropping from the street level into the basement. "We think their main data network is hidden down there."

"Why down there?" Jax asked.

"There is a quantum internet that connects all of Gaia's governmental buildings. A self-contained quantum data system. One of those nodes for that system is located under a corner of that room. That's where we think they have military access. Also, a good place to store their data center." Commander Lewis pointed as the image stopped spinning and focused in on a small room at the end of a dead-end hall.

"To access the QNet, they would have to drill down several kilos to get to the node. Then they would have to figure out a way to access the qubit current without breaking the flow of information. That would set off alarms. Then they need a way to insert new cryptography code into the system, that the system wouldn't reject as false. Seems practically impossible by known standards. They have proven very resourceful so far. I'm not sure I could do it and I created it," Nath said. You'd think he would be upset at them for doing this, but he seemed excited by the possibilities.

"Great," Jax said. "So, get in. Let Nath do his thing. Get our info and get out. Still time to dance at the ball. That about sum it up?"

"That sums it up," Commander Lewis said.

"It's never that easy," Jax said.

"It's never that easy," the commander said. She locked eyes with each person. Nods of agreement came fast. Nobody talked about the consequences if they failed, or if they were wrong. They had chosen to be here, destiny be damned.

"Well, let's load up. I ain't getting any younger," the gunny said, his gruff voice echoed through the hanger. "I want Charlie on the *Reckless*. Alpha and Bravo are on the *Bucephalus*. Let's move like you understand what you're doing, people."

Jax smiled as she stepped to the boarding ramp. Stopping at the top, she turned to Nath and Chambers, who followed her up. Weighing Nath's current state, still that of a young child, concern grew. "Huh, Nath?" she said, exaggerating her look as she scanned him up and down. "You want to get some armor on?"

"No need," Nath said. *Blink*, he changed into an exact copy of Chambers, except his armor had a red tinge to it. "No matter my looks, I'm always protected."

"Great," Jax said. "Do you need a weapon?"

"Oh, no. I never carry a weapon, can't stand using the things."

"Aren't you a weapons manufacturer?" Jax asked.

"Of course, but I never let my personal feelings interfere with business."

Chambers stepped up beside Jax. Chambers asked, "If we get into trouble, how do you plan on defending yourself?"

"Please don't worry about me," Nath said. *Blink*. Changing into a huge boxer. His ensemble was complete with shorts, gloves, and a championship belt. "I'm very much an expert in hand-to-hand combat. I will be fine."

Both Jax and Chambers' mouths dropped open. At a loss for words, Jax turned to Chambers, a single eye going wide. He nodded to her unspoken plea for help.

"Serph," Chambers said. The private first class hopped out of her seat and moseyed up to Chambers. Jax caught a slight wink between the two, angled so Nath couldn't see. Chambers continued. "Serph, this is Mr. Nath. Nath, this is Private First Class Val Serph."

"Just Nath, please," Nath said, his face alight with a smile and a bow.

"Serph, Nath is G.I.B.J. and we want to make sure he has everything he needs. Can you be his assistant on this mission?"

"Roger roger," Serph said. "Nath, if you would follow me," the PFC said, ushering Nath deeper into the *Reckless*.

"Excellent an assistant. I love being part of a team. What is G.I.B.J.?" Nath asked.

"Well, you see," Serph replied. "G.I.B.J. is Government Issue Biotech Jobber. A jobber in Corps speaks means specialist. So, you see—" Val's voice trailed off as she and Nath walked away.

Jax's head leaned in and whispered to Chambers. "What does G.I.B.J. actually stand for?"

His wicked grin crossed his face. "Good Intentions, Bad Judgment. We use it a lot for tenderfoots who mean well, but you know it's going to turn out bad, or it already did."

"That's not encouraging."

"It is as long as you live to tell the tale," he said, making his way to his space on the dropship, his smile never wavering. Jax stood on the entry ramp for a moment, shaking her head. She didn't have an argument for that. The ramp started to close, and she made her way in.

The *Reckless* rattled and rambled as it left the hangar. A quick rise to twenty-five meters, a tilt of its nose and they were off. Flying through the city was fast and silent. Everyone, except Nath, was suited up with HUDs active. Serph had convinced Nath to don a combat helmet. He seemed to think it was all some kind of game and she had him happy to play. He had blinked into his business suit form. His dark blue suit with helmet was quite the fashion statement. He may not join them in combat, but at least communication would be easy.

"One minute to target." Hat Trick's voice crackled over the comms. "Prepare to deploy."

The *Reckless* zipped low and fast through the cityscape. Buildings blurred by in a kaleidoscope of steel, glass and green. On her HUD Jax watched the Bucephalus circle away. Their approach would be higher and on a different vector. If spotted, they would draw attention from the Reckless. The Bucephalus would drop off one fireteam on the roof and then circle around to the front. The second team would attack from the main doors.

Once last glance at the cityscape showed the setting sun. Red skies danced across the clouds and cast long shadows. Like a countdown clock, the sun fell as the *Reckless* landed. The back hatch popped and fireteam Charlie made a smooth exit. The straight column made a beeline for the building and pressed close to the wall. Glancing back, Jax was happy to see Nath, now back in his Chambers look alike form, falling into the column. From behind him, Serph gave a quick thumbs up.

Rook was running point, and after checking a corner called an all clear. Chambers signaled for advancement, and the team shuffled forward. Their entrance was a standard garage door with a security lock. Private Wocheck, slapped a disk next to it. Swiping a holoscreen on his wrist and in a second the door rolled open. The tunnel was empty as they pushed forward.

Down and around to an open parking garage. A single utility truck sat idle in a corner, the loading dock otherwise bare of vehicles or personal. Their suits muffled the sound of their steps, but they had expected some noise. It was deathly quiet and only the "pat pat pat" of footsteps could be heard. Doors were unlocked, and they made easy access to the heart of the building. Tensions were high as they prepared for resistance but met empty halls instead.

At a junction, Jax signaled for a stop. The team squatted and leaned against the whitewashed wall. She brought up her HUD to check on the other teams. All had made access into the building with no problems. A quick check on their comms chatter showed they were having the same go of it as Charlie team. The building was empty with no targets found. Alpha and Bravo continued to sweep and secure rooms, but found nothing. *Do we have the wrong place?*

Charlie team was also clearing rooms as they went. Their rooms comprised closets, forgotten dust filled spaces and utility rooms. They found piping for plumbing, heating units, qave cell backups and more, but nothing they were looking for. A nervousness was washing over the group as they eased up to their final destination. The unassuming door that could potentially be the answer to all their problems. A quick check on the other teams showed the front and top floors were all clear. Alpha and Bravo continued to make easy progress of the building.

Jax's hands gripped her NEW24 a little tighter as she gave Chambers a nod. Chambers and Rook took an extra moment to physically inspect this door. They could feel it too, the trap waiting to spring. Their inspection done, they found nothing and gave an all clear. Jax relaxed a bit but couldn't shake the feeling of unrest. She couldn't wait any longer and gave the go.

Chambers turned the door handle and Rook slammed into it with his shoulder. The two corps sprang into the room, guns at their shoulders, yelling for people to surrender. "This is Gaia Corps. Nobody moves!"

Jax followed, her NEW24 raised high, her lips pressed in determination. She scanned the room and definitely didn't find what she was expecting. The medium-sized room could hold ten people at most. A heavy wooden table sat in the middle. Large sheets of paper lay scattered across it. Paper weights, nothing more than rocks, held some down. While others were rolled up like scrolls or in stacks. Pictures and notes adorned the walls in the same manner.

"All clear," Chambers called as the fireteam occupied the room.

Jax let the energy strap swing her NEW24 to her back hip. "What in the abyss is this?" she asked.

The fireteam spread out across the room and started grabbing papers. Jax, Chambers, and Rook focused on the table while Nath and Serph scanned the walls. Wocheck stood guard by the door, his head darting from the room to out the door.

The large papers showed what looked like to her a flattened holo image of building schematics. The smaller papers were equipment manifests, weapons inventory, and company names. If there was a method of organization here, they couldn't find it. Each member of the team shouted out things they found. Pictures of the *Ares* crew, of politicians, business leaders, were all in abundance.

"How can you run an op like this nowadays?" Serph said. "This has got to be the biggest waste of time and energy I've ever seen."

"It's genius," Nath said. His visage was now wearing a business suit. "Pure genius. In a world where information is freely shared and accessed instantly, what better way to keep secrets? Frankly, I'm amazed Dakos came up with it. He's always struck me as having more looks than intelligence."

"Maybe that's an act too, then," Serph said, shoving her eyes into another document.

As they worked through the documents, pieces came together. Finding connections to businesses, fake ones, according to Nath. Used to funnel weapons and equipment away from military issue to shell corporations. This left him noticeably upset. Since it was Nath Industries that were largely affected. Jax could hear him muttering, "Oh, I'll shut them down. Wait till I get to them—" On a continual loop.

A comm channel beeped in Jax's ear and Commander Lewis' voice crackled across the line. "Jax, how's it going? You have any trouble?"

"Negative," Jax said and then broke down what they had found.

"Damn, what in the abyss is going on? This makes no sense; we've got nothing here. No resistance, no personnel. Just an empty building. Now with what you've found, there should be people here,"

"That's what we're trying to figure out. You're welcome to join us," Jax said.

"Yeah, we're on our—" the commander said. "Jax, do those building schematics say what structure they are for?"

"Hold on," Jax said. She pushed papers around, clearing the large schematic. A little hunting revealed a small corner box with details. "It says Helena Cristoforetti Hall. Isn't that one of the founders of Gaia?"

"Yes, it is. It's also where they hold the military ball."

"Oh, crap. You think they'll attack the ball?" Jax asked.

Before the commander could respond, Chambers joined the conversation. He pushed a large paper in front of Jax. "This looks like an attack plan." He said, pointing to areas on the map. "Secure points, troop movements, the works. Several lists of names are also attached. The names on the first one have to be a hit list."

"Why you think it's a hit list?" Jax asked.

"Well, your names on that one," Chambers said with a weary smile. "A red mark across the top."

"Great," Jax said. "What's on the other lists?"

"This one has Dakos and other representatives on it. It also has a black mark at the top." Chambers handed it over. "And this one has the Prime Representative with a gold mark and some big brass."

Jax grabbed the lists and read as fast as she could. She barely recognized the rep's names from watching the news. The High Marshal and Admiral Koonce were listed high on the list with the Prime. "Oh crap, Commander!"

"I got it. Double damn! We're in the wrong spot," Lewis yelled as she switched comms so all the fireteams were included. "Everyone, double time back to the dropships. We have to get to the ball!"

Chapter 19

ALL THEIR PROBLEMS

"Why are we taking off our armor?" Jax asked over the comms. Her helmet was the first thing off, so she, like everyone else, had attached comm clips to their ears. Like the ones she used in ENG, the small top of ear clip was transparent and would allow full comm ability. They were bumping into each other as they peeled sections from their bodies.

Commander Lewis echoed in her ear, "Comms into the ball, everywhere for that matter, are blocked. Issac set up our comms and they seem unaffected so far. But we are getting feeds out, like they want people watching. We know from the plans you found they're waiting for everyone, and by that, I mean us, to arrive."

"Right, so shouldn't we be getting their ready to fight?" Jax asked. Her final piece of armor hit the floor, and she did her best at straightening her dress blues. Grabbing her case and inserting work contacts.

"If we go in guns blazing, they'll open fire, and it will be a bloodbath. Instead, we go in for a party, contact the people on the hit list, sneak them out to the dropships, and arm them. Lilly will coordinate from there, get those that can fight to secure key points and get those that can't out. With a little luck, we can turn this all around."

"What if they start shooting before we get them?"

"They won't. We're making an entrance remember? They want us there. They'll wait till everyone is sitting for dinner, feeling good, drinking, not paying attention. Maximize the damage they can do."

Jax looked up and saw the rest of her fire team nodding. "This feels like one of my plans, made up on the spot and completely dangerous. I don't like it."

Gemma barked a laugh that echoed in the comms and said, "Now you know how we feel when you have control."

"So, no weapons at all?"

"Side arms only. We're coming in as the bloody war worn heroes of the *Ares*. A little showmanship shouldn't raise too much suspicion. Anything more might raise anxiety levels."

What about my anxiety levels? Maybe I can get them to stand still while I shoot at them with this thing, Jax thought, resting her hand on the holstered ASA.

"Okay, we are landing everyone on the same comms," the commander said. "Since they are broadcasting, we should keep tone once inside their jamming bubble. Don't rely on them too much, they've had an uncanny ability to manipulate comm channels. Keep your contacts HUD up and if you find a target, mark them. No heroics. Priorities are to get people safe, get people armed and find that rallitch Dakos." Shouts, applause, and some vulgarities, echoed through the dropships and over the comms.

Jax eyed her contacts, and the HUD came alive. Not as immersive as the combat HUD, but she could pull up information as needed. Small lists on the edge of her vision were the "Hit List", "Fireteams", "Map" and "Tagged". She moved the map to a small window on her right side, made it transparent, and added dots for each list. Enemies would be red when marked, fireteams green, and tagged people orange. She hoped that was enough.

Hat Trick's voice crackled in her ear that they were coming in for a landing. Her stomach lurched as the dropship shed altitude. The metal frame rattling and bucking as the ship dropped and turned. Curses were frequent as the turbulence shook them all.

Chambers leaned into Jax. "Hey, you have the dog tags I gave you?"

Jax touched her chest and felt the metal press against her skin. She rarely had the tags off, so much so that she often forgot they were there. "Yeah, why?"

"Wear them on the outside. It will make a statement. Few in the fleet have corps tags. If you run into any big brass corps, they'll know you're someone to listen to." He said, adding a wink to his grin. She gave him a nod as the ship landed, sending a jolt through everyone.

They made their egress down the loading ramp. Their first look at Helena Cristoforetti Hall was a grand one. Leading up to the building was a long bluegrass lawn. All around were well pruned bushes and trees. Flowerbeds were aglow with nightlights. Ahead of them, a grand house loomed. White brick, tall pillars and graceful steps leading to the double front doors. Across the lawn, small groups of people were enjoying the night sky. All eyes now turned from the great beyond to the arriving dropships.

The people stared and gawked and whispered in hushed tones. Little news drones left whatever they were watching and focused on them. The round camera balls came swooping in, dotting the sky, little lights shining like stars. They put a spotlight on the arriving fire teams. Having wanted to make an entrance, their wish was granted.

As they filed out of the dropships, they formed ranks. Fleet to one side and corps to the other. Side by side, they walked down that lane towards the hall. Heads held high, backs stiff, they created their own grand parade. As they moved from the hum of the dropships, Jax heard a music beat hit her ears. She wasn't sure if it was part of the party or something Commander Lewis had arranged. Either way, it's beat was heavy, and it matched their steps. The heavy bass add a grandeur to their entrance that none could ignore.

Jax allowed herself a moment to check out the corps lines. Gunny Sergeant Locklear, Corporal Chambers, Private First Class Sephra, Privates Rook, Wocheck, and from Alpha squad Privates Hanta and Pompey. It was the first time it struck her mind that the corps' dress uniforms were different from Fleets. At the memorial she had been too lost in her own mind, while now it was clear. A slick black jacket with red trim. A high stiff collar, white gloves, a thick white belt, and angular white hat polished the whole thing off.

The fleet group in their dress was impressive, marching in rank, if loser. Their deep blue, gold and silver buttons, with round white hats, still set a standard. The commanders of the *Ares*, Lewis, Moro, and Haddock all stood shoulder to shoulder. Commander Bard would be staying on the ship as planned. The Lieutenants Wisler and Jax, along with the younger Moro brother, fell into line easy enough. As they marched, faint clapping built. That soon gave way to full cheers.

They passed the doors and marched in step. The grand hall lay before them, and it dropped quiet. Their boots echoed in unison, announcing their arrival. They stopped as one, the last burst of noise reverberating in the ears of all who watched. From the back someone shouted out "Long live the *Ares!*" and the room burst into cheer. They stood at parade rest and let the adoration flow over them. When it died, Commander Lewis called for attention. The group snapped into form. A salute, so in sync, people would swear they had practiced together for years, snapped off to the crowd. A call to dismiss and the group separated to join the party.

Time was short, and they knew it. While they had several objectives: find allies, identify foes, Jax's mind settled on one primary goal. Find Dakos. Rather than joining the crowd, she had circled to the outer walls. Her eyes scanning the mass of people the best she could. Her hat was itching her head and was a distraction she just didn't need. She dropped it on a table as she passed and kept going.

The nature of this party was also messing with her ability to look. She remembered her parents attending these as a kid. Her dad treated the army ball like it was a grand party. Mom was always a little tighter lipped about it. One time, when she was ten, Jax had asked if she could go. Her mom had said she was too young, maybe when she's older. Much older.

The ballroom itself matched her imagination. High arched ceilings laced with ornate molding. Large round tables decorated with flowers and sparkling dinnerware. Everything that she had always expected, but it was the people that were unusual.

She had expected a sea of military uniforms. Yet for every dress uniform she saw elaborate, or even scandalous, dresses. Dresses that were no way in military code, with plunging necklines, mini cut skirts, the works. Some wore costumes from the past, historical military personnel, and a few fantasy characters. There seemed to be no rhyme or reason for the outfits chosen.

Military decorum was also lost. Jax passed by more than one person who could barely stand. Drinking had started early and while the night was young, they were already drunk. No, not drunk, what had dad called it—Army Drunk. Wobbly feet, heads down on tables, friends lifting them off the floor. Such a strange mix of those behaving properly and those over the deep end. It boggled her mind with what she witnessed, but she had to shake it off and stay focused. Focused on Dakos.

She made her way to the outer parts of the room. As her eyes drifted over the crowd, she saw the fire team members were already accomplishing goals. Conversations started, and some were even casually heading for the door. Outside of the *Ares* crew, she would need her HUD to match names with faces. Her contacts were having a rough time with the constantly moving crowds. They did not make the contacts for this kind of work. As she made her way around the room, a solitary figure caught her eye. Nestled in a corner, the figure stood stiff backed and held a drink in one hand. A drink that was untouched. It seemed like a bubble had formed around this man and the crowd's activity avoided him. Jax made towards him like a laser.

Slipping around the edges of the party, passing groups who tried to engage her, she entered the man's bubble. Seeing his uniform clearly, she pegged him as a general. His two silver major stars shining brightly. Her contacts got a facial recognition and filled in the rest of the info. Major General Gaia Terrain Corps, Nazir Jandro. His name wasn't on any of the lists, so her instincts said he should be fine. More than that, his stance, the look in his eyes, Jax got an impression of her father.

Jax marched up and gave her best salute. Major General Jandro saluted back, but his eyes looked past her. "The party is over there, Lieutenant."

"I'm not here for the party, Major General." Jax said.

His eyes pulled back and focused on her. "Lieutenant Brandt. I met your father once when I was young. Last of a breed he was. Not many come to talk to me at these events. Can't stand them myself, but I'm required to be here. Thankfully, people tend to avoid me. What was it you needed, Lieutenant?"

"We have a situation. I believe the term my dad would use is Charlie Foxtrot." Jax said.

Major General Jandro tilted his head. He's eyes started to weigh on her like she was drunk or crazy. Then he caught sight of her dog tags and a light came to his eyes. "Give me a sitrep."

Jax made the situation report as brief as she could. The Major General listened with a stone face. Deep lines on his jaw moving only to ask pointed questions for clarification. "Smart thinking by your commander. You continue on. I know who in the corps can be trusted, I'll rally them and well help secure this place. Let's go."

He was off before Jax could even think to salute him. As he pushed into the crowd, it parted for him. He was like a tornado as he caught specific people in his wake. He did seem to move with much subtle, but it was too late to worry about that now. She pulled up a building schematic and checked on everyone's progress. No enemies found, but they were having trouble finding allies. Too many came to celebrate and had started the party early. She hoped the Major General could produce better results, or they were all screwed.

The main hall was well covered. The fire teams, and now the Major General, were canvassing the room well. She picked a spot no one had cleared yet and made her way. Her HUD showed the area as a utility hall with closets and a back stairwell to the second floor. Used by staff to bypass the main avenues and stay unimpeded by guests.

A flick in her eye, barely a glimpse. She felt like someone was following her. Stopping short of the double doors to the back hall, she spun around. Her left hand reaching for a grip, right dropping to her ASA. A slim man matching her height, with a dark blue suit, and messy hair. Her muscles flared as the first thought to dance through her mind was that of the shadow, Esteban. The nose was off. This was someone else.

"Oh, that was very quick, Jax. Most impressive. Can I see you do it again?" Nath said. A childlike grin crossed the otherwise adult face.

"Nath! What are you doing?"

"Blending in. I thought this was a very stylistic choice. I considered something more metallic but—"

"Not the outfit. Why aren't you looking for more targets?"

"I'm not very good at that. I keep getting distracted by the party. So, I figured I could stay close to you. You can keep me focused. Rose is very good at that, one of those qualities that I find so intriguing about her." Nath said, a Cheshire-like smile crossing his face.

"Great," Jax said, rolling her eyes. She determined it was easier to agree than argue. "Let's go."

Pushing through the doors, they entered a long hallway. Simple doors lined the corridor. At the far end, two figures were turning a corner. First, Jax missed seeing the face, glimpsing only a gray suit. The second was instantly recognizable. Dog. "That's Dakos' bodyguard. That has to be him," Jax said, venom seeping into her voice. "Come on."

Her heart raced as she took those first steps to give chase. She eyed a message to the others that indicated she had spotted Dakos. Jax and Nath went spiraling to the floor. A large serving tray spewed across the hallway. Jax hopped to her feet and raised her hands to apologize to the capsized server, but she didn't have time to stop.

"Sorry, got to go—" she said, the servers' eyes wide in horror. He was halfway to his feet, but his hands scrambled at his side. She saw it the moment his fingers made contact. *Gun.*

Jax tackled the server as he tried to push away from her. They crashed through the door he had sprung out. His gun, it looked like a slim version of a NEW24, went skidding off. Her shoulder drove into his chest, her left hand secured his wrist, and a grunt issued from his lungs. She had him pinned and immobilized against a wall before anything bad could happen. That's when she realized her mistake.

From the corner of her eye, she saw the room. This wasn't on the schematics. They had knocked walls down to create a larger staging area. Seven more servers lined the room. The others were partially dressed, armor and outfits showing in different states of wear. In a few more moments, disguises would conceal them. Weapons lay on tables and chairs as each person changed.

"Nath run, get help!" Jax shouted, her muscles strained as her assailant struggled, gaining his wind back. Shouts of alarm as the terrorist registered that they had been discovered. Dropping disguises and running for guns. Nath ran too, but to Jax's surprise, he didn't run for help. Like lightning, he entered the room. She wanted to yell to tell him to stop, but it was too late as the enemy brought their rifles to bear.

Nath's speed surpassed what even full kit armor could do. He was a blur in the wind. His punches sent the enemy flying. He danced around their shots with unreal grace, his body twisting and turning. Nath's arms and legs extended to unnatural lengths, slamming his opponents. Bones crunched and heads cracked as his hands and feet made contact. Shots passed by him with no chance of making a connection. The enemy tried to dodge, to move away, but none was safe. His whirlwind attack left no one untouched.

Jax and her opponent were caught like deer in headlights, unable to turn from the grisly scene. Shaking themselves back to their own situation. Jax acted first, driving her head up into her opponent's chin, a deep groan greeted her. She pulled him off the wall, and hip tossed him into a corner. His head buckled as he hit awkwardly on the floor, laying still. *O-goshi, not a legal setup, but can't argue with the results.* She looked around and saw Nath standing in a pile of bodies. He was whipping his hands as if they had dirt on them. His head moved left and right, checking his handy work.

"Nath, that was amazing," she said.

"Really? I believe I informed you I was proficient at hand-to-hand combat. This was an adequate display, I would say."

"That it was," she said, shaking her head and activating her comms. "All teams, we have engaged the enemy. Targets dressed as servers, heavily armed, back hallway."

"What now?" Nath asked.

"We have to get Dakos. Let's go."

"After you," he said, ushering with hands to the door. Jax nodded and plucked the slim NEW24 off the floor.

"That's a cheap knockoff of my designs. I wouldn't trust it, but I do like the slim look. Maybe I should make a SLIM24?" He made a sad face as he eyed the weapon.

"Later, we need to move." She slid out the door. Dakos was to the right, and she glanced that way first. Hearing footsteps and the click of guns turned her back to the left. A group of twelve-armed terrorists filled the hallway. This group wasn't trying to blend in, no disguises, combat gear all around. She spun, to raise her weapon, when Nath pushed her aside and down the hall.

"I've got this! Go get Dakos!" Nath yelled. He launched into the new group of attackers. His form blinked, and he was a barbarian in a loincloth, smacking his opponents down. Shock and terror spread throughout the group as they tried to adjust to the onslaught. The halls rumbled and shots rang out. Bedlam ensued.

Her eyes were locked on the assault for a split second before her mind caught up and her feet turned to run. Random fire chased after her. She ducked her head and zigzagged as much as the hall allowed. Over the comms, voices lashed out. The main hall was now a battlefield. Terrorist and the small force Jax's friends had assembled clashed. Shouts and gunfire echoed in her ears. She quickly got the feeling her side was vastly outnumbered.

At the end of the hall, two paths lay before her. One to the outside gardens and nature walks awaited. The other path headed upstairs to the second level. Jax didn't break stride as she ascended the steps two at a time. *He won't go outside. He won't go outside.* She kept repeating it in her mind, willing it to be true.

She crested the second floor and slowed to a walk. Another hallway with a whole new set of doors. She extended the stock on her SLIM24, pressed it into her shoulder. Over the comms, the battle the main hall continued to play in her ears. She cleared the hallway of locked doors and rounded a corner. In the next hallway, she was granted a gift. The dog, Talbot Blocksburg, was at the far end of the hall. He leaned with his back against the wall. His head lolled into his chest like he was napping while standing.

She stepped smoothly, her gun sights locked in. She covered half the distance before the big lug roused.

"Huh? What's going—"

Jax raised a finger to her mouth and hushed him. Her voice was steel when she spoke. "Stay quiet. If you move, I'll light you up. Where's Dakos?"

"He's occupied. Call his office and get an appointment."

"I'm not messing with you, Talbot. Get your hands up and tell me where he is."

Talbot scoffed at her and said, "Or what? You'll shoot me? Please, we both know you don't have the—"

To his credit, he didn't yell when the red beam pierced his leg. His mouth opened and his teeth clenched as he dropped to the floor, but he didn't yell.

"I'll only ask one more time," Jax said, moving in close and aiming at his head this time. "Where's Dakos?"

Talbot's face pinched and fury burst from his eyes. The words came hard. "Next door down. But you don't want—"

Jax smashed the butt of her gun into his temple. He slumped to the floor. *I guess I should check if this gun has a stun setting, but I'm sure it wouldn't have been as satisfying.* She absently checked the control and sure enough, the setting was there. She stepped up to the next door; the handle moved easily, and the door swung open. Rushing in and while her gun swept across the room. "Nobody moves!" Jax shouted.

Dakos jumped off a woman and fell off the bed. Scrambling to his feet, he grabbed a sheet to cover himself. "What's the meaning of this?"

The girl screamed, sitting up in the bed, while also clawing for covers. Jax drifted the gun back and forth between the two. Her brow curled in confusion. *He's got to be leading this, but this is not someone leading an insurrection. That's not his wife, and this is all wrong. This was all wrong. We have it all wrong.* Dakos held his ground, the gun making him wary, but he yelled anyway. Threatening her career and her entire life. Jax wasn't listening to his words and found his prattle distracting. She stunned him. The woman screamed as Dakos hit the floor. So Jax stunned her, too. The woman's body spasmed, and the room fell silent.

Jax fell silent as if stunned herself. This was supposed to be the end. Dakos was the one behind it all. He should have been sheltering here for the attack—not this. Jax mind raced. They were missing something. What was it? Dakos had led the legal charges against the *Ares*. He could find out where she was living to plan that attack. He could get someone on base to sabotage the plane. It all made sense. Right? The attack at the park he left the stage, but not to save himself. *He left to meet his mistress. Damn. The evidence at the compound isn't his plan, it's him being framed. Dakos is an idiot.* It came to her that Dakos was a patsy in all this. It would take someone smart, more poised, more powerful, to run everything. *By the abyss, we've been fools.*

Jax sprinted out of the room without a care, a single question beating itself into her head. She activated the comms and, over the spurts of gunfire, shouted the question that could answer all their problems.

"Where's the Prime Representative? Where is Emma Gibson?"

Chapter 20

I'M A PRINCESS

J ax pumped her legs and leaned into her stride. "I repeat, where is the Prime Rep?" she shouted into her comms.

"I think I saw her with some of the big brass heading out to the ceremony gardens," Chambers responded.

"Yeah, her bodyguards were down, and they were taking her to safety," Brooklyn chimed in.

"Is she in some kind of trouble, Jax?" asked Commander Lewis.

"She is the trouble," Jax said, while checking the schematics for where the ceremony garden was. "Dakos was a setup. It's the Prime Rep, she's the one behind it all. I repeat, the Prime Representative is enemy number one." She hurtled down the stairs as the outside layout appeared on her HUB. The back door gave her a straight shot to the gardens. "I'm going after her. Send backup."

"Where on our way, but we're still finishing up. We're all pinned down. Double damn," Commander Lewis called back.

Slamming open the back door, she sprinted for the ne*ares*t garden. Trimmed hedges and flower beds we're all the greeted her. Mini light posts illuminated the walkways and cast an uncanny glow around the garden. It would have been peaceful if not for the echo of gunfire in the night. Looking at the map on her HUD too many options opened before her. They could head to the road, but that would mean walking or a pickup vehicle. There was a boathouse near a lake, maybe a watercraft? Or, back to the entrance for vehicle support, but that was into the fire. No, none of those felt right. "Why go to the garden?" Jax asked. "I got nothing here."

"There's an open field in the far garden. The Prime's personal craft is there," Lewis said.

"Got it," Jax said, finding the field on her HUD. She launched into a sprint, cutting across the lawn, and foregoing the walkways. The soft blue-grass squishing lightly under her feet. She passed under an ornamental arch as she exited the main garden. Nighttime shadows cast strange reflections as only path lights broke the gloom. She skidded to a stop. On the side of the path lay several dead bodies. Several Gaia First terrorists, a Corps private and the body of the Major General. *Damn.* Gunfire lit up the sky ahead of her and she was off again. Her path took her through an opening in a hedge wall and the field was laid out before her.

Over fifty meters out on her left was a beat-up utility truck that lay wrecked against a tree. Scorch marks battered the length of the truck. The driver had lost control and landed headfirst into the oak; the truck's front hugged the tree. Stooped behind it were the high marshal, Admiral Koonce, and a corps major that Jax's HUD identified as Major Took. She couldn't see the Prime, but her bright silver ship sat further out, idle on the field.

Across from the huddled group, Gaia First terrorists harassed the military brass. An enemy technical, with eight combatants, well covered the group. The heavy weight black truck had full armor and an enormous gun attached on top. The big gun sat empty while the eight terrorists fired pot shots at the utility vehicle. The shots would fly high or wide or hit the ground, sending dirt flying.

Jax shouldered her SLIM24, and once again ran into danger. She covered twenty meters before daring to open fire. Two of the enemies dropped from her red beam. Another target peaked around the truck, checking on their friend. Jax's beam missed, but her attack distracted the target and General Took shot true. The last four terrorists panicked from the unexpected assault. Scrambling to change their cover, firing shots off toward the new assault. The fire was careless, but still made her dive for cover. As she rolled up from the ground, the big brass dropped another one.

Showing they were more than just decorated uniforms; the big brass used the new distraction expertly. Two more targets dropped from their precision firing. Sheer luck saved the last target as his teammate fell in front of him. The teammate absorbed the shots that would have taken him in the chest.

He dashed to the big gun. Jax slashed her beam, but her targeting was low. His legs burned, and he screamed, but he still pulled the trigger. A single boom from the gun and shrapnel burst from the utility truck. A large hole impaling the battered truck clean through. Jax found focus for her beam. The big brass joined in and the technical exploded in rays of light.

Jax ran at the group, shouting at the top of her lungs. "Where's the Prime? We need to secure the Prime!"

"The Prime's fine!" Admiral Koonce shouted back. "We kept her safe."

"No, she's the threat. We need to—" Jax yelled, her face straining to make them understand as the Prime came into view. Her hair was golden, it glistened off the nearby lights. Behind the big brass, she fell out of the darkness. She had a militia chest piece over her silky black dress. She had a gun, a NEW9, in her right hand. The high marshal dropped, a pulse of light shattering his skull. General Took turned, and she left a hole in his chest. Admiral Koonce raised his gun, but she had the drop on him. Stepping in, she leveled the NEW9 at his eyes and tilted her head as if to dare him to try.

"Don't move. Either of you," the Prime shouted. Jax slid to a halt and brought her rifle to bear. The Prime had Admiral Koonce drop his gun and turn around. She pulled him back with his collar and put the gun to his head.

"Drop it, Emma. It's over," Jax said.

"Silly little princess, nothing's over. Drop the rifle. From what I've heard of your shooting ability, you couldn't hit me, anyway. But you might get noble and cut us both down, just to save the day. Can't have that now, can we, princess?"

Jax held firm and slid a little closer. Admiral Koonce barely nodded as if to tell her to go ahead, take the shot. The Prime's face contorted, annoyed that Jax hadn't complied, and used the gun to poke the admiral in the head. The admiral's eyes narrowed, but it wasn't worry, it was anger.

"Do it." The Prime spat the words. Jax relented and tossed her rifle aside. She flashed the Prime her hands to show they were empty, but otherwise maintained her stance.

"It's over, Emma. We know it was you behind Gaia First or Gaia Alpha, whatever you want to call it. Surrender." Jax said, willing her voice to stay steady.

"Nothing's over, princess. I'm in control of everything. I will give you some credit, though. All my clues should have led you to that fool, Dakos. What gave me away?"

"We came here looking for Dakos," Jax said. "When we found him, it was obvious he wasn't the one in charge."

"Let me guess, he was shacked up with that perky assistant of his? How'd you know about the attack?"

Jax nodded. "We raided his warehouse tonight. Once we had that info and realized it wasn't him, we just needed someone who was powerful enough to frame him. Short list."

"He truly is an idiot. That man can't do anything correctly, even get framed. I guess I have Commander Haddock to thank for that. Or Lillian," the Prime said with a little extra venom on Commander Bards' name.

Jax let the Prime talk and slid a few steps closer. The Prime likes to talk, let her waste time till help could come.

"That's far enough," the Prime said, pushing the gun against the admiral's head again. "No heroes here princess, I'm getting on my ship and leaving."

Jax gave a slow single nod and lowered her hands. "It's over. Why keep going? The others I came with already know you're guilty. Hurting Admiral Koonce or me will only add to your crimes. Surrender," Jax said, forcing her voice to be calm as possible.

"Silly princess, aren't you paying attention? I'm in control here," the Prime said, flashing a smile. "I control the media, I control the government, I control the military. I could kill you both on a live stream and still get away with it."

Admiral Koonce stirred, and the Prime pulled him back, the gun pushing harder against his skull. The admirals' eyes stayed locked on Jax. A push of the chin, a squint of the eye said she needed to push, not fallback. Jax thought he looked more bored than worried about the situation.

"What's wrong with you?" Jax said, letting anger seep in. "You're already the most powerful person on Gaia. Earth is far off. Why do all this?"

"It's not about power, princess, it's about what's right. Earth is a cesspool of corruption. You and your 'royal' family, leading your perfect life. You don't see it. My family did. They were working with Gaia to build this place. Something free from all the corruption, till the corruption caught us. Called my family traitors during the Keres incident! We completely left Earth after that. We came here and put a shine on this place, pushed them farther from Earth. Had everything where I wanted it, till you came along."

"What did I have to do with it?"

"They praised your family while they vilified mine. Then the precious royal daughter comes here and does the same thing to me. Destroying everything I built! They all think you're a hero, some kind of saint, but I know better. I'll turn them on you, then they'll follow me. A better tomorrow without Earth, without you. My better tomorrow." Emma's neck pulsed and her muscles flexed. Her hand was shaking with anticipation. Admiral Koonce's lips pressed together, his eyes sharp to the side, staring at the gun to his head.

Jax planted her feet and squared her shoulders. She let her eyes flare and the phoenix inside ignite. "You're whack," she said. "I might be a princess, but at least I'm not blaming others for the problems in my life. Maybe your whole family is just a bunch of ralitch, scum suckers. Ever think about that?"

"How dare you!"

"Oh, I dare," Jax yelled. "This princess dares to own up to her mistakes. I dare to stand up to monsters wherever I find them. And there's something I dare, a thing that you have vastly underestimated about me."

The Prime's laugh was angry. "Oh, please share before I end this whole awful affair."

In an instant, Jax calmed, and her body relaxed. One moment her breathing was tense, the anger flowing through it and now it was cool, even and steady. The change caused the Prime to pull back a step, dragging

Admiral Koonce with her. It didn't matter to Jax anymore; she was tired of these games. She had to act, make something happen.

"You underestimated how much this 'princess' is sick of your bull-shit."

The anger in the Prime's eyes flashed and changed to surprise. It was a blink of an eye, and she fell away from Admiral Koonce. He stumbled a step forward as the Prime's arm dropped from the admiral's collar. His head slowly swiveled from the dead body of the Prime to Jax.

Jax was locked in that moment in time. She had fired from the waist, left hand hovering over the Army Single Action. All the practice, all those emotions compacted in a single shot. Her mind clicked and every-thing started moving again. She holstered the weapon and stepped up next to the Admiral. The Prime's body lay lifeless on the ground. A shot pierced her forehead, dead center.

"Excellent shot, Lieutenant," Admiral Koonce said. "It seems the gos-sip about you lacking marksmanship skills is off base."

"I don't know about that. I've never made a shot like that off the draw before. I'm usually off to left or right by ten centimeters or so. I just wanted to distract her so you could attack." She and the admiral stared at the body, the moments stretching. It took a while before she realized the admiral wasn't staring at the body, however, and was rather staring at her. His mouth was gapping open, and he seemed in shock. She gave him a gentle smile to try to calm his nerves. It would be a while before she realized what the issue was.

Both the officers turned when a voice called from behind. Corporal Chambers and the rest of Charlie squad, the stone dogs, came running. Chambers' uniform was dusty, and he had bandages wrapped around his left arm. "Admiral. Lieutenant Brandt," Chambers said with a casual salute. "Commander Lewis sent me to assist and look for the High Marshal."

"The High Marshal is dead, as is the Prime Representative, so I guess you'll have to talk to me. What's the situation back there?"

"Under control, admiral. They got the jump on us, but once we got our heads together, well, superior training wins the day," Chambers said.

"Excellent Corporal. We're under control here too, thanks to the Lieutenant. Still, it's going to be a cluster frip untangling the mess made here today. Let your commander know we'll be along shortly. I'll want to debrief everyone."

"That's the thing Admiral, I think we'll need you to come now since the High Marshal is dead. It's the Screech you see. They found them, and it looks like they're headed for Gaia."

"How many Screech are we talking about, Corporal?"

"Pretty sure all of them, Admiral," Chambers said.

The Admirals' eyes narrowed on Chambers and then turned to regard Jax as well.

Jax licked her lips, let out a deep breath, and said the only thing that felt right. "Well, that's ominous."

Admiral Koonce, Chambers, and even the stone dogs nodded in agreement. They all turned and started the march back to the hall.

Act III

You'll probably think this story is about me, but you'll be wrong.
This story is about Gaia, a world at war.

Chapter 21

GROWING HEADACHE

Hopper was always on standby, so Jax shuttled them to Alpha Station. Commander Bard rode shotgun in the copilot seat. The commander would occasionally shake or nod her head, raise an eyebrow, or evoke deep sighs. It seemed to Jax that the commander was commenting on her flying, but she never spoke. Jax tried to stay focused on being the pilot but was generally annoyed by Lilly Bard.

In the back, riding the rumble seats, were Admiral Koonce, Commanders Lewis, Haddock, and Moro. The cabin was dead quiet. Messages had come flooding in for the Admiral from the moment they hit the air. He had asked Commander Bard to silence them all. Everyone on board seemed to take that as a sign to hold their tongues.

"Let them sort the chaos a bit before they waste time telling me what I need to know. Otherwise, they'll be changing the information every minute. Let's have some peace till then," was all the admiral said.

At Alpha Station, they wasted no time making for the command center. Jax had expected the admiral to break off and head for a meeting room. Instead, they gathered on the main observation platform. Another admiral, several captains with their XO's were there waiting with them. The holoimages of other captains, VIPs, and government officials also joined in. When everything seemed settled, the admiral took over.

"Let's get started. What's the situation?" Admiral Koonce said.

Captain Milan stepped forward; she was the commander of Alpha Station. A slim bordering on frail woman. Her dark hair had streaks of gray; she was well regarded for her organizational abilities. "Approximately an hour ago, a deep space survey ship, Lil' Seeker, detected an anomaly in space heading towards them. They were checking a rogue planet for possible mining. What they found was horrible."

Captain Milan lifted her chin and waved a hand. A holoimage blossomed in the middle of the deck. A deep pocket of space with a few twinkling stars. *The Lil' Seeker* sat center stage and was orbiting a dark planet. *The Seeker* was a class two survey ship; it looked like a metal tube with an engine strapped on. The image started moving and veered off the small ship, heading into deep space. A small distortion, like something out of focus, became the center of attention. With each moment and movement closer, ships came into view, clearer, more defined. Their hulls painted to blend in with the surrounding space, no edges to be seen, the Screech.

The numbers were increasing, a never-ending wave. A deadly formation of every Screech ship imaginable. Destroyers, frigates, and fighters moving in harmony like a grand parade. The ships filled the holoimage until there was room for nothing else. A hush fell across the command center. Captain Milan took a deep breath and swallowed a lump in her throat. She spoke. "*The Lil' Seeker* was spotted and destroyed a short time later. Since then, we have been scouting the armada from afar with —"

"Admiral! Admiral!" An Ensign came running to the group.

"I'm assuming this is important, Ensign Aloa?" Admiral Koonce said.

"Yes, Admiral. We're — We're getting a message. We think, well we think, it's strange but—"

"Spit it out, Ensign. What are you talking about?"

"We're getting a message from the Screech. It's on a channel we use for corps missions."

Admiral Koonce startled for a moment and tilted his head at the Ensign. "Bring it up Ensign, let's have a look at it."

The Ensign nodded and dropped his nose into a wrist holoscreen. A moment later, he flicked his fingers, and an image formed in front of the admiral. Everyone took a step back, gasps escaping lips. It stood life size, a half head taller than the admiral. Its armor was dazzling with colors, reds, blues, and greens. Sharp angles like blades on a sword, cut and projected around the creature. Etched engravings formed intricate patterns across its armor. The markings could only be called feathers. It bore no helmet, it's enormous eyes with dark plate like pupils scanned back and forth. Hairy feathers in its scalp were swept back and then up into a high brown crest. The Screech spoke, the grating noise echoed through the command center. The creature became animated with wild gestures. Its clawed hands waving and clenching. Its back bending and then straightening, head snapping left and right.

"Turn the volume down," Admiral Koonce bellowed. "Do we have any idea what it's saying?"

"No, sir," Ensign Aloa said. "We've had some success with a written language, but nothing for the spoken. Some of the technicians are trying to send holoimages. Written messages, but they seem to ignore them."

"Wonderful, then what are we—" The admiral's eyes went wide.

The cawing of the Screech stopped, and it held up its left hand. An image of the *Ares* floated above its palm. It rotated slowly, displaying every detail. The damage in the hull, the burn marks from energy beams, everything. Its right hand pointed at the *Ares* and then swept across the room. Raising the image in the air, it screamed. A new body stumbled into the Screech's holo transmission. Ryan Nelson.

Private First-class Ryan Nelson. Who had given his life on Nest I for the rest of his fireteam. At least that's what they thought had happened. Jax's heart wrenched. The Screech general pushed the battered man. He stumbled forward. His face was hallowed, eyes like a skull. Burn marks lined the left side of his cheek and down into his chest. Scratch marks and ill healed cuts littered his body. His right hand, missing from the elbow, was wrapped in what appeared to be his shirt. Only tattered pants, held by a thread, remained.

The Screech pushed him again, and he snarled. His eyes alight with anger. His voice was like sandpaper when he spoke. "I... I don't... I don't know what... what they want." He gulped. The Screech pushed him again. "They just keep showing me the *Ares* and yelling, always screeching—It never stops!"

The Screech clawed his back, and he dropped to the ground. His body rippled with pain, yet he still lifted his head. "Come get these bastards!

Blow them out of the ever love'n abyss!" The Screech general flung Nelson out of the holoscreen. The creature turned, its hands held wide, and its head dropped. Its rapid-fire wailing filled the room once more. The creature slammed its fist into its palm, destroying the image of the *Ares*. Then the screen blipped out.

The silence in the command center was deafening. Captain Milan broke it first. "We've never known them to take prisoners. This is unprecedented. What are we going to do?"

All eyes turned to Admiral Koonce. His stony visage unmoving against the weight of their gaze. He spoke. "We get to work. We need to explore options. Mounting a defense or evacuating the planet. I want options from all command officers in—"

"What about getting him back?" Jax burst out.

Before the Admiral could respond, Commander Lewis stepped forward. She put an arm around Jax's shoulder. "We'll do what we can, Jax," Gemma said. "But the Admiral is right. We need to mount a defense and work on possibly evacuating Gaia."

"We can't evacuate. We don't have enough ships or time. I've seen these numbers. You should all know them better than me. We—"

"Lieutenant Brandt," Commander Lewis said. Her look had changed from caring to command. "While your insights have been valuable in the past, here they are misplaced. You will hold the chain of command and await orders. Is that clear?"

Jax's phoenix eyes were ablaze, but she held her tongue. "Understood, Commander."

Lewis weighed her options and held her stance, as if waiting for Jax to attack. A moment passed, and she felt secure that the Lieutenant had control of herself. She gave a curt nod and turned to go. Admiral Koonce, the other admirals, and captains were off to continue planning. Gemma quickened her step to catch up. The holoimages of the other captains, XO's and VIPS, blipped out or stayed huddled in their little groups.

Jax stayed frozen for a brief instant. The fire that erupted from her core hardened into a single drive. Captain Moss once said captains have to be what they need to be. They need to laugh and smile. They need to inspire and command. And sometimes, they need to yell and rage. She turned and her boots sounded like thunder on the decking. Commander Bard tried to confront her, to hold her back. Jax was having none of it and gave Lilly Bard no more consideration than a storm would a blade of grass.

She approached a control consul and shouldered an Ensign out of the way. He tried to protest, but her look sent him scampering off instead. Her hands danced across the controls. She glanced at the primary image of Gaia floating in the middle of the command center. The multiple-story high image called to her, but she didn't have access to use that. Instead, she copied what Captain Milan had done. She opened the largest holoscreen she could on the observation deck.

An image of Gaia started it all. It grew exponentially as she added to it. The information on the Screech armada. The surrounding solar system, Gaia and all its resources, everything. She moved objects with a swipe of the hand. Tactical information overlayed the holomaps, hot points and critical points highlighted. Ship movements and time frames spelled out before her. Her mind was in overdrive, her hands desperately trying to keep up with her thoughts. Instincts backed by training acted automatically, guiding her steps. The pieces of the puzzle fell into place, but in the end, she realized there were still things missing. Her hands slowed and wavered. She was at the end of her knowledge. Her eyes darted across screens, looking for the right information.

"What in the abyss is this?"

The voice rumbled in Jax's ears and pulled her away from her action plan. She had finished what she could, fearing the missing gaps. Too many things she still didn't know. Turning, it startled her to find a crowd watching her. The admirals, ensigns, everyone available had gathered around.

"This is how we fight back," Jax said. "They are coming for the *Ares*. When they want something this bad, they go straight at it." She waved her hands, and the image moved.

The holo image of the *Ares* left Alpha Station and moved into a high orbit around Gaia. The gun platforms moved, two completed, and one under construction, boxed it in. Three more *Ares* class crafts flew into view, creating a wedge in front. Other Gaia crafts moved around the planet. The older ships, the smaller Gaia created craft, and the Earth ships retrofitted for combat, taking up guard positions. The sleek design of the Gaia craft arranged with the more saucer looking Earth craft created a strange kaleidoscope ringing Gaia. The Screech armada moved in.

"For defense, we create a kill zone focused on the *Ares*." The image shifted, showing lines of fire crisscrossing the space in front of the *Ares*. Counter beams from the Screech were also included. The holoimage flashed reds, blues and greens. "Our focus for attack should be on these three ships." Waving her hand, the holo zoomed in on three brightly colored ships. Hard lines and sharp angles, they looked more like crystalline spears than actual ships. "These are the command ships. I think if we can break those, we can—"

"How do you know they'll focus on the *Ares*?" Captain Milan interrupted.

"It's an established pattern. The Screech are hyper focused on goals. We've seen this on the *Ares* and from my research into other incursions with the Screech. All the information I could find from Gaia's records. There is ample support for it."

"How do you know those are command ships?" Admiral Koonce asked.

Jax was afraid they wouldn't listen. As she scanned the faces of those assembled, she saw interest, not doubt. "We've never seen these ships. No record of them in Gaia's files. I've been studying those. They match what we think were leaders of some sort on Roost I. Military records show that the Screech avoid sharp angles, preferring a more organic look. The creatures we encountered on Roost I were exact opposite. Sharp angles and larger in size. They were obviously in some sort of command position there. It's not a far leap to associate that to these craft—"

"This plan doesn't work. We don't have the crew for those three *Ares* class vessels," the other admiral said. His round face squinted at the holoimage details while shaking his head.

"Admiral Brass is correct," Admiral Koonce said, shifting his gaze to that portion of the plan. "We'd have to pull crew from most of these support ships to make it happen. That would leave considerable gaps in this setup. With that, the whole thing collapses."

"No, it doesn't," Jax insisted. "We have a whole academy of highly trained crew ready to go."

"They're trainees. They are not ready."

"They are more ready and better trained than I am," Jax said. She checked the eyes of all gathered, daring them to contradict her. "This is their world, their fight. They'll die on the sidelines or die fighting. I thought Gaia was about that choice?"

The room stiffened at her words. Some puffed out their chests, a show of pride. Some dropped their heads in contemplation, a few grew stern, eyes piercing at her.

"I'm not sure even that would be enough," Commander Lewis said. "We could crew one and maybe half a crew for two, but not all three."

"We have to protect *Ares* as long as possible, keep the screech focused. What if—" Jax paused, her mind racing for a solution to their objections. "What if we put EVE on each ship? I know Gaia doesn't like them, but we have Earth craft here. Surely there are EVE units on them we can use. We can pull them, let them run what the crews can't cover, then we could get by with less than a skeleton crew, right?"

A few of the captains visibly stepped back at that. Admiral Brass turned pale.

Admiral Koonce was rubbing his temple and shaking his head. "We do not allow EVEs on warships, Lieutenant Brandt. Even if we did, it still wouldn't work. It would take an EVE unit weeks, possibly months, to map and be able to use an *Ares* class ship's network. We have hours."

"Then let's just copy the one I have on the *Ares*. That will work, right?" Across the room eyes went wide. Jaws dropped and anyone not paying attention was paying attention now. An icy chill touched everyone's skin and goose bumps prickled their flesh.

"How in the abyss did you put an Enhanced Virtual Entity on the *Ares*?" Admiral Koonce said his face was bottled with rage. "Who authorized such a thing?"

"Huh—well, it was an accident," Jax stammered. The pulse of anger directed at her felt like a blow to the chest. Something had changed in the room. "It was from the *Indiana*, a gift. I just wanted someone to help me study. I don't understand, EVE has been fine. Earth has them on all their ships. Why is this an issue?"

"Why is this an issue? Why is this an issue?" Admiral Koonce said, his voice rising with each word. He began advancing on Jax. She backed up a few steps before Commander Lewis placed herself between the two officers. The admiral gained his composure and stopped, but his eyes were still ablaze.

"Let us talk for a moment, Admiral," Commander Lewis said. She cupped his arm and ushered him to the side. They began whispering in harsh tones. Other admirals and captains moved in and soon the arguments were a jumble as the words came back to Jax.

She looked around, hoping to find some grain of support. She found none as she moved her attention from one to the next. Heads looked away from her. Some stepped back completely. She found Haddock and Bard creeping their way to her side.

"Okay, what did I miss? Why is everyone on Gaia so against EVEs?" Jax asked.

"How can you not know? Jax, this is Keres," Commander Bard said.

"Keres? As in the Keres Incident? That was on Earth and finished before I was even born. My father handled it, doesn't make me some kind of expert. What does this have to do with Gaia?"

"Oh, Jax." Commander Bard's hand covered her mouth. "We just assumed you knew or would research it. I'm so sorry. We should have told you. With whom your family is, we just never... Oh, my—"

"What? What is it? What am I missing here?"

"Jax, Keres may have ended on Earth, but it started on Gaia."

Jax's eyes went wide, and her mouth dropped open. She couldn't find the words. Her gaze darted between the two commanders.

"It was a lot worse here. Our solution cost a lot more lives than what your father came up with. So many lives."

"We have a bigger problem right now," Commander Haddock said. "Putting an EVE on a warship is a capital offence. The sentence is a death penalty."

"What?" Jax said. "What is it with Gaia and the death penalty? Nobody uses that anymore."

"We do on Gaia. For this. Treason on board during wartime and a few other places. This is big trouble, Jax." The trio of officers dropped into silence. Heads bowed in thought, in worry. Jax's face darted back and forth between the officers, the group of admirals and Captains. Her mind raced and her lips stammered, but she couldn't place it all together. *What have I done?* The three officers stood; heads bowed. Minds lost in contemplation, searching for solutions. Nothing could be said to fix the situation. They waited in silence.

Commander Lewis marched over. Stone-faced and stiffed backed, her gaze cut down the other officers. "I don't know, and I don't want an explanation. Point of fact is that they've accepted your plan."

"What?" all three officers said at the same time.

"We're on the edge of the mat here and there is no going back. Last seconds on the clock," Lewis said. "We can't leave three *Ares* class ships on the sidelines. Jax's plan is the only thing that works in the time we have. Make no mistake, there will be consequences if we survive this."

"Now what?" Commander Haddock asked.

"They've started to work on logistics and filling in the gaps. They are contacting the academy and asking for volunteers. They will not make it mandatory. Only senior year cadets will be eligible, but I have a feeling we'll be fighting off more as they try to sneak in. I'm assuming Rose will know a way to copy EVE from the *Ares*?" Commander Lewis asked.

"She should. We'll have to ask her. I got the EVE in a vpet. She can probably use the same setup for a transfer." Jax said.

"Excellent, we'll get her on that immediately. That leads us to our last problem." Commander Lewis paused a moment, ensuring the other officers' attention. "I'll captain the *Ares*. For the other three ships, we need officers in charge. Officers, preferably with battle experience and serving on an *Ares* class ship. Since we only have our crew to pull from, I've recommended Commander Moro for one. Issac I expect you to take the second one." Commander Haddock nodded while Commander Lewis continued, "That means Lilly you're in charge of number three."

"No fripping way am I in charge of anything."

"Lilly, we need you."

"You need your best pilot flying a ship."

"Technically, with a skeleton crew, you can do both."

"Technically, you can kiss my ass."

"Lilly —"

"I will let the world burn first, find someone else."

Lewis's jaw set hard, and you could feel her planning her next move. She placed a hand on her head, a growing headache. "That's what I told them you'd say. Admiral Koonce is going to fripping explode. Jax, that means you're up."

It took a moment for it to sink in, a moment for her to understand what Commander Lewis had just said. She looked at Gemma and judgement met her. She looked at Issac Haddock and was met with a calm resolve. Lilly Bard tried hard to hide a mischievous grin, and then it sank in.

I'm a captain again.

Chapter 22

HEADED TO WAR

They had twelve hours to prepare for the end of the world. For Jax that meant everyone would jump onto the ships and be off, simple, easy. They put the plan into motion and the EVEs worked on the details. Except here, she had to remind herself, there were no EVEs. Even for the mundane, Gaia preferred the hands-on approach. Her plan was broad strokes. Now the managers, the organizers, real people had to step in. A drop of water placed in the ocean would become a ripple that hopefully became waves. It was slow, painfully so, since she was now a part of that process.

Jax sat in a meeting with the two other new captains, Haddock, and Moro. Their first task was to staff their own ships. Admiral Koonce, now acting as high marshal, had ordered that they could recruit only volunteers. That included retired personnel, civilians with proper training, and academy members in their senior year. Reserves were called up, but there was precious few of those. While they didn't lack volunteers, in fact, they had to turn some away. People that didn't meet the requirements or those without the proper training. Somehow, they made it work. Each ship got its skeleton crew, the bare number they needed to run with the help of an EVE unit.

The hardest part was filling in the command crews for each ship. For that, they were only choosing from the *Ares*. The *Ares* had no lack of skilled crew. Taking them for command positions left holes elsewhere. Some, while skilled, had no command experience or were ill-fitting for the service. It was a no-win scenario, no matter what they did. Commander Lewis had a roster from the *Ares* for them to review. From that initial list, Jax grabbed the Ratpack. Nobody fought her for this choice. They were the best fit for her. The rest became a back and forth of who worked best and where. Who couldn't be spared and who could. Opinions ran high on all fronts.

Jax stayed quiet through this process. It was so different from when she first took the position of captain on the *Indiana*. She never had to handle this kind of thing. Earth's International Space Agency hired each member of the crew. They determined the positions, pay rates and such. Assisted by EVEs, it was a well thought out, and more importantly, fast endeavor. It seemed to Jax a much more efficient method than what they were doing now.

"Lieutenant Brandt. Lieutenant Brandt!" The words snapped her back to reality. Commander Moro's brow furrowed at her. "This is important, Lieutenant'. We still have several spots to fill. You need a Weapons officer if you don't recall."

She did recall, but did it matter? Anyone they gave her would be highly trained and capable. She didn't know any of the names being offered, anyway. What could she offer? "What about Lieutenant Moro? Your brother? I remember him saying he was waiting for a position' and I've worked with him already."

"My brother is assigned to the Dark Hood. Providing a running protection screen for strays attacking the planet. He is not available, nor is he *Ares* crew."

"That's a good point though," Commander Haddock jumped in. "We've been focusing on *Ares* crew, but we have fully trained personnel assigned to support craft. They could be allocated better."

Despite Commander Moro's reservations, this set off a whole new round of staffing debates. Jax slumped in her chair, weren't they almost done? Now she had added more work for them. A few messages to the Admirals and they had approval to rearrange as needed. It felt like days, but was closer to forty minutes. Still, time lost when we should be moving faster. She had a headache as they exited the staffing room.

Moro bolted in one direction, heading to his next meeting. He would be in charge of their three-ship brigade, so he had strategy meetings to attend.

Issac was off in the other direction. He oversaw checking on all the ships' supplying them as best as possible before the battle. Even Commander Bard, who wasn't assigned as captain, had important duties to attend. She was setting up flight paths to defend the planet. A zone-style defense that maximizes coverage and minimizes chances of friendly fire. Even the *Ares* doctor, Jax could only think of him as Dutch now, was busy setting up medical teams across the planet. Jax too had another responsibility, but hers was nothing but busy work.

The top brass wasn't too happy with her. They didn't feel safe giving her anything she could mess up. So, she oversaw getting the EVE units to the warships. Once Rose and Nath were on the project, however, she hadn't even looked at it. Plus, Rose had buttoned up when she found out about the situation, which left Jax brooding. She really wanted time with her friend to work everything out. To talk and decompress, work through the stress. There wasn't time for it, and they had to press on.

Out into the public byways of Alpha Station, Jax made for the *Ares*. The station was like a beehive, with the people buzzing through it. No one was walking except Jax as she meandered her way through the halls. People had their noses buried in holoscreens as they zoomed by. So much red tape to get the military moving, you would think in a time of crisis they would forget it. Bypass all the checklists and protocols. Nope, it seems for the military it was even more important for some reason.

The airlock for the *Ares* was a bustle with activity. It startled her at first. Since living on the *Ares*, this had become her front door. This entrance allowed easy access to the bridge and her quarters. The work and repair crews used a different entrance, and she would rarely see them. It felt strange to share this space once again. Undaunted, she fell into the old groove of moving through the hall. The old rhythms of turning, giving way of passing through the tight halls. Sliding down stairwells, she angled for the main engine room. Entering the machine shop, she found Rose hunched over a worktable.

A mess of cables dangled from the ceiling. Some hung loose, their end caps moving like wind chimes. Others were plugged into a heavily modified vpet. Boxes and bars welded on, and around, the inactive hex ball. Scattered around the workbench were boxes of equipment, some open, some still sealed. Tools added to the jumble, as Rose picked and chose the way through her task.

"How goes it, mighty engineer?" Jax asked.

Rose cast an evil eye up from the table and then grumbled "Busy." before dropping her head back into the work. The vpet she was working on was anything but standard at this point. Normally hand sized, this one had grown to where you'd have to cradle it in your arms to carry it.

Jax rubbed her temple, the headache flaring up. "Rose, I'm sorry I was going to tell you. I just forgot."

"You forgot?" Rose said, her eyes soaring as she looked up again. "You forgot? I made that for you. Made it harmless, so you could have it on the *Ares*. Made it so, while probably not liked, it would have been tolerated. Then you went and integrated it into the *Ares*. I could be charged to Jax. Worse, you didn't tell me. I could have studied this, but no."

Jax plopped onto a work stool, dropped her elbows on the table, and pushed her hair back. Holding back tears. "I know. I messed up. I still don't get this EVE thing Gaia has. I grew up with EVE units. When I was a kid, we moved a lot. I always had EVE to study, play, or for company. It's natural to have one around. It felt right. I' didn't want to lose it. To lose any friends. Now, after all this, there's a death penalty? Sometimes don't know what to make of this world. It's like I belong here, but it keeps trying to kill me. I really need every friend I can get."

"Stop. I'm trying to stay mad at you. I am mad at you, but you're the best friend I've ever had. Frip Jax, before you all my friends were gears and wires and whatever tech head I happened to be working with. I'm mad at you but you're my big sister. I opened myself to you. No secrets, we share everything and then this. This really pisses me of." Rose paused and looked up at Jax. Rose's face started shaking, dropping her head again. "Why have you got to look so sad right now? I'll always be here for you. Please stop."

"Thank you,'" Jax said. Her voice was a little more than a squeak, she opened her arms for a hug.

Rose tilted her head up and away. Both hands coming up, fingers flayed and the middle one pulled down. "I don't think so, you miserable rat licker."

There was the slightest pause as the two friends broke out in laughter. They hugged and turned back to the table.

"So, how's this coming and why are you working on it by yourself? Thought Nath and the rest of the Ratpack were helping?"

"They are," Rose said. "Nath is installing a quantum coupling node in the *Ares* neural systems. The boys are running more cubic lines to handle the transfer data we'll need to make copies of the *Indiana* EVE" Rose connected another wire to the vpet as she spoke. She was going to continue when she looked up and saw the blank stare Jax was giving her. "You have no idea why we're doing this, do you?"

Jax smiled. "Nope."

"How are you, head of engineering?"

"I believe that was your fault."

"I guess we all have our ratchet head moments," Rose said, returning the smile. "Look, we can't copy only the EVE memory files in this case. The data isn't enough. We need the entire circulatory system that's been created. On Earth, transferring an EVE is simple. The core of all EVV's are the same and we could simply copy the memory files and bam, another EVE with the necessary data. But the *Ares* is using quantum relays, DNA memory cores, and any number of technologies that Earth hasn't adopted yet. EVE has literally grown into them. This has never been seen before. This EVE is different"

Jax smiled and raised her eyebrows. She was going to talk, but her look was worth a thousand words.

Rose shook her head, sighed a heavy breath. "Here, let me show you." She waved and a school grade calculator app appeared over the table. Rose picked up a scanning device and waved it over Jax.

"What are you doing?" Jax asked.

Rose held up a finger. A second image appeared that was a box with an AI symbol inside. A third box with a human shadow inside appeared. This was the standard symbol for an EVE unit. A holoimage of Jax appeared next to the EVE unit. Her image, clothes and skin were dropping out, until only her brain and circulatory system remained. Next to the images, streams of data started scrolling.

"This calculator represents standard computer code. Nothing fancy but limited to only what it's been made to do. If it hasn't been programmed, it can't figure it out. Standard AI is the same, just better code. It mimics thinking but still limited creatively speaking. This image is an EVE unit and all the code that makes it up. It thinks and makes decisions based on feedback. It can learn and adapt, even develop what we humanize as personality traits. It can have feelings. It can create and come up with unique solutions to problems."

"I hadn't really thought of that. EVEs are natural for me. That's why Gaia will use basic AI like in med packs, but not full EVE doctors? They don't like, what, the emotion? This is so backwards from Earth. They like the personal touch EVE gives."

"Correct. Besides Keres, it's another reason Gaia doesn't want EVEs on warships. What kind of personality would they develop?"

Jax cringed at the mention of Keres but decided to ignore it for now. "It's still computer code, though, right? More complex, but what are we talking about here?"

"We're not talking code here anymore. Let me show you." Rose paused, her hands working the table. The image of the calculator and EVE dropped out. Jax's image took center stage and data started flowing around the representation. Jax recognized a DNA double helix and assumed it was her own. Information from her military personal file also scrolled past. "This is you, or a small part of what makes up you. You can learn and adapt like EVE's can, but there is another element. Feelings, previous experience, pain you felt can alter everything. A sentient being."

"Displayed like this, it still looks a lot like computer code to me."

"For the most part, it is. The human DNA code only takes about one point five gigabytes of data. We can copy that, remake it, but the other part, the feelings and such are still hard to quantify. What makes you, well, you, is a complex makeup of things that includes everything. Thoughts, feelings, experiences and more. We could copy you, make a clone, but it wouldn't be you without all that other information."

"Okay, I'm following that. What's that got to do with the *Indiana* EVE? It's simpler code than me."

"That's just it. This is what EVE looks like right now." Jax's image shrank, and an image of the *Ares* appeared. It faded away the same way Jax's image had earlier. The vast network that made up *Ares'* artificial circulatory system. The wires and computer equipment that let it work were all that was left. It should have the constant glow of machines, of processes running, but it was like a star field. A star field that pulsed and moved along pathways. Energy shooting around lines of light that pumped like a heartbeat.

"Wow. That's gorgeous. I thought EVE was disabled."

"EVE is disabled. At least we thought EVE was disabled. The first thing top brass made us do when they found out. With this, I don't know. This isn't how EVEs work on Earth ships, this isn't how EVEs work anywhere. This network is far more advanced than anything we've seen with EVEs, on Earth or even Gaia tech. I think this EVE could adapt to anything. Normally, that's not the case. You can't take an EVE that's been a tutor for children its whole life and ask it to run a starship, for example. They don't adapt well, and it would struggle. That's where humans still have some advantages."

"Some humans, anyways," Jax said.

"That's a different topic. Let me stay on track. *Indiana's* EVE is something different, both scary and amazing. We could copy the memories, but that would leave a calculator. We could copy the original EVE unit itself, but that couldn't run an *Ares*-lass ship. For this to work, we need everything, and I'm both excited and scared at what that means."

"We are walking the unknown, setting new standards."

"That's putting it mildly. Plus, there's no reference for doing anything like this. On Earth, EVE's can be transferred through a dedicated virtual network designed for that. We don't have that here, and it wouldn't handle all the quantum pathways that have been established. If we weren't under the gun to get this done, I might question whether or not we should even be doing this, anyway."

"We're finished!" A call came from the hall. Rose dismissed the holoimages as Coleman, Freddy, and Nath stepped through the hatch, joining the two friends.

"Hey Jax is here," Coleman exclaimed. "Great timing. We should be able to finish this all up."

"Most undoubtedly," Nath said, stepping next to Rose and admiring her work. His current form had long dark hair, a deep tan and square jaw. His clothes mimicked the Rat Packs, with work jumpsuit and vest. "Oh, I see you removed the gravitational controls and flight systems. Brilliant idea, we won't need them, and allows for more DNA memory cores. We'll need those. Your mind is truly amazing, spectacular to see it in action."

Rose seemed oblivious to Nath's ravings and dropped back into work mode. "Yeah, taking those out gave me a place for a direct hookup to the enhanced mother board I installed. Inside should be a working virtual *Ares* class ship to imprint on. Adding all the DNA memory and portable qave battery core makes it bulky, so we'll have to carry them, but it should work." Rose put a hand pm the vpet and gave it a small shake. "Should still be pretty durable, too." The vpet wobbled a bit but was otherwise stable.

"Damn right it's going to work! Right Freddy?" Coleman said, bumping Ensign Frederick Ambrose in the shoulder.

Freddy's eyes were glistening as he leaned in to inspect the work. A straight lipped smile and nod of his head was the only response. From Frederick Ambrose, this was high praise.

"How long will this take?" Jax asked.

"The copying process should be fairly quick. Assuming it works. Then we'll have to make two more of these. Maybe an hour with everyone pitching in. Three if you decide to help." Rose grinned.

"Ha. Ha." Jax grinned back. "Is there something else we need? Or shall we give it a try?"

"Your wish is our command, fearless leader," Rose said, nodding at the crew. Coleman, Freddy, and Nath activated holoscreens and their hands flew, eyes blinking. Jax stepped back as the table started to hum. The table began vibrating and holo light lines flashed on and off across its surface. The vibration became full shaking as the table tried to break loose from its bolting on the floor.

Steam hissed from the vpet, the attached cords strained to break free. The light of its hexagonal surface flickered and danced, a prism of color basking the room in its glow. The table and vpet seemed at war with each other, each one trying to out hum, light and shake the other. A pop and a flash brought it all to a halt.

The holoscreens all winked out. The lights in the room flickered out and came back on. Rose brought a holoscreen back up while everyone watched in silence. Screens flickered past her eyes and a smile formed on her lips. "It's working. The full EVE matrix is growing and expanding inside the virtual shell. If it maintains this rate, it will take about an hour and sixteen minutes," Rose said, looking up from the table. "This is going to work."

There was no cheer, but the crew all nodded and patted each other on their backs. Jax held back, thoughts of Rose's and her conversation clouding her mind. She shook it off and joined her friends in congratulations and heavier thoughts. It was hard maintaining a joyous attitude. They had accomplished the first major hurdle, but they had more work to do. In the back of their minds, they all knew where this was going.

This was work was headed to war.

Chapter 23

CHIMING IN

Jax pushed *Hopper* as much as the little ship could handle. They had assigned her the Segomo and the trek to the shipyards seemed impossibly far. She knew the push wasn't accomplishing much, but anxiety drove her on. Time was running out and they all knew it. In their minds, the Screech were descending like a tidal wave, a galactic tsunami. On board, Rose sat next to her in the copilot seat. Rose couldn't fly, but neither could anyone else on board, so it didn't matter. In her lap, Rose held the vpet cradled in her arms. This was the first copy of the *Ares* EVE they had created, and she had laid claim to it. A mother duck and her little chick, or was it more security blanket?

In back Brooklyn, Freddy and Coleman worked from holoscreens illuminating their faces. They were working remotely and helping as they could. Everyone was suited up in spacesuits, helmets secured, but faceplates open. These were the work suits like what they had on the *Ares*. Form fitting, they didn't hinder their work but didn't help either. Military procedures were in full effect. Flying on anything smaller than a battleship during battle conditions required them. Nobody was happy about that, especially the engineering folks. They liked to feel the work beneath their fingers and suits stopped that. Even more grumbling happened when they found out they couldn't take them off when they got to the Segomo. Not Jax's call. The top brass had decided for everyone's safety.

The skeleton crew for the Segomo was already in place, but getting it ready for battle was taking time. The checks and protocols for activating the engines, bringing gravity, life support, weapons and all operating systems online were designed with actual people in mind. Depending on the readings, decisions had to be made at each stage and okayed. With a full crew, this took time. With a skeleton crew, it was painstakingly slow. EVE would change all that, but they had to get the virtual unit their first. Till then, all they could do was review procedures, create new ones, or okay requests from those on board and working.

Rose hated remote work and avoided it whenever possible. She contented herself with shouting out answers to anything Coleman or Freddy deemed necessary to ask. Brooklyn never spoke, her eyes lost on her screen, her usual blunt attitude held in check for now. Occasional muttering could be heard, a curse here and there, but that was it.

Lieutenant Moro, the only member of her command crew not on board, was already at the Segomo. When his change of orders had come in, he was already serving on the Dark Hood. They were one of several ships running skeleton crews to the three *Ares* class vessels. He had disembarked on his last run and took over organizing the WEP station.

"There they are," Rose said, pointing out the window. They were still twenty minutes out; the massive shipyard was a mere speck at this distance. Rose zoomed in on her side of the window and the three *Ares* class ships took center. Nestled in their space docks, the scaffolding crisscrossed the ships. "Glad we got the Segomo out of the three."

"How come?" Jax asked.

"Mom and Dad worked on that one. Dad installs qave drive cores and mom handles installations of control systems. Two things I won't need to worry about. I'd trust those installs with my life."

"That's good, because you know you're going too," Jax said.

"I'm still not sure about this. These ships have been sitting in space docks. No shakedown cruise, no pressure testing, any number of things can go wrong. Now we're installing an unknown EVE unit into the mix, too many untested parts, too many failure points. I like knowing how things are going to function before I put my life on the line. This is not the *Ares*."

"No, they're not, but they are *Ares*-class ships. We have a good crew, a good team. We'll make it work. That's what you've all done since I've known you. This is just another day," Jax said, turning her most confident face to her friend. From the corner of her eye, she saw Freddy and Coleman pause from their work to listen in. She couldn't see Brooklyn directly behind her, but from the way the boys glanced, she was sure she had her ear too. Jax felt them relax and they went back to work.

Arriving on the Segomo, they all darted off to their stations. No time to rest and no seconds to spare. The last of their hours fell away, and the deadline ticked near. Reports of the Screech were coming in by the minute. A harrowing force of Gaia ships were performing hit-and-run raids in an attempt to slow the massive force. Hitting with long range torpedoes and then rushing off, trying to pull part of the force. They were successful, but it was a drop of water compared to an ocean.

The massive Gaia weapons platforms surrounded the *Ares*. Huge long-range missiles were constantly being launched. The platforms had sets of weapons based on interstellar distances. Rose had tried to explain the technical aspects of it, but Jax had gotten lost in the minutia. In Jax's mind, she shortened down the complex formula to far, medium, and close ranges. Far was light years away, medium was under a light year, and close was in your face.

Currently, the Screech were crossing the threshold of the far distance and moving into the medium. They had easily avoided the far distance attacks. Moving and changing directions like a flock of birds. The murmuration would have been beautiful to watch if you didn't understand the force behind it. The medium distance was of greater success for Gaia. While still a light year away, qave drive missiles, rail guns that made what the *Ares* had look like pea shooters, began to have an effect. No longer a drop of water, they had moved up to buckets.

Still, the Screech advanced as the three *Ares*-class ships sat in their births. They had to leave now if they wanted to be there when the Screech entered close range. Push as they might, this deadline pushed back.

Jax stepped onto the bridge, savoring the moment. Since arriving on the Segomo she hadn't been here. Up and down the ship she had run, lending a hand where needed. Beginning with the installation of EVE, checking energy relays, targeting sensors, any place, an extra set of hands was necessary. She had been a whirlwind of activity. This is something she wanted, something she had worked towards, and now it was here. She was once again the captain of her own ship. She wanted to enjoy it but found that emotion missing.

"Captain on the bridge," Lieutenant Moro bellowed.

"As you were," she responded. It wasn't needed as only Moro and Brooklyn were there and neither had so much as blinked from their duties. Moro's had to be Moro's however, and following protocol was always on the list. Jax stepped up to the command table and scanned through all the checklists and data waiting for her approval. She was happy this bridge was an exact replica of the *Ares*, even if it had that new car smell.

"Weapon systems are primed and ready to go. Torpedoes are available in tubes one to four. We only have twelve, so we'll run out quick," Lieutenant Moro said, sliding a holo report over the table to her.

"Twelve per tube?"

"Twelve total. Priority was for stocking first contact ships, the weapons platforms, and the *Ares*."

"We'll just have to make them count," Jax said. *Damn.*

"Shields, active and passive scanners, tactical interfaces are all go. Systems check on the NAV station is also showing all green. You're welcome." Brooklyn said.

Jax shot a quick eye at her new OPS commander, but didn't linger. Besides being captain, Jax was serving as pilot and NAV commander. Checking those systems was her responsibility. From the sound of her voice, Jax wasn't sure if Lieutenant Wisler was being helpful or condemning. She turned on a comm channel and called out. "Engineering, EVE, how are we doing?"

"Wonderfully, Captain," EVE'S voice rang through the bridge. The cheerfulness of EVE seemed alien, out of place, on the warship. EVE wasn't talking as much as when on the *Indiana*. The virtual entity had confided in Jax that it seemed to make some folks uncomfortable. "Though Lieutenant First Class Koike has taken to calling me Segee. I believe it to be a combination of EVE and Segomo. I find it more fitting given our situation and would request all crew members to do likewise."

"So be it. Segee it is," Jax said with a smile. However, when she looked at Lieutenant Moro, his face looked on the edge of nausea. Brooklyn's nose seemed to push harder into her work.

"Engineering is ready to go, Captain." Rose's voice echoed over the comms. A slight echo sounded as if Rose was in a tube somewhere. "We have a secondary hum in the qave engines we can't identify, but all tests are green."

All qave engines had a hum to them; so that wasn't a worry. A hum that Rose couldn't identify. That was something to keep an eye on. "Understood engineering. Keep us informed." Jax said, moving to the NAVpod. "Begin launch procedures. We're as ready as we can be and maybe we can be first out the gate."

"Sorry, Captain, the *Manrva* and *Perun* reporting. They are clearing moors," Lieutenant Wisler said.

Double Damn. "Let's double time it then. We don't want to be left behind."

Normally, the launching of a ship would be met with a lot of pomp and circumstance. Long-winded ceremonies marking the day. There would be none of that on this occasion. In her NAVpod the disembarking checklist for captain and NAV were displayed. Jax ran through them with a practiced hand till all were green. The docking clamps released, and the Segomo moved forward. Jax let the Segomo drift out for a few yards and then eased into the cruising engines. The NAV pod was alive around her. Light rippled up her arms as the ship responded to her movement. Gravity wave feedback pushed against her hands as the ship slowly took its first steps.

Clearing the space dock, the *Ares* class ship pushed its acceleration. Half cruising speed till a hundred meters out, where they could engage the qave drive. Clearing the safety zone around the space dock, she did a quick check. "We're clear of space dock. All stations report in."

"All clear. Systems are go." The response was repeated by both the WEP and OPS stations.

"I too am all clear. Systems go," Segee chimed in.

"Engines are good to go captain," Rose said. "Whatever that hum is, it doesn't seem to be affecting anything."

"I'm sure you'll monitor it." Jax said. "Bringing us up to two-thirds qave drive. Let's get in formation."

The Segomo bridged the distance to the others in a short time. They were waiting for her. The plan called for them to work together. She dropped speed, took position, linked tactical, and the three ships convey became a single entity.

The Screech had entered close range. It was the tip of the spear, but warnings and dire communications came flowing in. The main force, like Jax had predicted, drove straight for the *Ares*. Two splinter groups, broken off from the main, were pounding the weapons platforms. Platform three, the one not yet finished, was reporting heavy damage.

Jax's nerves twitched with each update. A small holoimage in her pod played out in real time the attack on Gaia. The *Ares* looked like a minnow to a whale, weapon platforms, that surrounded it. The force that was the Screech streamed in, a never-ending line of attack. Space was ablaze with light surrounding the *Ares*. Bursts flashing, explosions igniting, shrapnel from busted ships swirled around.

Jax longed to go faster, to get in the fight, and wondered why they weren't increasing speed. As she was about to contact Captain Moro, Brooklyn called out. "Communication from the *Menrva*, it's Captain Moro."

"Put him through." A full bust avatar of Captain Moro appeared in her pod. Even this shrunken avatar of the man seemed to stand ten feet tall. Another avatar of Captain Haddock also appeared. "Gaia Military Command has changed our orders. We are now to stay outside the main battery and assault their larger ships. Take targets of opportunity, but we will hunt their command ships."

"What about the *Ares*?" Jax asked, her eyes glancing at the live battle.

"Command doesn't want to risk our biggest, mobile heavy hitters. The *Ares* has the weapon platforms for cover."

"Bull crap," Jax said. "*Ares* is already taking hits. We're to be there for cover. She doesn't have a good portion of her hull Terrance, once the shields are gone, the *Ares* won't stand a chance."

"Captain Brandt," Captain Moro said through gritted teeth. "I do not have time to educate you on the strategy laid out for us. GMC has placed me in command of our battle group, and you will follow orders. Am I clear?"

Every muscle and thought in her body ached to punch him. To tear into him, break everything she could get her hands on. He said the strategy they had laid out. This was their plan, and they didn't tell her. They we're leaving the *Ares* as bait, to fend for itself.

"Yes, Captain," she said and then bit her lip to stop her from saying more.

"Very well. We engage in ten minutes. Good hunting," Terrance Moro said, and his image blinked out.

The bust of Issac Haddock lingered for a bit. His face was heavier than Jax had ever seen. "It is for the best, Jax. *Ares*, Captain Lewis, the crew, they're survivors, they'll make it." Then Issac blinked out.

Jax yelled and slammed her fists into the pod. The holoimages that wrapped her hands blinked out and the autopilot kicked in. She hopped out of the pod and went to work on the command table. Brooklyn and Sebastian both stopped and stared. They shot glances back and forth, but neither spoke. They had heard the message and it was easy to guess where Jax stood with it. Brooklyn opened her lips to break in when a whistle, sounding a ship wide announcement, broke in.

"This is the captain," Jax said, standing at the command table. "We've just been ordered to change our objective. No longer are we assisting the *Ares*, providing cover, so they can survive the battle. Strategically, this is the right call. Our three ships can be of much more use and effective harassing the enemy forces. However, I intend to disobey this order."

"The *Ares* and its crew, no matter what ship they are on, are the only friends, the only family I have. I cannot, will not, abandon them when I can help. I don't know the penalty for the action I'm about to take, but it can't get much worse for me. I won't drag anyone else through this, though."

"There's time if you wish, you may take a ship or lifepod and disembark. You will still be able to join one of the ships assigned to protect Gaia. You can still fight and will be able to make a difference. If you choose to stay, I ask that you send a formal complaint to me objecting to my actions. I have already entered a formal statement in the ship's records, taking full responsibility and I will add your denouncements. I'm sorry I can't give you more time to decide. You have five minutes and then we're going in." Jax turned off the comms and looked at the other bridge officers. Sebastian looked across the table at her. His body was a statue, but his eyes were enraged. Brooklyn's head was pulled back, her lips pricked in surprise.

Before they could speak, a chirp sounded on the table and an avatar of Rose popped up. "Engineering isn't going anywhere, Captain. We might be on this ship now, but *Ares* is ours and we take care of our own. Long live the *Ares*." A round of cheering could be heard before the comms dropped.

Jax looked back at the other two officers. "This is whack. You are more out of your mind than I realized. *Ares* is my first officer posting, but I don't know about disobeying orders." Brooklyn shook her head and Jax held silent. A moment's pause as Brooklyn studied her screen. The small group handling OPS were not wasting time chiming in. Brooklyn looked up again. "It looks like all of OPS agrees with you, however. I might not like it, but I think I do too. I guess we're all wack. Like the little lady said, 'Long live the *Ares*.'"

Jax gave a nod of her head, one that read absolute respect. She turned to Sebastián Moro.

"My brother is right about you. You have no respect for chain-of-command. You're wild and dangerous. My brother isn't wrong about these kinds of matters. You're going to get us all killed," Sebastian said.

"Then I take it you're leaving?"

Sebastian's eyes narrowed, and he glanced down. His own board had to be littered with messages. His jaw clenched as he said. "It seems everyone in WEP has elected to stay. I will not abandon my post, but this is the most foolish act I have ever seen. You will pay for this."

"I'm sure I will, but it really can't get much worse for me. I don't expect you to understand. You haven't been through what I have with the *Ares*. That's only a fraction of what all these others have. Your brother should understand it. He should know better." Jax didn't wait for his reaction. She turned and hopped back into the NAVpod. "I expect your letter of objection in the next few minutes, Sebastian. We're about to be very busy."

She didn't get a response, and she didn't bother to check if he got back to work. He was a Moro. He'll do the job. She brought the NAV controls back up. The light gauntlets formed around her hands. The grav pulse giving her feedback, the Segomo came alive once again in her hands. Activating the ship wide announcement again, she gave the only motivation she could think of. "Let's go save the *Ares*."

Chapter 24

IMMOVEABLE OBJECT

The moment the Segomo veered out of formation, comm messages came rushing in. The *Menrva* and the *Perun* were both sending inquires on the "why" she was breaking ranks. Jax was pondering responses when Brooklyn jumped in. She answered each incoming question with a broken, garbled voice only message. Jax glanced out of her pod to see the lieutenant tapping the command table. Her face became animated as she created her own sound effects. If she hadn't seen it, Jax would have thought it was real, too. While she didn't catch everything being said, she caught enough. Pieced together, Lieutenant Wisler's messages said something about comms being bugged. She went on about rudder control and more. That these new ships always had bugs to work out, and they were working to fix it. Jax grinned before turning her focus to the task at hand.

The *Menrva* and the *Perun* were circling to avoid the bulk of the Screech attack. They would look for the path of least resistance. An opening to cut through and assault the Screech command vessels. They had orders and no time to follow up on Jax's problems. The messages stopped coming, and she was free from distractions. Jax angled the Segomo the other way, inwards toward Gaia and the awaiting *Ares*. This vector would bring her in over Gaia's North pole, behind weapon platform two. The *Ares* was in an area catty-corner to that platform. Keeping to a designated area between all the platforms, it stayed an active moving target. These comprised random direction changes and rolling to keep *Ares'* hull away from the enemy fire. The weapon platforms handled countermeasures to stop incoming missiles and beams. Anything that got through the *Ares* had to deal with, unfortunately, that was happening more and more.

For being the tip of the spear, the onslaught was incredible. Dueling beams, bursts of energy, and torpedoes from the Screech and Gaia forces blanketed the area. The weapon platforms unleashed beams larger than the *Ares*. The Screech countered with numbers uncountable. Explosions and light crisscrossing in a deadly game of move and countermove. Through it all the *Ares* flew and survived. Jax would have sworn it was Commander Bard at the helm, but she was on the Perun. This was Hat Trick working magic. Gums would do the same for the *Menrva*. Despite all the fancy flying, it wasn't enough. It was like trying to run naked through a monsoon and expecting to not get wet. Sparks flew off the *Ares* shields, which so far still held. The weapons platforms spewed death at the enemy, but still they came. Still, the spear pushed forward. The comms chimed and this time Brooklyn let the audio only signal through.

"Jax, what are you doing?" Captains Lewis shouted as rumblings, pops, and bangs pushed to drown her voice.

"Following the plan." Jax said. Small fighters from both sides whipped by now. Enemy fire targeted her as the Segomo entered the danger zone. Small Screech fighters reigned blue and green light at the Segomo. Shields reflected the light beams off without a care. Larger, more numerous fire, continued to harass the *Ares*.

"I thought the plan changed?"

"I've never been good at changes. I prefer to stick to the book."

The comms filled with laughter as Captain Lewis said, "Thank you, Jax. Thank you."

"My pleasure, Captain. Sending tactical link up to Hat Trick. We'll move the Segomo into position to cover your damaged hull. Hopefully, draw a little of those fireworks with it."

"Link secured *Segomo*. We have the yolk." With that acknowledgement, Hat Trick was now flying both vessels in tandem. Jax could override and make independent movements if necessary. Trusting Hat Trick's skill was easy, so she turned to her captain's roll, free from NAV for the moment. In the pod, she minimized the NAV controls and brought up the overview of battle. It wasn't going well. The Screech formation was too tight, two in sync for the Gaia forces. The half-built weapon platform was incapacitated. Sections of it floated in space, plasma and wreckage leaked into the void. The other platforms were heavily damaged. Shielding busted craters and rifts burned into their hulls. Small Screech ships and Gaia fighters danced like fireflies across their surface.

The *Menrva* and *Perun* were having success in the outer ranges of the Screech attackers. Several Gaia warcraft, modified Earth designs that had weapons modded on, joined in. They were supposed to be in a position guarding Gaia but plans rarely followed form. Wherever they roamed, they cut a deadly path. They weren't enough to break the mighty spear of the Screech attack. The Screech moved where they wanted to move. Where there was resistance, the Screech threw overwhelming numbers. Gaia technology could be better, stronger, faster, but in the end numbers mattered. Beam for beam, blast for blast, Gaia had the bigger guns, but the Screech had more. Torpedoes were evenly matched, except once again the Screech had more. More, more and more.

Massive energy hit the Segomo's shields and warnings flew across Jax's board. The Segomo's qave engines struggled to dissipate the barrage. Rose's harried voice rang in Jax's ear. "That blow strained our shield emitters. We got the energy to handle it, but if the emitters go, we don't have the personnel to replace them."

Damn. "Got it." Jax yelled back. Jax opened a comm channel back to the *Ares*. "Captain Lewis, our defense is crumbling. How can we get on the offensive?"

"We can't," Captain Lewis called. "If we had space and could break their formation, maybe. Get them off balance by attacking the command ships, breaking up their game plan. Then our technology could even the odds. Put us a point up in the match. But those large command vessels are keeping them on target."

Double damn. They were done. Everywhere she looked on the board, Gaia was losing ground. The numbers were against them. Bigger mattered in this case. What they really needed was something bigger on their side. Something they could throw and overwhelm the Screech with. Get them to react instead of act. Like an ember igniting into a flame, it came to her. "Captain Lewis, how many torpedoes do you have?"

"We're stacked. Stopped launching when they got closer, and they were intercepting them, anyway. Why?"

"I've got a plan. Follow me and prepare to launch as we go."

"Jax! What are you doing?"

"I'm going to take a page from your book. When I want someone to move, I move them." Jax said and cut the communication.

Before it cut, echoes of "Oh fripping aby—"

"Commanders!" Jax sent orders to her ship. "All stations prepare for extreme conditions. Batten down the hatches and buckle up your space suits. Time to get on the offensive."

To their credit, no one asked what was happening. Affirmatives came rolling in as everyone prepared. Jax double checked her helmet and dropped its mask. She dropped the tactical link to the *Ares* and sent Hat Trick a message, daring him to keep up.

Segomo once more in her hands, she said, "Attacking now!"

She turned the nose of the *Segomo* towards the nearest Screech command vessel. Locking on, she increased speed. The Screech must have been caught off guard by the change in tactics. Shots continued to fire into the zone where the warships had been passing them. A slight pause and a new volley of energy fire erupted. The Screech attack split now between the *Ares* and the advancing Segomo. Not as skilled as Hat Trick, Jax kept her attack pattern simple. Weaving back and forth, flowing up and down, she dodged the big stuff and ignored the inconsequential. A small thought whispered in her head that this plan might have been better with Hat Trick in the lead. That wasn't what the situation had given them, however. All she could do was accept the situation and dive in.

Smaller Gaia ships were blocked to the outside. Unable to penetrate to the location of the Screech command vessels. The *Minerva* and *Perun* were being careful to avoid damage, to stay in the battle. Jax and Gemma didn't have that option. They were already targets. So, they headed where other ships feared to go. Where only fools would follow, they dove deep into the nose of the spear. Jax mind flashed to her time in the simulator working through Screech attacks.

Screech fighters bounced off their shields and exploded harmlessly in space. When they realized their futility, they began strafing runs, their energy weapons doing nothing. The larger battleships moved to intercept or ram. *Ares* class ships have always been faster and more agile. The Segomo and *Ares* avoided them easily. Weapons flared from all sides, a swirling kaleidoscope of power in space. Screech attacked as if panicked. More and more ships converged on the two Gaia craft as they pursued their target. The maelstrom intensified, battering the two ships. Then they hit a calm and all the aggressors dropped away.

The Screech command ship sat in the storm's eye. Other Screech vessels circled out and away. None of the other Screech dared enter the eye. The *Segomo*, with the *Ares* hot on its tail, squared up with the gargantuan command craft. Sharp angles glared at them from across space. Screech ships avoided sharp angles, but here they embraced it. Spiked edges and wings that looked so sharp they would cut skin should you touch them. Not painted to blend in with space, bright reds, blues, and golds were embossed across its hull. The three craft were hanging there in space, taking each other's measure. Then the Screech opened fire.

The command ship, easily five times the size of an *Ares*-lass vessel, had the power to match. The blue and green rays lashing out, the first volley rocked the Segomo. Jax rolled to avoid the fire, her team keeping pace and returning their own shots. The *Ares* was no longer linked but kept step. Torpedoes, now with a clear target, were let loose. The *Segomo's* small supply was gone in an instant, but the *Ares* rapid fire was seemingly never ending. The command vessel struggled to intercept them all. A few were caught early, the blasts pummeling the ships that launched them. The *Ares*-class ships shook it off and kept fighting.

They closed the distance, the *Segomo* covering and the *Ares* firing torpedoes. Energy weapons flared as they raced to engage the enemy. The single command vessel kept pace, intercepting torpedoes, shields turning away energy attacks. With each move, the Gaia craft hammered their target, but it wasn't enough. The Screech's shields held, and torpedoes were swatted away. The command vessel cruised forward, and its fire intensified. The Screech's counterattack was frantic, missing as many times as they hit. The accuracy didn't matter, it would still overwhelm them. It was an immoveable object in space and their force wasn't enough to match it.

"Hang on!" Jax yelled at no one in particular. Dodging a burst of beams, she lined the *Segomo* and Screech vessel nose-to-nose. Staring at her enemy, Jax accelerated.

The enemy had been splitting its fire between the *Ares* and the *Segomo*. A few moments after Jax's maneuver, the Screech's targeting changed. Their beams swept together and coalesced into a single tight target, the Segomo. The blue and green beams increased in size, the Screech dumping power into them. Brighter till the colors were lost, a blazing white beam taking their place.

The shields on the *Segomo* fractured the beam and pushed into it. Jax's arms strained as the interactive grav controls in the NAVpod pressed hard against her arms. It was like trying to bench press the ship off her chest. Her muscles protested, threatened to give out. It was as if they begged to turn the ship and relieve the strain.

"The emitters are going to blow!" Rose shouted.

"Hold! Hold, damn you!" Jax shouted back, not at her friend, but at the *Segomo* itself.

The *Segomo* continued to increase speed while bombarded with the enemy's fire. Jax screamed as the shields dropped away and the *Segomo* quaked under the impact. Its nose began to bubble and crack, blazing like a star. The *Segomo's* own forward beams cut out, broken under the intense heat. They were no longer needed, Jax knew that. They weren't the threat the *Segomo* was. The *Segomo* was its own beam, its own torpedo. The biggest torpedo, the Screech, Earth, or Gaia had ever seen. If it struck home, the mass of the battleship, plus the speed of the qave engines, would obliterate everything it touched. A final desperate run in a final desperate situation.

Then the unimaginable happened and the Screech blinked. The Screech, known for their straight attacks, known for sacrificing themselves, changed course. Their beams dropped and their engines flared, turning hard to avoid the oncoming Gaia vessel. They were too late. At this range Jax could easily smash into them, ramming them and ending it all. Jax had something else in mind.

Jax saw her opening, had been ready for it, planning for it. She had won her little game of chicken and now was the time to turn course. Like in the simulator she saw her window, she angled away from the enemy. She pushed her engines, and she made her turn. This time she would hit that window, this time she would make the turn and win the match. She didn't make it. The screech vessel's shield flashed and disappeared as the *Segomo* slammed its broadside into them. A burst of shrapnel exploded from both ships as they were welded together. They spun like a giant pinwheel.

On the bridge of the *Segomo*, alarms blared as red lights flashed through every screen. Jax shook in the NAVPod and caught sight of Lieutenant Moro. He was grabbing the command table to keep himself upright. *Missed that damn window again.* Jax cursed at herself as she jumped from the pod.

"I take it you meant to do that?" Brooklyn waved a red screen away and attempted the next. Try as she might, nothing was working or fixable. The command table showed the two ships spinning in space. Real-life images were sputtering and had trouble maintaining their likenesses. The ships continued to spin. Debris ejecting from their hulls. Lights flashing as explosions rippled across the surface of the now fused ships.

"You are trying to kill us," Sebastián Moro added.

"Not exactly," Jax said to both officers. "And definitely not today. Segee, sound abandon ship. All crew seek the safest port. Remind everyone no lifepods, shuttles, and fighter craft only."

"Of course, Captain. Sounding abandon ship. All crew proceed to safest port," Segee paused and then said. "On a personal note, captain, I am sorry to see you lose another ship. If I was superstitious, I would think our pairing was not a good one."

"Thanks, Segee. I think our pairing has been great. This is the second time you've helped save me and my crew. I owe you," Jax said. "You're a good friend. We have to stop parting like this."

"Thank you, Captain. Never fear, I am not lost. All my data will be shared with the *Menrva* and the *Perun*. The communication and data systems on these ships are quite wonderful. Plus, my original matrix is still in the *Ares*. We shall meet again. Be safe."

"Will do Segee. Till we meet again. Alight everyone, let's get out of here."

Chapter 25

BRING IT HOME

The artificial gravity was still functioning as they ran through the halls. Jax wasn't sure that was a good thing. They wouldn't have to work so hard to keep their balance if gravity gave out. The walls shook and moaned; rumbles tossed them from side-to-side. Her HUD popped up green pings showing crew members exiting the ship. With this skeleton crew, the bridge had the furthest run to the hangar bay. Metal crunched behind them as they passed the portal into the bay. Jax spared a glance back. The hallway rippled, sparks blew, and the ceiling collapsed. In her mind, an image of Henry Rickson flashed, but she shook it off.

"Let's go, Jax!" Rose yelled over the comms. Turning back, she saw Brooklyn and Sebastian entering *Hopper* with Rose's help.

"You should have gotten out with one of the other ships."

"Like that was going to happen." Rose took Jax's hand and pulled her in.

They didn't have time for arguments or pleasantries, but she felt good seeing Rose, Freddy, and Coleman. Brooklyn was quick to settle in and Sebastian was in the copilot seat, already going to work. The cockpit lit up, all the gauges coming alive. The hum of the little shuttle's qave engine kicked in.

"Time to go," Jax said, jumping into her seat. Her safety harness automatically wrapped itself around her. A couple flips of controls, and the craft lifted off the hanger deck.

"Catapult systems are offline. We've got no assistance for launch," Lieutenant Sebastian Moro said. Even through the mask, Jax could see the worry on his face. His voice stayed icy, but underneath, he was desperate for answers. His hands kept trying to access the catapult systems. He punched button after button as if constant pushing would force the thing to work.

"We don't need it," Jax said, turning and flashing her most devilish smile. Once off the ground, she had been floating the craft into position. Normally a gantry arm would lift them and place them on the launch platform. The catapult would engage, and it would hurtle them down the runway. Segee had been operating those systems for the rest of the crew, but as with the rest of the ship, they were breaking down.

She lined *Hopper* up like a thread inserting into a pin needle. She pushed the engines to full and shot them down the launch tube. Under normal circumstances, you could never do such a thing. The energy coming off the small craft's engines, the speed of its acceleration, pulled panels off the tube. Instead of launching, they exploded out of the *Segomo*. An intricate array of debris and light shifted in front of their eyes. Jax banked hard to avoid a detached piece of hull. From inside, curses sang out. This wasn't the smooth ride of a warship. The internal dampers would keep you safe, but you were going to feel those turns. The hard turn brought the Screech vessel and the *Segomo* into their view. Like a daffodil blown on the wind, it twirled through space. Streaks of light pulsed from the command ship. Not attacking beams, but the Screech equivalent of shuttles. They too had abandoned ship.

She blinked on her HUD and brought up a quick sitrep. A small holoimage appeared off to her right, showing the surrounding space. The on-board tracking computer automatically assigns designations to each object. Common fields were friends, enemies, and the unknown. The unknown consisted mainly of damage from combat, debris broken off from ships. Jax made a mental note. The friends were in far too few numbers, while the enemies in far too many. Two large markers caught her attention. They were the other Screech command ships. They seemed startled, their usually flowing flight patterns were now wavering. Their perfect formation now broken; one ship was veering off. The other was turning and laying in what could only be called a retreat course. Where once they had moved as a whole, now they seemed unsure of themselves.

The *Ares* had circled to the far side of the of where the *Segomo* and Screech command vessel lay entwined. Batting away small enemy ships that insisted on attacking. Picking up escape craft from the *Segomo* as they went. Shielding any others they couldn't get to as best they could.

"*Ares*, all personnel are clear of the *Segomo*. Repeat all personnel clear," Jax said over comms. They didn't hear a response, but moments later the *Ares* answered another way.

A spread of torpedoes tore into the damaged command ship. Overwhelming force punched into damaged hulls and ignited both ships. The Screech ship split in two and the *Segomo* broke free. Capsized in space, rotating on its axis, as it drifted away. Jax pushed *Hopper* away from the bombardment as the shock wave burst out. She wanted to circle back and meet up with the *Ares*. "Damn! So much for that idea," she cursed. The empty area the Screech had allowed for the command ship was gone. Enemy craft came swooping in, both from outside the area and the enemy escape craft. Jax banked hard, cutting away from the incoming ships. Blue and green bursts crossed her bow.

"Head in the game, captain," Lieutenant Moro spat at her.

"I'm on it, I'm on it," she said. "We're heading to Gaia. Look for a clear path. You're on guns."

"Guns? The only guns this Earth antique has that are worth anything are the forward cannons. And those are line of sight. You should have requisitioned a better craft."

"I like this ship."

"Well, at least we all die knowing your personal opinion matters more than our lives."

Jax didn't have time to respond to the younger Moro brother as she rolled the ship hard. Three enemy ships crossed her flight path, beams tearing through space. They were faster and more powerful. *Hopper*'s only advantage lies in its smaller size and higher mobility. Jax banked and rolled, hit quick turns, dove, and rose. Randomizing each motion, each pull on the yoke, each change in speed through instinct. Thought to action became as one as she wound her way through the battle. She moved close to larger ships, both ally and enemy alike. Looking for obstacles to keep between her and her pursuers. Lieutenant Moro called out options and kept their guns blazing.

An energy shot broke their shields on the port side. The shuttle knocked sideways in space, sounded like metal tearing on the inside. The scar mark left on its outer hull was superficial, but sent alarms blazing in the cabin. Jax dropped and turned as two Screech fighters once again zeroed in on her.

"Give me a shot," Sebastian yelled.

"I'm trying." Jinking the plane again and Sebastian hit one of the craft broadside. The enemy craft turned hard but showed no signs of damage. Jax pushed to stay on target to give Sebastian a clean tone. A clear shot never happened as shots burst around them. The other enemy gained their aft and let loose a blitz of gunfire.

"Can't shake him!" She was out of tricks. The Screech pilot wouldn't be out flown. A blast hit and what was left of *Hopper*'s shields blew. Warning alarms blazed in the cabin; the flight consul turned red as if in despair. The rumble in the cabin left all of them exclaiming in fear. Both their pursuers disintegrated into fireballs.

A message shouted over the comms. "Make haste, Fire Fist. We've cleared a short path, but it's hairy." Four SAFI4s zipped by Jax's craft.

The comms showed a call sign, and Jax was quick to respond. "Roger that. Thanks for the save Tafi. We're out of here."

"Enjoy the blue skies and tailwinds, Fire Fist, Tafi responded. Jax smiled at the common phrase space pilots used to wish those returning planet side good luck.

The clear path was relatively straight, and Jax laid on the throttle. As the battle raged around them, the safe corridor collapsed after only a hundred meters. The Screech lines were split now that the *Ares* was no longer the focus of the attack. Battle lines were nonexistent as ships fought and wove together. The comms were amassed with reports from ships, weapon platforms, and Gaia itself. A few banks and turns brought them safely to the upper atmosphere of Gaia. Relief washed over the desperate group. The warming embrace of coming home, a place safe from the horrors of the universe. A section of hull was blown off *Hopper*, and the winds came in.

Jax fought the stick and forced the craft to turn. With alarms blasting and the ship spiraling, she knew she had to stay focused. Still, she glanced over her shoulder. Rose and Brooklyn strapped into their seats; their hands were locked tight on safety harnesses. Through their faceplates, their eyes bulged.

Jax couldn't see Coleman or Freddy positioned behind her. They had to be strapped in the same as the other two ladies, they had to be. For once, Jax was happy with military protocol, wearing the suits and being strapped in. Knowing they were all safe, her split second reassurance gone, she got back on task.

She flattened the ship, hit a victory roll, dropped back, and lined up one of her attackers. Lieutenant Moro was on pace and let *Hopper*'s forward cannons fly. They purged the enemy craft from the sky. The comms blasted her ears with cheers. Under her breath, Jax said, "I'm really starting to hate dog fighting."

"More incoming," Sebastian said.

Jax eyed the tactical display on her HUD. Dozens of enemy fighters entangled with dozens from Gaia. They performed a lethal dance across the skies. *Hopper*'s shields were gone, hull damaged. This was not a fight she could stay in. She needed to get to a safe harbor. The military installations outside the city were heavily fortified for that reason. From there, they could plan their next step, get back in the fight. *Come on, Hopper. Let's bring it home.*

Craft streaked by, rocking *Hopper* with turbulence. Shots exploded around them; the sound mired with curses from inside the ship. Jax leaned on the throttle, wanting to push past its max. No amount of willpower could push *Hopper* faster, however. A sharp turn to avoid blue and green streaks crisscrossing her path. A jolt slammed her forward, a gust of air pushed her sideways in her seat. She looked out the front window and the world was a blur of spinning shapes. Streaks of blue, green and browns rushed past her. She pushed the stick around, but all resistance was lost. It flopped around worthlessly in her hands. She screamed as the back of her craft, smoldering from where it had been cleaved, rushed by. Jax didn't see the ground as *Hooper* slammed into the terrain.

Chapter 26

THIS MOMENT

S he woke with a gasp, hands clenched, white knuckles on the joystick, head pushed back in her seat. The world fractured before her, the faceplate on her helmet bearing a lightning-like scar. She tried to move, but her muscles ached at the thought. A small holoscreen popped up on the flight dash, warning her to stay still, help was coming. She brought her hand up to brace her head; the throbbing was making it hard to keep her eyes open. The helmet blocked her, and she fumbled with the straps, trying to get it off. It clunked to the ground, and she rubbed her head. That accomplished, she waved the warning away with a hand and decided it was time to stand.

First, she had to figure out how to get up. Her feet wouldn't move. The lower half of her body was covered in impact foam. The light green material was a safety feature on Earth ships. On impact, the carbon nanotube foam expanded instantly and solidified. It would allow the person wrapped inside to handle over a hundred Gs of impact. Gaia fighter style ships didn't use it, preferring to eject for safety, but *Hopper* was an Earth passenger vehicle. As such, it had crash protection systems for everyone on board in case of a catastrophic event. Force fields would surround the cabin and the impact foam would fill it. Claustrophobic, and you couldn't move, but breathable. The body would take a beating, but you would survive.

Jax looked around. The foam that should have been covering her was largely gone. Lieutenant Moro lay slumped in his chair. His foam covered up to his chest from what Jax could see, but it should be covering the entire body. Just like it should for all the others.

Her head snapped around. There was nothing to see. The end of the cockpit ended in a gaping hole. Charred metal, small bits still glowing hot in places, was all there was of *Hopper*. Beyond lay a stretch of dirt and furrowed rock. She needed to get out. Her heart raced. She pulled harder on her legs and once again the emergency warning popped up in front of her. *Warning. Possible Injury. Stay still. Help is on the way.*

She eyed the holescreen to dismiss the message and then used her command codes to disable it. She pulled her legs again, but they wouldn't budge. The impact foam had solidified around her legs into a spongy catacomb block. She hammered her hands into it, and it broke away. The motion exhausted her and left her head spinning. When the spinning had passed, she steeled herself to rise again. Climbing out of the seat and was pulled back down. "Damn it!" She hissed and undid the safety harness. Her legs were stiff and sore as she pulled herself across the aisle to the co-pilot's seat.

She pulled on Sebastian to lift herself. "Lieutenant Moro? Sebastian? Can you hear me?" No response but she could see his chest rise and fall. She pulled a holoscreen off his space suit to read his vitals. Small warnings dotted the displays, but the most worrying one was on his head. He had slammed the back right of his head hard against the hull. The helmet, safety shields, and impact foam had saved him. Without them his head would have been crushed like a grape. Even with them, the injury was severe and would take time to recover. Each space suit had a medical AI built into it. She double checked it was working and then made her decision. There was nothing she could do here. "Rest well, I'll be back, or help will be here soon." She stumbled out the back of the now shortened craft.

Explosions echoed in her skull and she whipped her head around. Fireworks ripped across the skies. Red, blue, and green lights weaving a dangerous pattern. An explosion dropped her eyes down. In the distance, but still way too close for her, Jax saw the corps. Heavy vehicles she knew to be tanks floated forward. Their large cannons cracking like thunder, a never-ending beat. Full kit troops swarmed like upset bees. Rockets and sparks of light raced off into the horizon, where the Screech returned fire.

The Screech outnumbered the corps easily a hundred to one on all counts. Their vehicles were smaller, less armored, it seemed, but moved faster. Large groups of Screech soldiers ran the battle lines, moving in mass across the surface. They would meet the corps, overwhelm them, or bounce off and strike out again. A frenzied, never-ending combat.

Jax ducked as red, blue, and green sparks launched over her head. A check assured her it was random fire, but the reality of her situation sunk in. The battle looked to be shifting away from her, but could change course any minute. She checked her surroundings for clues. Something, anything, to point her toward her friends. The surrounding ground was burned and pocked marked, normally a tall grassy plain. It was cratered and muddied. It looked as if the battle had already rolled through.

She forced her mind to work. The angle of her part of wreckage, scrapes of soil, like giant footsteps, gave her a path to investigate. The cockpit had skipped along the ground like a rock thrown over a lake. It would impress her she survived if she had the time.

She stumbled as she scanned the area. She ached to rest. She forced herself to move, shuffling step after step. More blasts making her cringe. She fought to calm herself, pushing her sweat drenched hair from her face. Eyes on a swivel, she searched for her friends. All she saw were bits of *Hopper* littering the ground. Her eyes passed a piece of debris, only to realize it was moving.

She ran as best she could, her legs felt like iron. The image before her sharpened into Coleman Sales. His space suit was burned, muddied, and ripped. His helmet was missing, and his face matched his outfit. He walked stiffly through a score of wreckage. His eyes were glazed over, and he was repeatedly muttering, "Where are my kids? I just need—I'm here—Where's my kids? I just want to go home."

Jax gripped him both in a loving hug and for support. "It's alright, Coleman. I got you. Let's sit someplace safe," Jax said. She led him to a small patch free of debris and sat him down. "You rest, okay? Help will be here soon. I need to find the others."

"My kids?"

"Their safe in the bunkers Coleman, they'll be waiting for you when you wake."

"Okay," Coleman said. He laid his head down, but his eyes stared blankly at the sky. Jax brought a holescreen up from Coleman's suit. The medical read out showed multiple injuries, but all were being treated. He had a hairline fracture of his right arm, but everything else was superficial. The screen warned he was in shock and recommended a sedative. Jax glanced around and figured this was a safe a place as any right now and hit the accept button. Coleman gave a deep gasp and then settled back down.

Coleman's medical alert beacon popped upon the screen. "Emergency beacon activated. Help coming. Are you able to provide assistance?" She hit the "No" button. Cursing herself, she realized she had been approaching this search the wrong way. Crouching beside her friend, she bought a screen from her wrist. Flipping through a few menus and found the tracker for the emergency beacons. It flooded her with alerts. *Damn it.* A few more selections and she filtered out anything outside her proximity. Three red dots pulsed in front of her.

She ran and fell, crawled till she could gain her feet again and then tried running more. Her space suit caked with mud, more cuts opening with each fall, she pushed forward. Weapon's fire continued across the landscape, the ground quaking from explosions. A ship burst through the atmosphere, a Screech destroyer, engulfed in flames. Jax had stopped noticing any of it. Those red dots were her only thought.

She reached the next beacon and confusion washed over her. Part of *Hopper's* hull lay here, torn metal covering the ground, but nothing else. From the corner of her eye, the barest of movements drew her in. She turned and shuffled forward. The mud caked glove sticking out from a slab of metal twitched and then stopped.

Jax dropped to the ground, pushing her head into the dirt to look under. With the barest gleam of light, she made out Freddy's face through his helmet. He wasn't moving, and she couldn't tell if he was breathing. She grabbed his suit and heaved with all her might; he didn't budge. She grabbed the slab and tried lifting it, but it didn't budge. "Freddy!"

Whipping tears from her eyes, she pulled a holescreen from Freddy's glove. The built in med AI was working, but the vital signs were all jumbled. One moment his life signs were gone, then they would spike, stabilizing, and then do it all over again. Jax looked around for help, but none was to be found. She racked her brain for options, but her mind was jumbled. If only she wasn't so tired, so sore herself. The only option that continued to beat into her brain was the one she had already been using.

"I'm sorry, Freddy. I'm sorry, I can't do anything here. I'm so sorry. I'll find the others. Help is coming." She moved on to the next beacon. The last two beacons were on top of each other. Ten meters away with what was left of the rear hull. Jax stumbled, trying to quicken her pace. Her body ached and her mind felt numb. She wanted to collapse.

The rear hull had dug itself into the dirt, laying tilted. Stepping over torn metal and ducking her head, she entered from where the cockpit should have been. Beams of light cast in from the gaps and holes blown in the hull. Flashes of light and thunderous booms breaking the bright blue day. The noise seemed to get softer, or perhaps it was the hull blocking the sound.

Brooklyn sat impaled in her seat. A slim metal rod protruding from her left abdomen. She gripped it like she was trying to pull it out. As Jax approached, Brooklyn let out a large moan. Her hands slumped to her side and her mouth panted.

"You don't look so good Brooklyn," Jax said.

"You think? I always thought I looked good with piercings." Brooklyn's voice crackled as she spoke.

They both smiled as Jax checked the holoscreen for the wise cracking lieutenants' vitals. "The bar missed anything important, but it's entangled in something behind you," Jax said, pulling up an image to show. "We're not pulling it out. You also have a few broken ribs and too many lacerations to count. Medical AI is doing its job, but we'll have to wait for help. I've got nothing to get you free."

"Wonderful," Brooklyn said. "Don't suppose you have anything to drink?"

"Sorry."

"Wonderful again. Have the damn little nanites sedate me then. Sitting like this is just going to piss me off."

Jax gave a thin smile and keyed in the sequence. Glancing around the cabin before hitting the sedate button, she said. "Have you seen Rose? The last beacon is here, but I don't see her."

"She got thrown into the back," Brooklyn said, tilting her head. "Thought I heard her earlier, but my helm was damaged and too many explosions happening. I tried calling out, but my voice a little weak right now."

Jax nodded. "Sleep well." Brooklyn opened her mouth to respond, but her eyes closed. Her head dropped to her chest and deep breathing took over. Jax checked her harness to make sure she wouldn't accidentally shift. It held secure. Small flakes of impact foam were scattered around her. This entire cabin should have been filled with it, protecting Brooklyn and Rose. The rip in the hull filled her eyes, and she forced herself to stop analyzing it. She had better things to do.

Jax didn't look to where Rose would have been sitting. She knew she wasn't there now, so took steps towards the back. A collapsed panel barred her way to the last part of the ship. She gripped and pulled. It squeaked but went back in place. Planting her feet, she heaved again. The whine of metal bending filled her ears as she screamed to pull harder. The metal gave way with a crack and Jax tumbled backwards. She crawled into the new opening. She went cold.

Rose lay twisted, contorted on the floor. Partway down her right thigh, a triangular metal shard had merged with her leg. Her right arm disappeared behind her and her left broke at an odd angle. Her head lolling back, the helmet part way out of a hole in the hull.

Jax scrambled forward. "Rose! Rose! Rose!" She lifted Rose's head into her arms. Looking into the cracked visor, searching for any positive sign she could find. *No. No. No.* She popped the holoscreen of Rose's suit and gazed desperately at the medical readout. Red lights flashed in her face, but the only read out it gave was "Analyzing." *Come on, you stupid thing.* Slower and slower, it seemed to work. Split seconds felt like minutes until finally a blip. The tiniest, minimalist indication that Rose was alive.

Jax undid the connectors on Rose's helmet and slipped it ever so gently from her head. Sweat dampened Rose's hair. The shortcut had still managed to drop in her eyes. Jax pushed it softly aside and whispered. "Hang in there, little sis. I can't lose the only sister I've ever had. Please stay with me. Please."

Rose's chin lifted, and her lips trembled. Her eyes opened, like they were lifting a ton. Her voice was faint and breathy when she spoke. "I-I'm sorry."

"Sorry? You have nothing to be sorry for. Pretty sure I was the pilot. You just relax," Jax said.

"Th-the hum. Second one. Never—never did find it. You could've—could made— turn, if I fixed..." Rose said, her eyes closing, her head turning to rest in Jax's arms. A small moan lifted from her and drifted away.

Through the tears in her eyes, Jax smiled at her beloved friend, her sister. "Silly girl, you were awesome. Just rest. I'll make sure we're safe. I'll try to keep us all safe. You did your part. Just rest."

Jax held her friend as far in the distance rumbles filled her ears. Through the hole in the ceiling, lights flashed, and explosions lit the sky. In a moment, she would move and make Rose as comfortable as possible. She would check on the rest of her friends and do more to secure them, to do what she could. If she could. For now, for this moment, she knew she had reached the end of what she could do. Her body beaten, mind fatigued, all her options were gone. For this battle, this war on Gaia, she was done.

Chapter 27

NOT SUPERSTITIOUS

Jax marched the halls with a stiff back and eyes locked. Her dress blues were pressed, and her shoes shined. While she had spent a lot of time on Alpha Station, this part was unknown to her. This wing housed the administrative offices for the station. She imagined during normal times these halls were quite busy. The days after the battle for Gaia were anything but normal. Her footsteps echoed through the empty halls.

She had a hard time placing how long it had been. She remembered her dad once said that he didn't understand time like a normal person. Life in the military didn't work on a Monday to Friday schedule. When he worked, he worked. When he had furlough, he would enjoy the time until he returned to work. Days of the week, months, had no meaning for him. You were in the military every day no matter what, so the specifics of time didn't matter. She didn't understand him then, but she did now. Everything blurred together.

She knew the last time she wore this uniform had been at the military ball. The less she thought about that, the better. The battle came soon after, and so did their victory. It was hard for her to call it that, however, with all the tragedies associated with it. The waiting with her friends while the battle raged on without them. The cold, the unsure feeling that things would change, would go their way. She stopped and took a deep breath, shaking the feelings out of her.

They had won. Everyone said so. They completely routed the Screech forces. They seemed confused with their command ships pulling back. Some ships joined them, others worked into a frenzy and attacked harder.

Officially, the battle continued for a few days, but small skirmishes happened weeks later. The threat of the Screech was their vast numbers and synchronicity of movement. That gone, Gaia's better tech, high-capacity weapons, and maintained battle lines won out.

Gaia was nothing if not efficient and the recovery had started immediately. The gathering of damaged ships, the repairing of buildings and landscape. Accounting for the dead, so many dead. While civilian casualties were low, thanks to protective bunkers. Everyone on the planet, civilian and military alike, had joined in the relief effort. Jax didn't remember the emergency crews picking her up. She did remember waking up and ignoring the pleas to stay in bed. She had spent every waking hour since then on that relief effort. Till she was called, ordered, here to Alpha Station. It had taken her two days to make it here, waiting for transport. So many lost ships, so many lost people.

Both branches of the Gaia Military had been hammered. The Gaia Terrain Corps had fared better of the two. The corps, backed by the militia, had been on point for any incursion onto Gaia soil. Every landing the Screech had attempted was destroyed or turned back. The corps had deemed their losses acceptable. Better than expected, in fact, and congratulated themselves. Jax hadn't bothered to look up what those "acceptable numbers" were. She didn't want to know. Her "stone dogs" had made a stealth run on a Screech Command vessel. Focusing on Ryan Nelson's personal locator, they cut their way onto the ship. Freed him and got out. She longed to hear the story. *Semper Aduax*, the corps motto, made reality.

The Gaia Fleet had fared far worse. All the Earth based craft that were modified for combat were destroyed or damaged beyond repair. A majority of their crews lost with them. Only one of the weapon platforms was operational, barely. The platform under construction had been obliterated. The last platform was an abandoned husk. So heavily damaged by the Screech attacks, it now sat as a derelict mini moon in orbit. The corps had deemed their loss of personnel "near catastrophic". Jax had been afraid to look up what that meant.

She approached her destination and snapped her mind back to the present. She knew why she was here. She knew she should be focused on that, but it was so hard. She raised her hand to knock, but let it drop instead. Her life had changed so much since joining the Gaia military. It was never what she expected, but it was what she always needed.

Here she had found the best friends that she had ever had. While she and Rose joked about being related, in her mind, they were sisters. Jax realized she felt that way about everyone she served with. They were all her brothers and sisters. They were all her family now. Not necessarily a family she would have chosen, but a family she needed. A family that gave her purpose and a place to belong. A place aboard a warship of all things, the *Ares*.

The *Ares* had survived the battle for Gaia. Commander Lewis had used the wreckage of the Screech command ship and the *Segomo* to her advantage. Her hit-and-run tactics, along with the flying skills of Hat Trick, were magnificent. They used the wreckage as an ad hoc shield, letting it absorb incoming fire. They continued to take damage but were able to survive till help could arrive.

The *Menrva* and *Perun*, under the command of Commanders Moro and Haddock, were stars of the show. Working together, the two ships, and several smaller Earth based fighters, had cut large swatches into the Screech lines. After Jax rammed the one command ship, the two *Ares* class ships found an opening. They cut their way through two destroyers to the second Screech command ship. Together, the small battle group eliminated the destroyers and tackled the command ship. The return onslaught of the Screech destroyed the *Perun* and the Earth based fighters that had joined them. Moro had expertly used the Screech's focus on those ships to win the day. The *Menrva* terminated the enemy craft from the battlefield. While damaged, the *Menrva* came out of the battle relatively unscathed.

It was a hard pill for her to swallow. Her plan hadn't saved the day, Terrance had. If she had stayed with him, the three Ares-class ships would have been unstoppable. His plan, Gaia's plan, was the better option. Her rogue actions had put it all in jeopardy. They had lost the *Segomo* and the *Perun* because of her actions. They had seen the faults in her plan and adjusted, but she wasn't able to. She had been critical of the military's ability to think creatively, but it wasn't creativity that won a fight like this.

It was discipline; it was following orders; it was understanding that others could see things you simply don't understand.

She shook her head and straightened again. She knocked on the door and was instantly greeted with an "enter". The door slid open, and she marched in. A couple meters in, she snapped to attention and saluted. "Lieutenant Harumi Brandt, reporting as ordered." When no response came, her eyes darted around and scanned the room. This was not what she was expecting.

She had expected admirals and legal teams. A full military tribunal to try her for her crimes. What she got was a simple office with a sturdy metal desk. Behind which sat Commander Lewis, working through something on a holoscreen. A moment passed till the Commander put an eye on her. The Commander dismissed her screen and leaned back into her chair. "At ease, Lieutenant. Not what you were expecting, is it?"

"You read my mind," Jax replied, slowly lowering her hand. "I thought this was the formal inquest into my crimes."

"It is, but we've already deliberated on the outcome. You're here to be informed."

"So, I don't get a chance to defend myself? Pretty sure that's illegal on any planet."

"Probably, but this is how it's going to work, anyway. Sit down, Jax, and let's drop all the military protocol and talk. It was hard enough for me to convince them this would be the best way as it is. I don't need you getting your fury up. Your Jax, I'm Gemma, let's talk. Please," Gemma said, a gentle wave of her hand ushering Jax to a seat.

It took a moment, but Jax let the tension fall from her body and took the seat. "So, how bad is it?" she asked.

"It's bad. Everything changes after this, but I'm not ready to lay it on you yet. How's the Ratpack?"

"On the whole, they'll be fine given time. Rose's leg is gone, and she's currently arguing with the Doc."

"Arguing?"

Jax chuckled. "Yup. Doc wants to DNAfab a new one, but Rose is favoring the full synthetic."

Gemma barked a laugh. "I bet she thinks she can mod it herself that way."

"Yeah. Doc thinks she's crazy, but it's her life. The synthetic will get her back up and running in a few weeks. A DNAfab could take months. She wants to get back to work."

"That's Rose. Someday she will die with a wrench in her hand. What about the boys?"

"Coleman's got some PTSD. Physically, he's fine, but mentally he's struggling. He's got the meds to help, and he's working on the support programs. Taking time with his family. He says he'll be back, just needing the leave time for now."

"He's a good man. First time I think he's been in the thick of it like that. He'll bounce back. What about Fredrick?"

"Doc says he'll live, but beyond that..." Jax said. "He has extensive neurological damage. Possible feedback from the qave drive or maybe the Screech weapons. They're not sure. Anyway, they're having trouble repairing it. He wakes up occasionally, but he's heavily sedated."

"I'll stop by and visit him later today. I actually helped Fredrick pass his tests for Ensign. He is a brilliant engineer but freezes up on formal tests. I gave him some mental exercises to help him relax, to stay focused," Gemma said.

The two officers shared simple smiles. The silence fell into the room. Neither one wanting to break the small moment of peace. It stretched long enough for the tension in the room to rise.

"Now that the pleasantries are done, I suppose we should get down to business."

"They're kicking me out, aren't they?" Jax said.

"Oh, they're kicking you, but not out. This is a complex situation, Jax, with a lot of moving pieces. Each move affects the other. Some moves will gain reward and others will gain a penalty. Even some rewards will feel like a penalty. It's all going to hurt eventually, but some might take a while. A lot of these decisions are as political as they are military. You haven't been here long, but you've made quite an impact and that impact affects us all. You want the hard blow first or the softer ones?"

"When you're getting a beating, does it really matter?" Jax said, sinking into her chair. "Your choice I guess."

"Okay, let's start with my news first. I will not be taking command of the *Ares*."

"They're taking the *Ares* from you because of me? That's ridiculous!" Jax said, straightening. "I'm under your command, but it was my fault, my responsibility. You were marvelous during that battle. They have to see you're ready to be a captain. They can't do this to you."

"Calm Jax, this has nothing to do with you. At least not yet. Truth be told, that battle made me realize I'm not cut out for it. At one point, I thought that's what I wanted, being the captain of a ship. Being there, working at that level, I realize it's not where I'm at my best. Others do it better and want it more. It's not for me."

"So, what are you going to do?"

"It seems the battle left a vacuum in the upper ranks. Later today, they will make a formal announcement, several promotions will be given out. I'll be promoted to admiral."

Jax's mouth was agape, and she blinked a few times, taking it in. "Wow. Congratulations. That's quite a jump. You deserve it."

"Thank you, and yes, it is. War sometimes makes such things necessary. We put people where they do the best. I was always good at training camps for Judo. I can see the long-term goals that need to be accomplished. Given time to analyze a task, I can figure it out and make training necessary to succeed. Now I can put those skills towards the fleet and fixing the holes in our game that this attack exposed."

Jax nodded to that. She had experienced Gemma's training sessions since joining the *Ares*. Grueling on the edge of cruelty, she had to admit her own skills in Judo had progressed further than she ever thought possible. Killing time living on the *Ares*, she had even worked off Gemma's recorded classes in the VRpods. She could see Gemma applying the same structure of her classes to the Fleet, fine tuning it, making it better. It was a good fit.

"That means Terrance will be captain of the *Ares*, right?" Jax asked. It wasn't really a question. She knew the answer. Commander Terrance

Moro had lived up to all the mystique surrounding him in the battle of Gaia. He had earned it, but it wouldn't sit right with her.

"No, Terrance will be captain, but he'll be staying on the *Menrva*. He'll be assigned to protect our space shores while we rebuild. Several other *Ares* class ships will be permanently recalled and placed under his command. This will establish an in-system space guard. Terrance's actions during the battle provided enough evidence on how affective that can be."

Satisfaction washed over Jax, she couldn't accept Terrance in command of the *Ares*. She relaxed in her chair as her mind wandered.

"So, Commander Haddock then. I'm not sure how I feel about that. Now that I know him a bit better, not sure I'd want him in that position."

"Me either, truth be told. Thankfully, Issac has turned down the promotion. Being in the top spot would be a little too much spotlight for someone like him. He feels safer in shadows."

Her ideas had run their course, which left her with only one more sad thought. "Their scrapping the *Ares* then, aren't they?" Her thoughts spilled out loud. "Reassign the crew to the *Menrva* or spread them out on other vessels. Then they can drop me in some hole of a position, out of sight and out of mind. Military wouldn't have to deal with me causing trouble and politically nobody would touch me."

"You know, for someone with such a dynamic thought process, you can be really dense sometimes."

"What? I don't understand?"

Gemma shook her head and then said. "Jax. They're giving the *Ares* to you. You're going to be the captain."

The words hit Jax as if Gemma had picked her up and slammed her into the ground. Gemma continued, "Before the shock wares off and you get all happy. Remember what I said about some rewards being a penalty?"

Jax shook herself and forced a response. "What do you mean?"

"It's been decided we need to retaliate against the Screech. We don't have a fleet to do that, however. So, we're going to send a single ship to find the Screech and deliver the mother of all bombs. A bomb to deliver the message they we are not to be messed with. A world killer."

"The *Ares*."

"Yes."

"Why me? How does making me a captain solve anything?"

"You're a problem on Gaia now," Gemma said, her face as gloomy as the abyss. "I don't think the politicians lobbing for this care if you succeed. If you do, fantastic, they can take credit. If you don't, you die defending Gaia, and they can say they tried. It also removes you taking any sides in Gaia politics. It's a win—win for them. Plus, I think they're all a little worried about you since you shot Emma."

"Well, in my defense, the Prime deserved it."

"That she did, but the political spin has some doubting that. Plus, in a month there will be a new Prime. Any guesses on who the front runner is?"

"Damn. Dakos. You've got to be kidding me."

"Unfortunately, not. He's getting a big sympathy vote. People are wondering if all the negative things about him were manufactured by Emma."

"Double damn. How does this fix the trouble I'm in with Fleet?"

Gemma let out an enormous sigh. "I told you before, the military has a history of promoting its problems. You've proven you're capable, don't get me wrong, but you don't work well in the military structure. They can't give you the death penalty after what just happened, so they do the next thing they can."

"They give me a suicide mission."

"Point and match. The worst part is you must take the *Ares* and her crew with you. Everyone gets penalized for this. I'm sorry Jax, but this is on your shoulders."

"What if I quit? That removes me as a problem and then they don't need to send the *Ares*."

Gemma shook her head. "That would be bad. The military gives you a certain level of protection. Also, they'll send the *Ares* anyway, but they'll work hard to make sure its captain doesn't have a chance of succeeding. Normally we could stop that, but not right now. With the Prime dead and so many high-ranking officers gone, things are decided by a joint council. Much as I hate to admit it, the civilian council is better organized than we are."

"Is there a triple damn?"

"Don't joke about this. We've been trying to fight this, but politically we're being overrun. The politicians are pushing for this, Dakos is pushing for it. He wants everything to do with the *Ares* gone. Since the military is in shambles, he's getting his way. Losing the high marshal and other senior staff has us off balance. We'll get it back, but it's going to take time. Admiral Koonce is already working on that. It will be easier once he is officially sworn in as the new high marshal."

"Oh, that's good. I like him."

"Me too. You will be happy to know he thinks highly of you. He's still pissed about the EVE units, however."

Jax sank into her chair and started to speak in her own defense, but Gemma cut her off. "Don't. It worked out, which is what's giving you a chance. It's also started a discussion about EVEs in Gaia society that may change the way we do things. Lot of big debates are coming up. Dakos is already swing his political club where he can. We are living in interesting times."

Jax recognized the old Earth proverb and couldn't help but shake her head in agreement. "So, where do we go from here?"

Gemma held up a finger and then swiped a few screens on her desk. "Normally, a captain can request or recruit their own command team. I hope you'll forgive me for taking a few liberties on your behalf," Gemma said and gave a flick of her hand. Two images flew from her desk and floated midair. A picture on one side and a scroll of personal data on the right. Issac Haddock and Lilly Bard. "Commander Haddock will make a good XO and Lilly is, well, Lilly."

Jax paused, studying the two files for a moment. When she turned from them, she locked eyes with Gemma. "I have questions about Commander Haddock. Some of the things I've learned about him, I don't know how much I should trust him. Can I trust him?"

Gemma held up a finger, her eyes darted around the room as if looking for something. "Yes. It's complicated, but yes. Keep an eye on him. I can't say what I know. He's dangerous, but I think you can trust him. On this mission, at least. Lilly's probably the more immediate threat."

"Why is that?" Jax raised an eyebrow.

"She's mad at you for killing Emma. If anyone was going to do that, it was supposed to be her."

"Admittedly, I've only seen her a little since then, but she didn't seem upset with me."

"That's not how Lilly works. You should realize that by now. Anyway, be ready. I've talked to both of them, and they've agreed to the position. You can choose others if you'd rather, but I doubt you'd find better."

Jax shook her head. "I'll take them. I'd be a fool not to."

"Good. This next one I figured you would want to ask. Also, it would come with a nice promotion to lieutenant commander." She waved her hand and the two images faded away. Replacing them was a face similar to Jax's own, but with short, cropped hair. Lieutenant Second Class Rosita Kioka.

Jax smiled. "No doubts about this one. I can't imagine anyone else I'd rather have at my side."

"I figured as much. That still leaves openings for OPS and WEP. Commander Haddock had mentioned Lieutenant Wisler for the position. I haven't had much experience with her, so that will be your call."

Jax chuckled. "She'll be interesting. She is a lot like you, but without all the refinement."

Gemma laughed. "Your screwed, then. I can put together a list of candidates for WEP if you want?"

"Maybe. I have an idea, but I think I should approach them first. I want to make sure he wants to come and not be bound by duty to follow orders. It will require another 'nice' promotion if that's alright?"

Gemma stared at her as if reading her mind. "You're crazy."

"Maybe, but it's a crazy situation."

"Your funeral. Terrance will be less happy with you than he normally is."

Jax shrugged and asked a final lingering question: "What about EVE? I know I'm pushing it here, but having an EVE around really made the difference. It doesn't seem right to deactivate them. On Earth, EVE units have basic rights. I like having an EVE around."

Gemma's face tightened and she shook her head. "This isn't Earth. Arguments are ongoing. Strange enough, we have a lot of transplants from Earth who feel the same as you do. Sentiment you could say is about fifty-fifty. Nath has some interesting ideas on the subject, so we'll see how it plays out. Best if you stay as far from it as possible."

Jax nodded and asked. "Is that it then?"

Gemma nodded. "That's more than enough. You have time to prepare. We'll move the *Ares* to the shipyards in a couple of days. Work orders give it six months till space worthy. Nath said he'll have it done in four. We'll get a full crew for you and stack the deck as best we can before you leave. There's always a way to win if you plan for it, always."

Jax stood and offered a perfect salute. Gemma rose, walked around the table, gave a bow, and then offered her hand. The two officers shook hands and embraced.

"Be good Jax, be better than good. We know you're not supposed to come back, so prove them all wrong. Work the impossible," Gemma said.

"Coming back is definitely in my plan," Jax said. "The good part I'm not too sure about. Seems like every time I do something bad, I get promoted around here. You're starting to give me bad ideas."

Gemma laughed as she turned back to sit at her desk. "As an admiral, I must officially dissuade you from such thoughts." The new admiral paused, looked into Jax's eyes, and grinned. "Unofficially, I'm reminded of something Captain Moss once told me. When in deep space, captains make their own rules."

Jax returned the wicked grin, gave one more nod of her head, and walked out the door. She wandered Alpha Station for a while, her mind flooded with thoughts. She tried to push the idea of a suicide mission out of her pondering, but it kept popping back up. Like Gemma, she focused on the words of Captain Moss, "Every time we accomplish the impossible, we simply set a new standard." It became her mantra; it hardened her resolve that she could survive. Set a new standard.

She ended up where she always seemed to, the bridge of the *Ares*. She couldn't live here right now. There was too much damage. She had been staying in Rose's house while Rose was in the hospital. While she felt comfortable there, it wasn't her home. This was, this was where she felt the best, the safest. This is a place where she could get to work.

Checking in on the command table, her registration popped up as Captain H. Brandt. She was positive when they announced the promotions later today that hers would be conveniently absent. That didn't matter to her; however, she had her prize. She wished EVE was here, but all the EVE units were disconnected the instant they declared the battle over. She had a few thoughts about that herself, but she would talk to Nath and Rose about it later. She'd have to keep her distance, but it didn't mean she couldn't filter things through others. That was for later, however, right now her mind rested on something else. Something that might make a difference in the days to come.

She would be given Operational Orders, an OPORD, in a few days. These would detail her mission and what they expect the result to be. She had enough information to get the gist of it now. The idea was simple, yet broad. She would have to find the Screech home world first. Figuring out where to start that goal would be the most challenging, impossible challenge. It would be like finding a needle somewhere in the universe. The second part would be the more dangerous attacking said world. They expect her to run into the abyss, guns blazing and die in some grand gesture. At least she thought that's what Dakos wanted. An end to her, the *Ares* and all his troubles, while still glorifying Gaia. She had other plans.

A star chart formed over the table. A miniature version of the one she had first seen when she had arrived on Gaia. A string of purple dots moved around the table and became her only focus. She had been told that each of these dots represented a world the Screech had conquered. Not just conquered but conquered and wiped from the universe. There was limited information available about each. Possible levels of technology, similar structures and so on. The people on Gaia kept this information as a reminder of what the Screech were capable of. That the Screech had exterminated so many races. Whole worlds of equal or greater development than themselves. Or had they?

For in Jax's mind, these little dots showed a different pattern. Not one of destruction, the way Gaia tended to look at things, but rather of hope. She overlay her map, the one she had slowly been building in her time living on ship. Lines connected planets where similarities suggested a connection. Little dots that created a pattern, a pattern that reached deep into space. A space beyond the Screech. This pattern created a picture in Jax's head. A picture of a race that stayed at least one step ahead of the Screech. A race that had beat the Screech at their own game and survived. If the Screech had other enemies, maybe, just maybe, Gaia would have allies.

Jax wasn't superstitious, but as she looked at the image, it was hard for her to ignore. Those dots, those six little dots, gave her a direction. A path that didn't lead to destruction, but rather to hope. *Lucky number six.*

This ends Warworld Gaia
Captain's Fate Book 2

Next

The story of Jax and the crew of the *Ares* continues in
Book 3 of Captain's Fate:
Warcaptain Brandt!
The thrilling conclusion to our epic story!
Coming Soon!

From the Author

H ello wonderful Reader!

    Thanks for taking the time to read this, my second novel. I hope you enjoyed reading it as much as I enjoyed creating it! If you could please take just a few minutes of your time, I would love a review. Reviews are the life's blood of self-published authors. Even a brief review of a few words will help me reach new readers and encourage me to continue to enhance my craft.

    I thank you for your support!

    -Skip Scherer

About the Author

S kip Scherer lives in Washington State with his lovely wife, daughter, two dogs and the ghost of an immortal fish.

Before he started writing, Skip got a degree in computer graphics and design. After working as a freelance artist for many years, Skip made a huge life change and opened a martial arts school. That career choice led to a way of life for over two decades. He continues to run that school to this day, writes at night and continues to take on new challenges.

If you want to know when Skip's next book will come out, please visit his website at, where you can sign up to receive an email when he has his next release.

You can also join him on social media:
https://twitter.com/skip_scherer
https://www.facebook.com/WarShipAres

CPSIA information can be obtained
at www.ICGtesting.com
Printed in the USA
BVHW040950060623
665471BV00011B/49